Praise for *A House With Good Bones*

"T. Kingfisher's *A House With* [...] and (c) charming. You will gulp t[...] day."
[...] [...]lling
series

"*A House With Good Bones* grapples with a thorny family legacy with heart, wit, and creeping horror. I was compelled to read the book in one breathless, white-knuckled sitting. Vultures, ladybugs, and underground children, oh my!"   —Paul Tremblay, author of *A Head Full of Ghosts*

"An eerie Southern Gothic that still has Kingfisher's trademark humor."
—*BuzzFeed*

"Impressively weird, nerve-wracking but still laugh-out-loud funny, *A House With Good Bones* is another horror hit from T. Kingfisher."
—*BookPage* (starred review)

"Wickedly witty and intensely scary, *A House With Good Bones* is a thoroughly modern take on the Southern Gothic, about thorny family secrets that refuse to stay buried. You'll be feverishly turning the pages, so engrossed you won't notice the vultures circling overhead. . . ."
—Rachel Harrison, author of *Cackle*

"This magical book somehow manages to be laugh-out-loud funny and completely terrifying at the same time—and I could not put it down! It's immersive and entertaining, and the cleverly imaginative storytelling mixed with an oh-so-memorable voice will have you racing through the pages. I absolutely loved this!"   —Hank Phillippi Ryan, *USA Today* bestselling author of *The House Guest*

"Kingfisher goes Southern Gothic (Waffle House visits included) in this hilarious and gruesome contemporary horror novel. Horror fans who like a little whimsy on the way to a chilling climax won't want to miss this."   —*Publishers Weekly* (starred review)

"T. Kingfisher has mastered her own special blend of horror and snarky mundanity, wherein the not-so-dearly departed demand half-frozen ham, terrifying abominations hunger for blood, and the vacuum is full of ladybugs. A creepshow in taupe with extra vultures. I loved it."
—Travis Baldree, *New York Times* bestselling author of *Legends & Lattes*

"*A House With Good Bones* is a dark, eerie fantasy that creeps through your skull and covers your brain like rose vines, tightening with every strange reveal. Despite the looming dread, T. Kingfisher weaves incredible wit and humor through every passage, crafting a tale of mystery and horror well worth sinking into." —Chuck Tingle, author of *Camp Damascus*

"*A House With Good Bones* had me nodding and laughing in recognition at the family dynamics and eccentric Southern neighborhood and then full-out shrieking at the bugs and buried secrets. No one blends humor and creeping dread as satisfyingly as T. Kingfisher."
—Gwenda Bond, *New York Times* bestselling author of *The Date from Hell*

"T. Kingfisher continues to establish herself as one of the freshest voices in horror! Samantha grounds this story in a normalcy that is so approachable and understandable that it only heightens the horror. You'll be reading underneath a blanket with a flashlight!"
—Katee Robert, *New York Times* bestselling author

"For fans of stories that take the haunted-house trope and overlay occult themes with generational trauma, like *The Good House* by Tananarive Due and *How To Sell a Haunted House* by Grady Hendrix." —*Booklist*

A

HOUSE

WITH

GOOD

BONES

T. KINGFISHER

NIGHTFIRE
Tor Publishing Group
New York

A HOUSE WITH GOOD BONES

Copyright © 2023 by Ursula Vernon

A Nightfire Book
Published by Tom Doherty Associates / Tor Publishing Group
120 Broadway
New York, NY 10271

www.torpublishinggroup.com

Nightfire™ is a trademark of Macmillan Publishing Group, LLC.

The Library of Congress has cataloged the hardcover edition as follows:

Names: Kingfisher, T., author.
Title: A house with good bones / T. Kingfisher.
Description: First Edition. | New York : Nightfire, 2023. | "A Tom
    Doherty Associates Book."
Identifiers: LCCN 2022041387 (print) | LCCN 2022041388 (ebook) |
    ISBN 9781250829795 (hardcover) | ISBN 9781250829801 (ebook)
Subjects: LCGFT: Novels.
Classification: LCC PS3611.I597 H68 2023 (print) | LCC PS3611.I597
    (ebook) | DDC 813/.6—dc23/eng/20220829
LC record available at https://lccn.loc.gov/2022041387
LC ebook record available at https://lccn.loc.gov/2022041388

ISBN 978-1-250-82981-8 (trade paperback)

Our books may be purchased in bulk for promotional, educational, or business use.
Please contact your local bookseller or the Macmillan Corporate and Premium Sales
Department at 1-800-221-7945, extension 5442, or by email at
MacmillanSpecialMarkets@macmillan.com.

First Nightfire Paperback Edition: 2024

Printed in the United States of America

0 9 8 7 6 5 4 3 2 1

This is for my grandmother,
who was actually pretty awesome

The First Day

Winchester Cathedral: An old-fashioned English shrub rose. Grows to four feet high and four feet wide. Produces masses of large, loose-petalled white roses, occasionally with a touch of pink. Fragrant. Repeat bloomer.

CHAPTER 1

There was a vulture on the mailbox of my grandmother's house.

As omens go, it doesn't get much more obvious than that. This was a black vulture, not a turkey vulture, but that's about as much as I could tell you. I have a biology degree, but it's in bugs, not birds. The only reason that I knew that much was because the identification key for vultures in North America is extremely straightforward. Does it have a black head? It's a black vulture. Does it have a red head? It's a turkey vulture. This works unless you're in the Southwest, where you have to add: Is it the size of a small fighter jet? It's a California condor.

We have very few condors in North Carolina.

"I bet you have some amazing feather mites," I told the vulture, opening the car door. The vulture tilted its head and considered this, or me, or my aging Subaru.

I took out my phone and got several glamour shots of the bird. When I tried to upload one to the internet, however, my phone informed me that it had one-tenth of a bar and my GPS conked out completely.

Ah yes. That, at least, hadn't changed.

My mother lived on Lammergeier Lane, which made the vulture even more appropriate, although we don't have Lammergeiers—"bearded vultures"—in North Carolina either. They're a large species of vulture from Africa and Eurasia that eats bones. Why would you name a private road after a bone-eating vulture from a different continent? I looked it up one day when I was bored, and discovered that the developer of the subdivision had been obsessed with birds. His first project had been Accipiter Lane, then Brambling Court, then Cardinal Street, and so on through the alphabet until Whip-poor-will Way, whereupon he died, presumably so that he would not have to come up with a bird for X. (The correct answer is Xantus's murrelet, but I admit it doesn't exactly roll off the tongue.)

Lammergeier Lane was a type of subdivision that we have all over the South, although I don't know if they've migrated out to other areas. You'll be driving along a rural road, surrounded by trees, cow pastures, and the occasional business that sells firewood, propane, and hydraulic repairs. Then you'll see a dilapidated trailer and a sign for a private drive. You turn onto the drive and suddenly there are a dozen cookie-cutter houses lining the street, all with neat lawns. The road either terminates in a cul-de-sac or links up to another, even more rural road.

You are required by tradition to have the dilapidated trailer, which is generally owned by a grumpy survivalist who refuses to sell. Otherwise the residents will have nothing to complain about and will become fractious.

My grandmother, that odd, frustrating woman, had bought the third house on the right side of the street and lived there for a number of years. We moved in with her for a year when I was ten, then Mom managed to get us an apartment and we moved out again. Then Gran Mae died when I was fourteen and we moved back in. Now I was thirty-two and here yet again.

The subdivision looked exactly the same as it had when I left. It had hit that stage where all the covenants have lapsed and someone has put in a chicken coop and someone else's lawn is going to seed—I approve of this, it supports far more insect life—and there's a truck on blocks tucked almost out of sight behind a shed. Subdivisions can persist in this particular developmental stage for decades before they finally pupate into their adult form and become a neighborhood ripe for parasitizing by developers.

I looked across the street at Mr. Pressley's house. Was he still alive? He had to be in his eighties by now.

Yep, sure enough, the curtains on the big window were just slightly cracked, and I could make out the outline of a pair of binoculars. Mr.

Pressley was a one-man neighborhood watch, whether the neighborhood wanted it or not. He was convinced that rural North Carolina was a hotbed of murderous activity. If I didn't get moving soon, he'd probably call the cops on me.

"Put out an APB on the fat woman with curly hair," I muttered to myself. "It was malicious standing, Officer, I saw it with my own eyes! And parking her car with intent!" There aren't many social advantages to being fat, but I'll give it this, nobody ever thinks you're a cat burglar.

So Pressley was still alive and the trailer was still there. Cell coverage still shaky. My grandmother's front yard was still covered in roses. (Despite my mother having lived here for nearly two decades, I still thought of it as my grandmother's house.) About the only thing that had changed on Lammergeier Lane was that the Bradford pear trees had mostly died and been replaced with crepe myrtles.

And, apparently, vultures.

The vulture in question was still sitting on the wooden crosspiece behind the mailbox. I had no idea if it was hostile, nervous, or about to launch itself at my head. They don't have facial expressions like mammals. Mind you, I'm not that great with mammals either.

The screen door slammed and I heard my mother calling. "Samantha! Samantha, you're here!"

"Hi, Mom," I said, not taking my eyes off the bird. "Did you know you've got yard vultures?"

"Don't mind them. They belong to the lady down the street," Mom said.

I turned to stare at her. "They *what*?"

"Well, not *belong*, exactly. There's a tree." She waved her hands toward the end of the street. "Oh, never mind, I'll explain later. Don't worry, they're harmless."

"Don't they puke when they get upset?" This is just about the only fact I know about vultures, and only because an ex-boyfriend of mine got too close to one once and found out the hard way. In retrospect, the vulture may have had the right idea.

"Oh yes!" Mom beamed at me. "One threw up all over the Goldbergs' beagle."

Fortunately, this vulture did not seem particularly inclined to vomit. I backed away until the car was safely between us, then turned and hugged Mom.

"It's so good to see you, honey," she said. I didn't say anything, because I was just realizing that she had dropped a scary amount of weight since the last time I'd seen her. The women in our family are either fat or skeletal, and it felt like she had switched sides in the last year. I could feel her ribs and the knobs on her spine.

"Good god, Mom," I said, stepping back. "Are you okay? You don't have cancer or something, do you?" (Tact. I do not have it.)

"No, no." She smiled, but her face had gotten as thin as the rest of her, and I couldn't tell if she looked worried or if it was just the new lines around her mouth. "I'm fine. Do you know how long you're staying?"

"Haven't a clue," I admitted. "They found human remains on the dig, so we're all furloughed until it gets sorted."

"I'm so sorry." She grabbed one of my duffel bags out of the car. "I know you were excited to work on this one."

"Eh, they've promised to bring us all back on. Hopefully it won't take too long."

I'm an archaeoentomologist. It's fine, you've never heard of me. I study insects in archaeological remains. Actually, if you're in the field, you probably *have* heard of me, because there's hardly any of us. You've almost certainly heard of Dr. Wilcox, my boss, who did all that amazing work with sawtoothed grain beetle larvae found in food storage from the Viking era.

Anyway, my job is mostly spent either sitting in a room sifting through dirt from digs looking for dried-out insect husks or staring at photos somebody else took of dried-out insect husks, fiddling with the brightness and contrast to see if I can make out any details. Occasionally I do get out to dig sites, which I enjoy a lot more. My particular specialty is Pacific Northwest Paleo-Indian middens, but I get dirt samples from all over because, as I said, there aren't that many of us.

It was a dig that had brought me back home. Start of the season, the promise of a whole lot of hands-on time in the dirt instead of staring at photos. I'd told my roommates I wouldn't be back for six months, shoved my furniture into storage, and went off to play in the Paleolithic midden. And then, like I told Mom, somebody found human remains. On the *third day* of serious digging, no less.

Well, that was the end of that. The whole project was on hold until the Native American Heritage Commission could sort out what tribe the bones belonged to and if they had any living relatives who would want them back for burial. Some archaeologists get bitter about these sort of regulations apparently, but I personally don't want to muck around with anybody's ancestors. It seems rude, and just generally tacky.

Anyway, give me a trash heap over a grave any day. A grave tells you how people act when they're on their best behavior in front of Death. Trash heaps tell you how they actually *lived*.

The problem was that I'd announced a six-month absence, and my roommates had already sublet my bedroom to an exchange student. Also, I had no real idea when the litigation would get resolved—sometimes they can sort these things out in a couple of weeks, if all parties are trying hard to get along, and sometimes they drag on for years and the person in charge of the dig tells us to take other jobs and they'll call back. So, I called up Mom and told her I needed to come back home for a bit, and of course she had alternated between concern and enthusiasm, which is Mom's normal state of being.

"I'm so glad to see you, honey," she said again, giving me a worried look over her shoulder. The line between her eyebrows had grown deeper since the last time I'd seen her. "I just wish it didn't have to be here."

"Here?" It seemed like an odd thing to say.

"Oh, you know." She opened the door and waved me inside. Laden with all of my clothes and about half my worldly possessions, I inched past her and set my duffel bags down with a grunt.

"Uh . . ."

"Well, just because your dig was canceled." She hugged me again. I had a feeling that it wasn't what she'd planned to say.

My brother, Brad, had said that he thought we needed to check in on Mom more often. At the time, I'd thought he was just worrying too much. Now, seeing how thin she was and how harried she looked, I started to think he should have called me sooner.

"Are you sure everything's okay, Mom? I don't mean to impose, it's just that Brad and Maria have no space, and I figured it had been a while . . ."

"No, no! You know this is your home too." And she hugged me again, which is Mom all over—always anxious to make sure that no one feels unloved for even an instant.

"Sure, but I don't want to interrupt any hot dates." I grinned at her. "If you need me to get lost some evening . . ."

She swatted clumsily at me with a duffel bag. "Pff! Thank you, no. All the single men my age want either a trophy wife or a housekeeper, and I'm not doing either."

"Awww*right*," I drawled. "Two sexy single ladies living the fabulous single lifestyle, then."

Mom gave me a droll look. "So . . . boxed wine and binging British crime shows?"

"It's like we're related or something." I turned toward the stairs and stopped. Something had been bothering me since I stepped in, but it wasn't until I saw the wall over the stairs that I realized what it was.

"You repainted everything."

Mom has always loved bright colors. We'd painted almost as soon as we moved into the house after Gran Mae died—bright yellow in the kitchen, lime green on the staircase, deep blue in the downstairs bathroom. In a way it had primed me for living in Arizona, with all its rich terra-cottas and turquoise. But now I was standing in the house and the walls were . . . white. Eggshell. Ecru. All the various shades that are just white under different names.

"Oh. Well," said Mom, sounding embarrassed. "I thought it was time for a change. And you know, all those colors, some people might think they were a bit much."

"It's your house," I said. "Who cares what other people think?" Then it occurred to me that there's usually only one reason you repaint all the walls white. "Are you thinking of selling?"

"*No!*" said Mom, nearly a yell. I blinked at her and she flushed. "Sorry, honey, I didn't mean—I'd never sell. Of course I wouldn't."

"Okay. That's fine."

"I'm sorry. That didn't come out like I meant." She was getting flustered, and I tried to salvage the situation.

"No, Mom, really, I wasn't judging. It just surprised me, that's all. It looks very bright and airy." I also thought it looked very generic Suburban White People Chic, but I kept that to myself.

She led the way upstairs to my old room and pushed open the door. I paused on the threshold. She'd repainted here, too, but not ecru.

"Antique Rose," Mom said.

"It's almost the same color as it was when we moved in when I was a kid, isn't it?"

"Is it?" She frowned. "I don't remember."

"I think so." I set my bags down on the bed with a *whump.* "It looks nice," I added, since Mom had the line between her eyebrows again. I actually preferred the old color, which had been a restful blue, but I hadn't lived here for years. It wasn't my place to police what color Mom painted her guest bedroom. Or the rest of her house, for that matter. Still, *ecru.* It's like if you couldn't decide on white or beige and combined the two for maximum blandness.

There was a doily on the chest of drawers. I eyed it warily. I have nothing against doilies, but they're a slippery slope. You start with doilies, then pretty soon it's crocheted table runners and then it's a short step to antimacassars. As if doilies are some kind of larval form, and the table runners are an instar in their development. But then are the antimacassars the adult form, or just a later instar? Perhaps the adult form of the doily bears no resemblance to its juvenile stages.

"Mom," I said, cutting off this chain of thought before it got any weirder. "I love you to pieces but I've been driving for three days and I think I need a nap. I'm getting loopy."

"Oh honey, of course. You must be exhausted."

"Eh, you know." The one good thing about the dig being put on hold only a few days in was that I hadn't yet made the drive up from my apartment in Tucson to the dig site in Oregon. (The phone call had literally caught me heading to the car that morning.) So instead I'd taken my already packed-up car and driven from Tucson to North Carolina, which is a longer trip, mostly involving Texas.

God, there's just so *much* Texas. I could handle all the other states, but Texas lengthwise really breaks you. I attempted to express this to my mother, which mostly involved wild arm gestures and the words *El Paso* uttered at intervals.

"Take a nap," Mom advised. "I was going to order a pizza for dinner."

"You are a saint," I said, collapsing onto the bed. "An absolute saint. Did someone start delivering way out here?"

"There's a place in Siler City that will. Do you still like ham and pineapple?"

"Very much so."

Mom closed the door. I rolled onto my side, still thinking vague thoughts about doilies pupating. I had just gotten to the point of wondering if I could get a grant to study the life cycle of crocheted tablecloths when sleep overtook me.

CHAPTER 2

For a moment when I woke, I had no idea where I was. No, that's not quite accurate—I had no idea *when* I was. I knew that I was in my bedroom in my grandmother's house, but the rose-colored walls meant that I must be ten years old and Gran Mae was alive and I would go downstairs for breakfast and Mom would make eggs and Gran Mae would look disapprovingly at me and ask if I wouldn't like some nice low-fat yogurt instead and I would shake my head and eat my egg. Brad would sit across from me, sixteen and already nearly six feet tall, shoveling in three eggs to my one, but Gran Mae never asked him if he wanted yogurt. Sometimes I wished I was a boy.

If I didn't answer her, she eventually stopped talking at me and started talking to Mom, saying that maybe she shouldn't feed me so much. That was easier. I could pretend they were talking about some other girl and it had nothing to do with me. Mom would say that the other girl was growing and needed protein, and then she'd put the pan in the sink and wipe her hands and say that we had to leave for school. Unless it was Saturday, and then Brad and I would watch cartoons and Mom would be at her other job, so we ate cereal. Mom hadn't come to wake me up, so maybe it was Saturday, and I could go watch *The Smurfs* and *The Real Ghostbusters*. I wanted to be Egon when I grew up. Egon was *cool*.

I stared at the rose-pink wall and part of me was ten years old and another part of me was thirty-two and had a doctorate and had written a thesis on the spread of seed weevils through North American sunflower crops. I had a sudden horrible fear that maybe the ten-year-old was the real one and I had just had a particularly vivid dream and now

I would have to go and live my entire life all over again. I put my hand to my forehead and said, "Fuuuuck..." which ten-year-old me would not have said.

Gran Mae did not teleport to my location to say, *Samantha Myrtle Montgomery, you know what happens to little girls who swear.* (Yes, Gran Mae, I know. The underground children get them.) This was proof positive that she was dead.

I sat up, looked down, and saw that I had breasts bigger than my head, which ten-year-old me most definitely did not have. Right. Thirty-two. Did not have to rewrite my thesis. *Thank you, Jesus.*

I slid out of bed and staggered down the hall to the bathroom. The underground children. Heh. I hadn't thought of that in years. Gran Mae's personal answer to the boogeyman. The underground children got you if you swore, if you disrespected your elders, and possibly if you didn't clean your room, although demands that I clean my room had usually been met with the aforementioned disrespecting of elders, so I wasn't entirely clear on that one.

I pulled open the bathroom drawer, looking for aspirin, and caught a whiff of my grandmother's scent. Something powdery and floral; not roses, but something else. Freesia, maybe. Some of her powder must have spilled in the back of the drawer years ago. How strange that I'd lived in the house for years and it had been our house, not hers. And now, with one coat of paint and a remembered scent, it was like being back at her house all over again.

Getting maudlin, I thought. *Must be low blood sugar.* Dry-swallowed the aspirin, grimaced, reminded myself for the hundredth time to never ever do that again. Blech. I straightened up and saw a note on the mirror at eye level, in my mother's neat handwriting: REFILL TP BEFORE SAM GETS HERE.

I chuckled. My mother leaves notes to herself everywhere. She is meticulous and keeps a planner for work, but at home, the entire house becomes her planner. My brother and I grew up surrounded by her notes to herself: on the refrigerator, on the bathroom mirrors, on end tables and nightstands and tacked to the back of the front door so she'd remember before leaving the house. I checked the strategic toilet paper reserves and found that they were indeed low.

I looked past the note to my reflection in the mirror. I looked pretty rough by my personal standards, but pretty good for having driven across Texas, so I'd call that a win. I tucked a couple stray bits of hair behind my ears. They wouldn't stay. They never do. My hair is a comb-eating monster that is technically "curly," in the same way that a cassowary is technically a bird. It's factual, but leaves out a lot of the kicking-a-man's-bowels-out-through-his-spine bits. Not that my hair has ever done that. To my knowledge.

I galloped downstairs. My legs still remembered the rhythm of the stairs, *tha-thump tha-thump tha-thump*, which my grandmother had always said sounded like a herd of mustangs in the house. Brad had started it, but I picked it up from him out of a combination of sibling hero-worship and solidarity, and here I was, thirty-two years old, doing it again instinctively.

"I'm in here," Mom called from the living room. I swung by the fridge to grab a can of something cold and carbonated and admire the notes currently adorning the door. CHECK WATER FILTER FEB/AUGUST. GET MONEY FOR PHIL. DON'T BUY HUMMUS W/ RED LID—EVIL!

I knew that Phil was the guy Mom hired to cut the lawn, who I'd never met, and the water filter seemed self-explanatory. I was contemplating the potential sins of hummus as I stepped into the living room, then I stopped dead and stared.

There was an old painting over the fireplace, one that had hung there as long as my grandmother had been alive. It was oil paint, or at least trying to look like oil paint, and featured an old-timey bride and groom standing together under an arbor of pale pink roses, gazing into each other's eyes with expressions of wistful bliss or blissful wist or whatever the hell you call that particular sappy expression.

This would have been merely tacky if it had been an ordinary bride and groom, but the groom was wearing a military uniform in Confederate gray, which made it tacky *and* racist. My most vivid memory of the painting was the day that my mother and I moved into the house after Gran Mae died, when Mom took it down from the wall and replaced it with a large woodcut of a fish.

"Mom," I said, struggling with that same sense of double vision, as if I was seeing the bones of my grandmother's house under this one. "What's with the painting?"

"Huh?" She looked around, puzzled. I pointed to the Confederate wedding. "Oh." Her eyes slid away from mine. "Well. Your grandmother loved it, you know . . ."

"Yes, but you *hate* it. You called it Lost Cause bullshit. I thought you threw it away."

"I'm sure you must have misheard me," she murmured, looking into her wineglass. "I wouldn't have thrown that away. Not when Gran Mae loved it so much."

She looked so worried that I tried a different tactic. "What happened to the fish?"

Her gaze sharpened unexpectedly. "You remember the fish?"

"Of course. It was a great fish. And there was a hellgrammite in the stones, and nobody ever draws hellgrammites."

Mom's whole face lit up. I don't know how, but suddenly she looked a decade younger and much more like her old self. "I can't believe you remember that! My friend Theo made it in college, and I carried it around for years." She beamed at me. "It's still in the attic."

"We should put it back up."

"Would you like that?" A trace of the worry crossed her face again. "Well, I . . . well, let's see if I can find it again, maybe we can figure something out . . ."

"I'd love that," I said, deciding on positive reinforcement. Was I doing this right? I strongly believe that you have to confront your older relatives about racist behavior, but I admit, it seemed this was a much easier position to hold before I actually had to do it. Mom was deeply, profoundly liberal, and the Confederate wedding painting shocked the hell out of me. A couple years back, she'd driven the thirty minutes to Pittsboro to join the protests demanding they take down the Confederate veteran statue. So what the hell was this painting doing hanging on her wall?

"Pizza should be here soon," said Mom. She raised a wineglass in my general direction. "I'll be out tomorrow night. I have a client coming in on an early flight the next day, so I'm going to spend the night in Raleigh. I ordered enough pizza for leftovers, but you might still need to go to the store."

"No worries. I'll make a grocery run tomorrow so I'm not eating you out of house and home. Enjoy your escort mission."

Mom is quasi-retired, but she isn't good at it so she works as a media escort these days. Media escorts are basically people wranglers for minor celebrities, keynote speakers, lifestyle gurus, authors on book tours, that sort of thing. Anybody who has a publicist but not a personal jet. She meets these people at the airport or the hotel, has their itinerary all printed up, and drives them to where they need to be. She also handles emergency laundry, makes sure they've got bottles of water, mails packages, makes sure they eat, things like that. Then she drives them back to the airport and sees them off to the next stop. It always struck me as a weird job, but Mom is very good at mothering strangers and accommodating their various requests, and she can make small talk all day long, which is a skill I did not inherit.

"Anybody exciting?" I asked, meandering into the kitchen and locating the box of wine. "Martha Stewart? Salman Rushdie?" She won't gossip about her charges, but I do get tidbits occasionally. Apparently motivational speakers are the absolute worst. Her all-time favorite was a man who wrote a book on bondage for beginners, who she said was genuinely delightful and made his audience give her a round of applause for all her help.

"No, no. A celebrity chef. He's doing a cooking demo and a radio interview, and he specifically requested a case of Cheerwine."

"His funeral." (I know, I know, many North Carolinians will go to bat for Cheerwine. I am not one of them. The stuff tastes like carbonated maraschino cherries.) "Well, good luck. They can't all be Bondage Guy."

Mom giggled, sounding much happier than she had a few hours ago. "He really was just the sweetest. And he still sends me a Christmas card every year."

"Ask if he's single!"

"He's not even forty."

"So?" I squeezed out a generous portion of the finest Malbec cardboard can buy.

"Someday you'll get to an age where you die a little whenever someone doesn't get your movie references." Mom sighed. "The last time I went on a date, I said something about *Silent Running* and he thought I meant the one about the Jamaican bobsled team. I could actually feel the gray hairs sprouting."

"Heh." I dropped onto the couch, checked my phone, remembered that there's no signal worth a damn on Lammergeier Lane, and spent five minutes trying to make it talk to the house internet. (Which is also terrible out here, don't get me wrong. Nobody is running cable down rural roads unless they have a pressing reason.) My phone informed me that it was absolutely talking to the internet, it was happy to talk to the internet, it loved talking to the internet, then as soon as I tried to check my email, it told me it had never heard of the internet and wasn't entirely sure it existed. I dropped the phone on the coffee table and tried to remember how to make conversation like a normal person.

"So what was the deal with the vulture?" I asked.

"Oh! Gail, the woman who lives just around the bend at the end of the road? She does wildlife rehab, or she used to, I think. She says a whole flock lives in a tree on her property. A roost tree, she called it."

"That's cool. A lot of people would freak out having vultures living in their backyard." As a biologist, I disapprove of those people on principle. Scavengers are essential to a tidy planet. Do you really want all the deer that get hit by cars to lie around in the ditches for months on end? No, of course you don't.

"She's an interesting person."

Something clicked. "Wait—the woman at the end of the road? Who owns the big property there? Not the one Gran Mae used to call the old witch?"

Mom stared into her wine. "I'm sure she never said anything so unkind."

"Yes, she did! Don't you remember? She was always saying that her garden was a weed pit and . . ." I trailed off because the expression that had crossed Mom's face was actually scaring me. She had looked worried before, but for a moment, she looked genuinely frightened.

"I *said*," said Mom, in the tone that she used when I was a small child and was Not Getting The Hint, "I'm sure Gran Mae never said *anything like that*."

I swallowed. That tone of voice was the parental equivalent of a shotgun being cocked. Mom hadn't used it on me since before I was old enough to drive. "Uh," I said. "Maybe I'm misremembering." But I wasn't. I knew I wasn't.

She slugged back her wine like a frat boy chugging vodka. "I should check and see if the pizza guy is on the road."

"Maybe I'm misremembering," I repeated, trying to sound conciliatory. Jesus, this was strange, though. Mom hanging up Gran Mae's old painting, and now trying to pretend the "old witch" stuff hadn't happened? Gran Mae had *hated* that woman. I'm fairly certain she only called her an old witch because *bitch* was not a word that Gran Mae allowed to pass her lips, or anyone else's. (Brad had once engaged a family friend in conversation about his dog-breeding business, specifically to watch her flinch at the dinner table.)

Mom couldn't possibly have forgotten. It was one of Gran Mae's favorite topics of conversation. If you mentioned that Gran Mae's roses were looking nice, she'd tell you it was all down to bonemeal and careful tending, which is what it took to make a garden, not just letting it go wild like *some people* did. "Why, Father would never have stood for it for a minute, rest his soul!" she would say. And if you even so much as grunted in a conversational manner at that point or, God forbid, said, "Oh?" she'd be off and running about the woman at the end of the road who called her garden "cottage style" but it looked more like a trailer park what with all the junk in it and the weeds everywhere and at that point you might as well just grow geraniums in a toilet and embrace that you had no class at all.

Gran Mae felt very, very strongly that the world was divided into those with class and those without. I can't remember if she believed in the Rapture, but if she had, only the classy would be saved. I don't know what happened to the non-classy in her cosmology. Possibly the underground children got them, or possibly they were just doomed to live out their days in a giant Walmart of the Damned.

I stared at the Confederate wedding and thought dark thoughts. Gran Mae had been racist, in that Southern heavily-in-denial way, where you think watching Oprah counts as having a black friend. When I had been doing my history homework at the dinner table once, she'd muttered that Dr. King was "just a rabble-rouser," and Mom had given me a grim look over her shoulder and mouthed, *That's not true.*

Fortunately the pizza arrived before I could go too far down that unpleasant memory lane. Mom seemed relieved that I didn't press the issue of the old witch but devoted myself to appreciation of pineapple on pizza.

I had a slice halfway to my mouth when Mom said, "Oh! We should say grace, I think."

I paused. A piece of pineapple slid slowly from the tip of the pizza and landed on the cardboard. "Really?" I said.

We are not a family that says grace over food. Gran Mae always insisted on it, but Mom's Christianity has generally been limited to a fondness for *Jesus Christ Superstar.* I couldn't remember the last time I'd sat at a table where someone prayed over the food. No, wait, I could—it was when Brad's in-laws came to dinner one time in Tucson and they'd done it, while Brad and his wife and I sat around trying to pretend that we were absolutely devout people who prayed all the time, yes sir, no heathens here.

"I'd feel better," said Mom firmly.

Right. Okay. Brad had said there was something odd going on with Mom, and apparently he didn't know the half of it. I set the pizza slice down and folded my hands.

"Lord, bless us for this food we are about to receive . . ." Mom intoned.

As a child, when Gran Mae would say grace, Brad and I would stare at each other across the table. This is why one has siblings, after all. Without Brad to look at, I stared at my folded hands and wondered what on earth was going on.

Had Mom gotten religion suddenly? Was that why Brad thought she'd been acting oddly? It was possible. Still, Christianity doesn't make you repaint the house ecru, as far as I know.

"Amen," said Mom. We carried the boxes into the living room and sat on the couch, eating pizza.

"You told me what a hellgrammite was once, but I forgot," said Mom, as we munched straight from the box. "I know it was the larval form of . . . something." I'd just taken a bite of pizza, so she continued. "Hellgrammite. It sounds like something out of a horror movie."

I swallowed. "Looks like it too," I said. "Very chompy." I made clacking mandible motions at her. "Helllllgrammiiiiite." Mom grinned and refilled my wine. "The adults are dobsonflies. They're pretty freaky too, if you're not a bug person." Normally I'd have pulled up pictures at this point, but I'd have had to get my laptop out to access the internet. It was probably just as well for Mom's digestion that my phone didn't like the Wi-Fi. Dobsonflies are glorious, but not exactly an entry-level species.

She shook her head, clearly bemused. "You got your father's hair and his sense of humor, and I like to think you got my brains—"

"And stunning good looks."

"—but I have no idea where the bug thing came from."

"Clearly a recessive gene. An extremely cool recessive gene." I considered this. "Of course, I also had to get my love of dirt from somewhere. I spend enough time in it. Did Dad . . . ?"

"I assume he made mud pies as a baby, but no, not that I know of." She smiled fondly. "He used to say that he could kill a plastic houseplant."

Dad died when I was nine, which was why we eventually moved in with Gran Mae. You don't have to feel sorry for me, it's fine. I mean, obviously it sucked, but I lived through it and it's ancient history now. Mind you, I had a counselor at school who always wanted me to talk about my feelings, and my feelings even then were pretty much "yeah, it sucks." I'm not great at performative emotions.

"Well, maybe it was Gran Mae, then," I said. "All that gardening was bound to have involved dirt in some fashion."

Mom's smile slipped and she stared into her wine.

Dammit, I'd said something wrong again. Should I just not talk about Gran Mae? But she'd hung up that damn painting, which might as well have been a portrait of the old woman. And she'd defended her commentary on the vulture woman at the end of the road. That didn't sound like she was upset with Gran Mae. Unless she really truly had forgotten about the "old witch" thing. *And* she'd painted the house the same colors that Gran Mae had, and was saying grace just like she had . . .

Good lord, was Mom somehow in belated mourning? For a mother who had died nearly twenty years ago? But why? Granted, she was about the age that Gran Mae had been when she died, that might have shaken something loose, but still . . . (Now *I* sounded like the school counselor.)

The thing is, Mom survived the loss of her husband and raised two kids, lived through her childhood with Gran Mae, which could not have been terribly easy, had a career, took early retirement when the factory shut down, and then started a second career. Successfully, no less. Mom is tough. It's easy to think that sweet people are weak, but if you look at all the stuff Mom's lived through, she's nearly indestructible.

Mourning for Gran Mae? *Now?* Really?

Was *this* what Brad had meant when he said that she was acting odd?

I refilled my wine from the box and wondered what to do. Did I bring up Gran Mae more, try to see if Mom was having genuine lapses in memory or was just seeing everything through rose-tinted glasses? Did I not mention her at all? I didn't want to upset her. She is a genuinely kindhearted person and a champion worrier. If there was an Olympic sport for worrying, Mom would win the gold and then give it to the silver medalist because she was afraid that they might feel bad for losing.

Either way, I wasn't going to do it tonight. I was tired, and I was probably going to be here for weeks. I had plenty of time to get to the bottom of things, hopefully without upsetting Mom.

"So how about a nice British murder?" I said. Mom turned on the TV and we spent the rest of the evening saying, "Oooh! I bet *he* did it! Because he's holding a grudge about the car accident twenty years ago!" and, "She had to kill him to cover up the way she'd tampered with the wine bottles!" and thoroughly enjoying being proved wrong.

The Second Day

Beverly Jenkins: Superb hybrid tea rose, with fine light pink color and exceptional fruit fragrance with notes of apple and plum. Full, mostly solitary blooms, on a tall, upright plant with clean dark green foliage. Excellent resistance to black spot. A superior rose for Southern regions.

CHAPTER 3

"I was thinking," said Mom the next day, in the diffident way she had when there was something she really wanted to do and was hoping that you would also like to do it, but didn't want to make demands in case you didn't, "maybe if you aren't too tired, we could check up in the attic for the fish print you like."

I could have been at death's doorstep and I would have crawled up the stairs to the attic if it meant getting rid of the Confederate wedding. I snapped my laptop closed. "Sure. All I'm doing is reading forums that are two years out-of-date."

The door to the attic looked like all the other doors upstairs, except that it was about six inches off the ground. Mom opened it and we navigated the steps up, which were cluttered with boxes of coat hangers. (Forget maggots; I am convinced that boxes of coat hangers are the real proof of spontaneous generation.)

The attic was frightening, but not in the ghost-and-goblins way. Mostly it was a testimony to your elderly relatives dying with a whole household worth of *stuff*. Picture the warehouse scene in *Raiders of the Lost Ark*, only a lot messier and with boxes labeled KITCHEN and SENTIMENTAL CRAP. (I recognized my own handwriting on that last one.) Gran Mae had died with an attic full of stuff and Mom had only gotten about half of it cleared out. The back of the attic was hidden behind ramparts of boxes and there were old cedar chests that were probably antiques, but getting to them would have required moving so many boxes that both Mom and I would be antiques ourselves by the time we got there.

Horizontal stacks of framed art leaned against one wall in long lines that stuck out at least three feet. Mom cleared a path to them by shoving more coat hangers out of the way, and we both picked a pile and began flipping.

Mine was a mixed bag of old posters from my childhood bedroom and framed samplers of indeterminate origin. They had to be gifts. I couldn't imagine Mom buying a BLESS THIS MESS sampler. Mom was not a "Bless This Mess" kind of person. Nor was she a "Live, Laugh, Love" person, and definitely not a "Prayer Is a Family Value" person. On the other hand, she hadn't been a "Saying Grace" person either, so maybe things had changed.

"One of my coworkers back in the day," said Mom, when I held up PRAYER IS A FAMILY VALUE. "She made everyone in the office one for their birthdays. She meant well. And it's so hard to throw out something handmade."

"I'll throw it out for you right now," I offered. "All part of the service I provide."

"No, it's fine. One of these days I'll clear all this out . . ." She waved aimlessly at the piles of boxes. I accepted this fiction politely.

Once I'd gotten past the sampler layer, I hit a rich vein of embarrassing childhood art, and then got into family photographs. I flipped past my baby photos, my brother's baby photos, my mother's wedding pics—god, she looked so young! And her hair was nearly as big as she was!—another stray sampler, a set of very seventies psychedelic posters, and . . .

"Is this Rasputin?"

"Eh?" Mom looked over. I held out the photo, which was an old-style sepia photo of a bearded man gazing intensely at the camera. She took it, frowning, then her face cleared. "Oh my! No, that's your great-grandfather."

"Looks like the mad monk to me." I took the photo back. My great-grandfather had the same burning gaze with a little too much white around the pupil and the same shaggy beard. He obviously went to the same tailor as Rasputin too: Dusty Black Suits "R" Us.

I flipped the photo over and read the back. "Elgar Mills . . . Hang on, this can't be right. It says 1917. Are you sure this wasn't *your* great-grandfather?"

"Oh no." Mom had finished her stack of art and started on the next one. "He was born in . . . god, I can't remember. 1870-something. He was over sixty when your grandmother was born." She frowned down at the art in front of her. "I got the impression it was a bit of a scandal at the time, but Mother would never talk about it. You know how she hated gossip."

This was not strictly true. Gran Mae was a great fan of gossip about other people. It was only when it got close to home that it became a problem. "Father," she would say, in a tone so Southern that it could have fallen straight from Scarlett O'Hara's lips, "would say that you must never allow your good name to be sullied by other people's mouths." I have no idea how Father was supposed to stop this from happening, mind you, but she would utter this phrase as if it settled the matter, and then usually sweep dramatically out of the room. Gran Mae had an extraordinary capacity for dramatic sweeping.

"So wait a minute," I said, staring into the burning eyes of Elgar Mills, "this is 'Father'? Of 'Father always said' and 'Father would never have allowed' fame?"

"That's the one."

I shook my head, bemused. I hadn't ever given much thought to my great-grandfather, or even my grandfather, who had died before I was born. My interest in my ancestors is on a rather longer timescale. You want to talk about the Saxons, I'm here for it. Immediate ancestors, meh. Once you get to flush toilets, they don't even leave a good midden.

On the other hand, "Father" certainly appeared to have predated the flush toilet, and possibly the Saxons. "How long did this guy live, anyway?"

Mom frowned. "He died when Mom was a teenager, so he must have been in his eighties, I think?"

I wondered if he'd still had that intense gaze in his eighties. The man in the photo was definitely not young. Gran Mae had never talked about "Father" as being an old man.

On the other hand, looking at him, you could certainly believe that "Father would never have allowed" a lot of things. It was hard to imagine him doing any of the social things that Gran Mae had considered important. Charity suppers. Debutante balls. That sort of thing. Elgar looked more like the type to organize a cult meeting, or maybe bump off a Russian tsar.

"He certainly looks . . ." I tried to find a diplomatic phrase. "Formidable."

"Oh yes. And quite a character too. There were all sorts of rumors back in the day, that he was a wizard or warlock or something like that."

"Huh," I said, mildly surprised. I typically associate wizards and warlocks with Dungeons & Dragons, not with my maternal relatives. "What, did he go around turning people into toads? I can't imagine Gran Mae would have approved of that."

"Well, obviously the rumors weren't *true.*"

"Good to know!"

"I just think he was old and eccentric and a bit of a hermit and you know what people were like back then."

Generally I would condemn the superstitiousness of small-town folk, but I have to admit that it wasn't much of a leap, given Elgar's appearance. If you had to pick a warlock out of a lineup, you'd point at that guy every time.

"Here we go!" Mom crowed, lifting out a frame. The fish glared out, wearing the angry expression common to most large freshwater fish.

I cheered and set down Father aka Rasputin. "There's my hellgrammite!"

We tromped downstairs with the woodcut. "Shall we take down the Confederate wedding?" I asked.

"I . . . oh . . . well . . ." She stared at Lost Cause: The Matrimony Edition. "I suppose no one would mind for a little while, would they?"

"Who is going to mind? It's your house."

28

"And you love that fish." Mom pressed her lips together, then rushed into the kitchen and came back with a chair. I helped steady her while she took down the Confederate wedding and handed up the woodcut, wondering why it seemed like such a big deal. Was she afraid of someone seeing it? Was she dating a KKK member and didn't want to tell me?

No, that was ridiculous. So what the hell was going on?

She hefted the painting. The groom gazed wistfully over her shoulder as she went down the hall, and I heard a door opening upstairs.

Well, small victories. I gazed up at the hellgrammite with great pleasure. They're a monstrous little creature that will bite your toes if you stick them in the water, but they're also very useful for assessing water quality. You just don't get them in polluted water.

Mom came back down a few minutes later, carrying a suitcase. "All right. I'm off to Raleigh. Call if you need anything, honey."

"If I can get the phone to work. Text if you think of anything I can pick up at the grocery store." We exchanged hugs and off she went. I sank down on the couch to read forums and bask in the warm glow of a marvelous and underappreciated arthropod.

I put my feet up on the coffee table. In the back of my head, a little voice whispered, "Father would *never* permit it . . ."

Screw you, Rasputin, I thought cheerfully. *And Gran Mae too.* The dead have to keep their feet on their floor. Let the living put their feet on the table if they feel like it.

CHAPTER 4

The grocery store in Pondsboro had changed since I was a kid, and mostly for the better. It used to be a Piggly Wiggly. I know people get extremely nostalgic about Piggly Wiggly, but it was basically a gas-station convenience store writ large. The lighting always had that peculiar jittery fluorescent quality that you get in gas stations, and the frozen pizzas should have been banned by the Geneva Convention.

The replacement, Food Lion, is still a midrange Southern grocery store, but it's several steps above the Pig. I loaded up on frozen pizzas that did not count as war crimes, bagged salads, and another couple boxes of wine. If I had to get Mom drunk and giggly to get her to tell me what was going on, that was a sacrifice that my liver was willing to make.

The vulture was back on the mailbox when I got home. I stared at it. It stared back. I wondered if I should offer it a frozen pizza in return for not vomiting on me. Then I wondered if I should get the mail, or if the mail truck would even deliver if there was a vulture on the mailbox. Rain and snow and sleet and hail were one thing, but large scavenger birds was quite another.

"Hi," I said.

The bird did not reply. Mind you, I'm not sure what I would have done if it had. The breeze tugged at its feathers, but it remained as still as a statue.

"I'm . . . just gonna . . . go inside, here . . ." I said, giving it the widest berth I could. It turned its head to watch as I went up the walk to the front door, which I did sideways, in case it began to make vomiting motions.

I had one foot on the doorstep when it half-spread its wings, and I nearly jumped out of my skin. Then it settled, turning away as if it was bored now. How did you get rid of nuisance vultures? They were undoubtedly protected by the Migratory Bird Treaty Act, which meant you couldn't kill or harass them, or disturb their nest sites. Would an air horn count as harassment? How about yelling "Shoo!" really loudly, while wearing a hazmat suit against vulture puke?

These are the questions that try women's souls. I went inside.

It was very quiet in the house. I'd forgotten how quiet it was in the country. My apartment in Tucson is smack in the middle of the city and there's always an underlying hum of traffic. I set the grocery bags on the counter and began unloading them, making as much noise as possible with the cupboard doors and the refrigerator drawers, but it only made the quiet feel louder by contrast.

It was just a little bit creepy.

Which was ridiculous, of course. Creepy is for old Gothic mansions and run-down cabins out in the woods, not cookie-cutter houses in the middle of a subdivision. Hell, Lammergeier Lane wasn't even cookie-cutter enough to be *Stepford Wives* material. If a serial killer tried to break in, he'd be up against Mr. Pressley, and my money was not on the serial killer.

No, it was all perfectly normal. Normal house. Normal everything. Normal colors on the walls, even. Gran Mae would have been pleased by that. She'd always wanted everything to be normal. "Nice and normal" was one of her favorite phrases. When Mom came home from work late and asked how we had been, Gran Mae would say, "Nice and normal!" every time. It didn't matter if Brad had been blasting music through the door until Gran Mae yelled at him to stop that god-awful racket, or if I was crying because I was ten years old and life was a lot, it was always "Nice and normal!" when Gran Mae was watching us.

(I'm pretty sure Mom didn't actually believe this, but Mom was stuck, and all she could do was work two jobs until she had the money to get us out of there. Like many family dynamics, it didn't have to be healthy, it just had to work.)

I left the kitchen and went to the living room. Still too quiet. I could hear the clock on the mantel ticking, and the grinding sound of the air conditioner running upstairs. I opened my laptop but found myself staring at the fish instead, eyes tracing the swirling lines of ink framed by the blandness of the white wall.

The ecru and eggshell was bothering me more than I expected. More than I wanted it to bother me. It wasn't my place to judge the paint. Mom will always bend over backward to accommodate her family, way more than is healthy, and Brad and I have gotten in the habit of trying to be gently supportive of anything she does for herself. If she liked those colors, I was going to be gently supportive if it killed me.

They say you can't go home again, but of course you can. It's just that when you get there, somebody may have repainted and changed the fixtures around.

The clock ticked.

Ecru. Jesus. Mom had never been an ecru type. Of course, she'd never been a Confederate-wedding-over-the-mantelpiece type either. That was all Gran Mae.

Ironically, even Gran Mae hadn't had the photo of Great-Grandaddy Rasputin out on display. Possibly he wasn't nice-and-normal-looking enough.

Another tick.

"Right," I said out loud. "If I'm going to be miserable, at least I'll be productively miserable."

I looked back down at my laptop and set to work on The Project.

Oh god, The Project.

To give you the very quick version, museums and colleges and other institutes that keep insect collections for entomologists are almost always strapped for cash and, more importantly, for space. Whenever they want room for a new exhibit or a new lab or whatever, they look for things to toss out, and sooner or later, they trip over drawers and boxes and bulky cabinets full of bugs on cards and they say, "Isn't this all on the internet now? Why are we keeping it here? Who cares about dead bugs anyway?" (This is why entomologists drink.) Cue dozens of frantic scientists trying to tell them that it's actually really important and some of these are the type of specimen that defines the entire species and they say, "Okay, so find someone to take it."

For years, that someone was Rudd College, a dinky little liberal arts school in Michigan, which, for reasons known only to their donors, had a gigantic entomology department. They probably took in half the orphaned collections in the country.

And then they had a fire.

What the flames didn't get, the sprinklers did. Complete loss. Absolutely irreplaceable specimens, some of which went extinct before we even got around to assigning them a genus. (This is also why entomologists drink.)

But! All was not lost! Rudd College had conscientiously documented each and every specimen that passed through their doors, taking multiple photos of each one. Great! Wonderful! We could salvage something!

Then somebody actually looked at the collection, and it was on about a hundred little unlabeled data cards and the file names were all DC1247.JPG and DC9495.JPG and so on and so forth for *thousands* of photos. So if I wanted to go look up, say, the type specimen for *Vostox apicedentatus*, the toothed earwig, I would have to trawl through all these photos until I actually saw it, and hope that its label was still attached and legible in the photo, and also reckon with the fact that it would probably have been labeled *Spongovotox apicendatatus* because taxonomy is a harsh mistress. (This is why biologists of every stripe drink.)

Dr. Wilcox was bound and determined that these photos be useful again, so whenever we caught up on our current projects, she'd tell us to go work on The Project. Pull up a photo, stare at it, check the ID label, check to make sure it was actually correctly ID'd, change the file name to the species, put in a note that said what collection we thought it was from, if we knew. Pull up another photo, rinse, repeat.

It is *exactly* as thrilling as it sounds. But I was on furlough and unemployment doesn't cover a lot and Dr. Wilcox was willing to fudge the budget a bit and pay me under the table to work on The Project.

(Also, the toothed earwig doesn't actually have teeth. The male's got one little pointy bit on his forceps. That's the only way to tell them from other earwig species. [This is yet another reason why entomologists drink.] Anyway, they live entirely inside rotting cacti, so you are unlikely to run afoul of one unless you spend a lot of time kicking over dead barrel cacti, in which case you probably deserve the occasional earwigging. That's a technical term. Trust me, I'm a scientist.)

I spent probably two hours pulling up photos and changing file names. Some of the photos would require a specialist—don't ask me to do ants, ants are *hard*—and one had a label that was, shall we say, a triumph of optimism over reality. I figured two hours was enough to earn my pittance for the day, stood up, stretched, and decided to go wander around the garden for a bit.

The sliding glass door from the living room let out onto a small deck. There was an oval of lawn in the center of the yard, and the rest was taken up by roses. If it had changed since my grandmother's day, I couldn't see it. The roses were still thick and lush, hugging the wooden fence and running riot across the small white shed in the corner. A climbing rose had spread into the cedar tree in the back corner and I could see a spray of pale yellow roses dangling thirty feet above the ground.

I was struck again by the same feeling I'd had yesterday when I woke up, that I had somehow stepped back in time. The garden looked exactly as it had when Gran Mae was alive. We hadn't done much to change that, admittedly—a few large containers with tomatoes, the obligatory potted basil. Now even those were gone. Perhaps that wasn't that strange. Mom had never been much of a gardener, and certainly she had never been one for garden gnomes or anything like that. (Gran Mae would have had apoplexy if a garden gnome appeared among her roses. Cement garden statuary was not *classy*.)

I brushed my fingertips against a pink rose by the deck railing, inhaling the scent when the memory appeared in my head, clear as day, of my grandmother cutting one and nipping the thorns off the stem with a pair of pink-handled pliers. She wore light green gardening gloves and the sun shone through her white hair like a halo. She tucked the pink rose behind my ear and smiled. "You could be so pretty at your coming out."

Gran Mae believed strongly in coming out and debutante balls. I couldn't have been much more than eight or nine at the time, but I was a child of a different era entirely, so I had a vague notion that Gran Mae thought I was a lesbian. I hadn't given it a lot of thought one way or the other. I didn't think I was a lesbian, but then again, the boys in my class were gross, so being a lesbian might be the sensible option. (Fortunately for all involved, I asked Mom about it, not Gran Mae, and when Mom had finished laughing herself sick, she explained that no, Gran Mae meant an entirely different kind of coming out, and I didn't have to decide on boys or girls or both or neither any time soon.)

It was warm and humid and just as silent in the backyard as it had been in the house. I couldn't hear any birds or katydids or frogs. The air didn't have that oppressive feel of an oncoming storm, but it felt . . . I don't know, *flat*, like a soda that had been left out too long and lost all the carbonation.

I stepped down off the deck. I heard a car passing, and either it was very far away, or sound really was muffled back here. But it wasn't until I wandered up to the roses against the fence that I finally put my finger on what was bothering me.

There were no insects in the garden.

Yes, it's impossible. I know it's impossible. I am telling you this, knowing that it was impossible. The impossibility is the point. There were no honeybees rolling around in the golden sepals of the single rose blossoms, no flower longhorn beetles dusted in pollen, no aphids coating the stems. There were no hoverflies, no fat bumblebees or blundering carpenter bees. No buzz, no cricket chirp, no hum or wings. There were no insects, *period.*

I started checking everywhere. I examined the undersides of leaves, I separated petals looking for crab spiders lying in ambush, I scuffed the leaf litter under the rosebushes looking for stray millipedes. *Nothing.*

What the hell kind of spray was Mom using on these roses? DDT? Mom belongs to the generation that believes if it's organic, it's probably safe, but you can pack a lot of evil into organic chemistry. And if it wasn't Mom, was it the mysterious Phil, who cut the grass and raked the leaves?

I was gonna have a word with whoever it was. This was an entomological Superfund site.

"There used to be bugs," I muttered, standing in the middle of the garden. "I remember them." Gran Mae showing me ladybugs when I was small. A praying mantis balanced on a stem. A wheel bug, with its prehistoric-looking fin and tiny head, packing a bite that would send you screaming. I had been outside with a field guide and a camera regularly from sophomore year on, making up spreadsheets of every insect I could find on Lammergeier Lane. (Possibly this tells you something about the kind of teenager I was. No, I did not go to prom. I did, however, photograph the only funereal duskywing ever recorded in the county, so there.)

Now there was nothing. I could not have checked one box of those long-ago spreadsheets. The roses exhaled their perfume into the humid afternoon air, and the only living thing around to smell it was yours truly.

"There used to be . . ." I said again, frustrated and alarmed, and went back inside to text my mother to ask what she was spraying.

⌒

Of course my phone didn't work. Right. No signal. It assured me that it was definitely talking to the house Wi-Fi, provided I didn't ask it to do anything like actually use said Wi-Fi. My laptop confirmed that the Wi-Fi did indeed exist, even if it was slow. I grumbled and went out front.

The vulture was gone, thankfully. I wandered up and down the road, holding my phone in the air, trying to get a bar of signal. I'm sure Mr. Pressley loved that. ("That's her, Officer! She was meandering! *Meandering in the first degree!*")

Finally, halfway down the road, I got a bar of signal, and then my phone beeped as texts piled up. Mom, saying she'd gotten to the hotel. Mom, asking if I was okay. Mom, asking if I was okay again. Mom, telling me to call her when I got the message. Mom, remembering that my phone wasn't working.

I called. She picked up immediately. "I can barely hear you, honey. Are you outside?"

"It's the signal," I said, hearing static building on the line. "I might cut out. I'm fine."

"Oh *good*." Did she sound more worried than usual? I couldn't tell, between the bad connection and anxiety being Mom's middle name. "Did you—*zzzt*—groceries?"

"Yeah, I'm stocked up." I resisted the urge to yell into the phone, since that wouldn't help. "Mom, I have a question!"

"Yes?"

"What are you spraying on the roses?"

"What?"

"The roses! In the garden! What spray are you using on them?"

"I don't—*zzt*—thing."

"Really?" I was pretty sure she was telling the truth. Mom knew about my feelings on insecticides, but she wouldn't lie to my face just to avoid conflict. That left the mysterious Phil. "Gotcha."

"Can't—*zzt! zzt!*—row night. Will you be—*zzt garble zzt hssshhhh!*"

"You're breaking up, Mom. Text me, and I'll try to check in."

"*Zzzt!* Love you!"

I hung up. A minute later, my phone buzzed with a text. Mom saying she loved me again, she was sorry she wasn't home, and if there was any problem at all, I could come and stay at the hotel with her. In fact, I could come and stay even if I didn't have a problem. I rubbed my face wearily. This is why Mom is great at her job, but it's a little overwhelming to be one of her kids. I texted back that I was completely fine and was probably going to turn in early because I was still tired from driving. This diverted her concerns into a different, easier to handle channel, and I agreed that yes, it had been a long drive and I would get some sleep, yes, and then mercifully was able to type, "Talk to you tomorrow!"

It was late afternoon. I leaned against my car. I could hear a frog calling somewhere nearby, and a couple of katydids beginning their repetitive *zeee-dik! zeee-dik!* sounds. (Oblong-winged katydids, in case you're wondering. Get enough of them together and it sounds like the shrubs are full of maracas.)

There *were* bugs out here. That was a relief. It wasn't some kind of massive pesticide drift from a farm or something. (I had been skeptical, since we don't have big farms anywhere in the immediate area, but that stuff can travel.)

I wanted to call Brad and talk to him about Mom, but I'd need much better signal. I suspected that it was going to be a long phone call, and discussing whether your relatives are acting oddly is hard enough without constant static interruptions. So in the end I just texted him that I'd gotten in safely and I'd talk to him tomorrow, and went back inside to break into the boxed wine.

⌒

It was too quiet all evening. I ate cold pizza and drank too much wine. The box said that I should pair it with chimichurri sauce and salsa dancing. The box was going to get British murder shows and like it. Tonight was *Inspector Lowell Mysteries*, which features a gruff DI solving crimes with his sarcastic assistant and his lovable Scottie dog, Magnus. I have seen every episode at least twice, but fortunately there are nearly a hundred episodes and I'm bad with faces, so I had about a 50 percent chance of remembering who killed who on any given one.

"Don't trust that guy," I told Inspector Lowell. "He's got an alibi. People with alibis in the first half of the show are always suspicious."

Even with the TV on, it was still too quiet. When I had to pause the show to go get more wine, I felt like I was standing in a mausoleum.

I missed my roommate's cat. Salem is a demanding jerk, but having a cat around means that there are never any unexplained noises. If something crashes or thumps or goes bump in the night, you think, *It's that damn cat again*, and don't worry about it. Not that anything was crashing or thumping, but the house had that sort of fraught silence that magnified any noise that did occur. The ice maker in the fridge came on with its horrible grinding noise while my back was turned and I nearly jumped out of my skin.

"This is ridiculous," I muttered, when I had recovered from the ice maker's attempt to give me a heart attack. I grew up in this house, for Christ's sake. I couldn't really be thrown this badly off-kilter by a paint job and a fucked-up old painting, could I?

And Mom losing all that weight. And the way she seems more anxious than usual—although she might just be getting older, that happens to everybody. And . . . dammit, no, there's nothing wrong, why am I acting like this?

I went and checked the locks on all the doors. We never used to lock the doors, but it was reflex after living in the city. The sliding glass door was unlocked. I locked it. Then I unlocked it, and locked it again, just to be sure. I went back to the wine and the murders.

I was right about the guy with the alibi, who had given his wife sleeping pills so that he could go out and strangle the vicar. (I am still not entirely sure what vicars are, since we don't have them over here. I think they're like cozy priests? As far as I can tell, they primarily exist in order to solve murders or be murdered on British crime shows.) I was wrong on the next one, where the person who looked guilty was cleared and then had the temerity to turn around and actually *be* guilty. How dare he?

By nine thirty, I was ready to call it a night. "I'm a wild woman," I told Inspector Lowell. I drained the last of my wine and put the glass in the sink, then went to bed.

Nothing tapped at my window or clawed at my door. There were no mysterious footsteps in the attic or voices in the hall. I pulled the covers over my head to keep away monsters and listened to the silence until I fell asleep.

The Third Day

Ladybug: An eye-catching striped rose featuring velvety red single blooms stippled with white. This vigorous, disease-resistant climber is covered in deep green foliage that sets off the multitude of small blooms produced in large sprays. Fragrance is sweet and contains notes of apple and grape.

CHAPTER 5

I slept late, but at least when I woke up, I didn't have the weird moment of dislocation where I might have been ten years old again. I made coffee, scrolled around on my laptop until social media had made me sufficiently angry, then wandered out into the garden with my coffee cup.

The roses were beautiful, they really were. It wasn't too hot yet, and the humidity helped spread a light, delicious scent. The garden was lovely, just as Gran Mae had designed it. I just would have thought it was a lot lovelier if there were insects in it. I sipped my coffee, then padded over to the little white shed in the corner.

The door wasn't locked. I pulled it open, wondering if there was a clue inside as to the Mystery of the Nonexistent Arthropods. A leaking barrel of DDT, say. A promotional flyer from Permethrins Forever. *Something.*

All I found was a potting table covered in dust, some old terra-cotta pots, and a row of garden tools, most of which were now 50 percent rust by weight. "Come on, there's got to be some cobwebs at least . . ." I muttered, checking the corners.

There were not. I was standing in the one shed in the universe that was not inhabited by cobweb spiders. (Family *Theridiidae.* I don't actually know every arthropod family, but I always kinda liked that one's name because of the double *i*'s in the middle.) This was deeply weird. There are cobweb spiders in *everything.* Every continent, pretty much every human dwelling, if you build it, a cobweb spider will show up. A dusty shed without them felt deeply unnatural.

I moved a stack of pots. Old newspapers spread over the table, yellowing with age. From 2003, according to the dates. Not long before Gran Mae died. She'd kept puttering around in the garden until the end, although she never planted anything but roses.

A flash of pink caught my eye. I picked up a small pair of jeweler's pliers, the plastic handles still bright. Gran Mae had used these to break the thorns off rose stems. I'd just been thinking of them yesterday, hadn't I?

There was nothing that immediately indicated why there wouldn't be any insects in the garden. No conveniently leaking pesticide barrels. I rubbed my forehead, probably leaving a smear of dust behind. The dusty shelves were full of glass jars. Could one be unlabeled DDT? Seemed unlikely, but you do find really weird stuff in people's sheds. Job security for future archaeologists, anyway.

I poked around. The dim, dusty light made it hard to tell what I was looking at, but there were no jars of strange liquid or suspicious granules. There was a baby food jar full of nails, which is possibly the only thing more common in sheds than cobweb spiders.

A small wrapped bundle looked promising until I unrolled it and found a dozen candles. They'd been partly burned down, but were otherwise just ordinary white candles. For use in case the power went out? Maybe? I had no idea why Gran Mae would keep them in the shed, though. If a tree's come down on a power line, you certainly don't want to go fumbling out to the shed looking for candles.

There was a bag of rock salt next to the candles. Hard on slugs and snails, but it didn't explain the insects. A quantity of salt that would damage insects would have also killed the roses, I imagine.

I stepped out of the shed and pulled the door closed behind me. While that had certainly been an exciting diversion, it didn't get me any closer to figuring out why the garden was an ecological dead zone. Salt and candles may ward off evil influences in some cultures, but I'm pretty sure that they weren't keeping aphids at bay.

I was halfway back to the deck when I saw a spark of red on the petals of a rose and peered closer. My heart leapt. An insect! They weren't completely gone from the yard!

Granted, it was an invasive Asian lady beetle, not one of my favorite leggy friends. They bite and they tend to swarm buildings, although you can't really blame them for that last one, because most ladybug species will swarm, given the right circumstances. But it was alive! It was here! (Mind you, I still didn't want to get too close. Asian lady beetles secrete smelly goop as a defense. They're no brown marmorated stink bug, but it's still not a terribly pleasant experience.)

"Ladybug, ladybug, fly away home..." I murmured. "Your house is on fire, your children are gone." Gran Mae used to sing that to the ladybugs. I remembered her pulling down a rose and showing me the ladybug, then singing the song. I must have been young, because I started to cry at the thought of the ladybug's house burning down. "It didn't really," she told me. "It's just a silly rhyme. Ladybugs don't live in houses. They live in the garden, and we want as many as we can get."

She had always liked them. She said they were the one good insect. She even bought bags of them to release in the garden to eat the aphids. Which made me wonder what this little guy was eating, or at least, what its larvae had been eating.

"Did you fly in from somewhere? There's no aphids for your babies here." I tilted the rose, watching the lady beetle climb between the petals. The stem between my fingers was absolutely clean, not a tiny green body in sight. I shook my head. "There should be a lot more of you," I said, "but there's nothing for you to eat. Or if not you, at least... you know. Two-spotted. Nine-spotted. Something." (Yes, I was standing here talking to a ladybug. I do that. Don't judge me.)

The ladybug was unimpressed. It reached the edge of the rose and its carapace snapped open to reveal the delicate wings underneath. "Why aren't there more of you?" I said plaintively. It didn't answer. I tilted the rose, jabbed myself on a thorn, and cursed. The rose snapped back and the ladybug flew away while I was sucking on my finger and thinking dark thoughts.

I went out into the front yard to check my texts. It was easy to tell when I got into a patch of good signal because my phone started chirping madly. Five texts from Mom, asking if I was okay, how I slept, if I was okay, to ping her when I got the texts, and apologizing for having bothered me.

Even for Mom, this was special. She was definitely more anxious than she had been. Either something was bothering her, or . . . well, I couldn't say for sure. I reassured her that I was alive, threw on clothes, and got my car keys. It was time to call my brother and get to the bottom of this.

⁓

Pondsboro has one good coffee shop. It probably has a name, but more importantly, it has the word COFFEE in large letters over the door. I went in and ordered something extravagant in the mocha genus, with extra whipped cream.

The barista was a woman so goth that she probably bled black mascara, but her coffee was top-notch. I sagged into a chair. "You have saved a life," I said.

"It's what I do." She sized me up. "New in town?"

"Visiting my mom. I grew up around here, but it's been a while."

"Well, we're open until seven on weekdays. *And* we have reliable Wi-Fi."

"You know your clientele." I set my laptop to download the next batch of photos for The Project, a task that would have strained Mom's house Wi-Fi to its limit, and went outside to make a phone call. (People who talk loudly on the phone in coffee shops are one of the minor banes of existence.) The street was deserted. I leaned against my car and punched the contact button.

It was still early in Arizona, but Brad answered the phone anyway. "Sam?"

I considered various greetings and methods for easing him into the conversation, but settled instead on, "Brad, what the hell is going on?"

He groaned over the phone line. "I have absolutely no idea. You see it too, though?"

"She's . . . jumpy. I don't know. Anxious. More than usual, I mean. Not just anxious that everybody's happy, but *really* anxious."

"Yeah." Brad sighed. "That's what I thought."

"And she's lost a lot of weight."

"I know. She says the doctor says she's fine."

"They always say that when you lose weight," I said grimly. "You could be shooting heroin twice a day and if you lost weight, it'd be 'Just keep doing whatever you're doing!'"

Brad made a noncommittal noise. The men in my family all have fully functioning thyroids and never put on a drop of fat until they hit forty. I resent it greatly.

"Do you think something's wrong? Like, somebody blackmailing her or something?"

I stared at the sky. "Blackmail Mom? What kind of secrets could she have?"

"How should I know?" He sounded exasperated. "Okay, maybe not blackmail. Maybe she's got a stalker."

"She still leaves the front door unlocked," I said. "But okay, yeah, maybe."

"Do you know, she told Maria not to visit?"

"Whaaaat?" I actually pulled the phone away from my ear and stared at it, as if that would make the statement make sense. "But she loves Maria! She says she's the best thing that ever happened to you!"

Brad's voice softened. "She's not wrong there. I don't know what I'd do without her."

I grinned despite everything. My big strong he-man brother, former marine, had fallen in love with a tiny little Latina woman from Tucson, who he could pick up with one arm and who doted on him utterly. (And if you've never heard a man with a rural North Carolina accent speak Spanish, it is a feast for the ears.) "How *is* Maria?"

"Oh, she's doing great. But Mom doesn't want her visiting."

I leaned against the car, trying to make sense of it. The Confederate wedding flashed across my mind. "Is it a . . ." I looked around, making sure no one was around to hear me say something terribly shameful about my mother. "Is it a racist thing?"

"I don't *know.* That was my first thought, but it's *Mom.*" His frustration came over the line loud and clear. I could practically see him dragging his hand over his jarhead haircut.

And he was right to be frustrated. Mom *loved* Maria. We'd had Thanksgiving in Tucson a couple years running, because I was working out of ASU and it was just easier for Mom to fly out to Arizona. Every time it had ended with Mom and Maria in the kitchen, drunk on wine and cackling together like loons, while Maria taught Mom all the really foul swear words in Spanish. Frankly, if Brad and Maria ever divorced, I was pretty sure Mom would keep Maria and tell Brad he was out of the will.

"What does Maria think?" I asked, staring up at the sky. A vulture circled overhead, probably wondering if I was dead yet or planning to become so in the near future.

Brad sighed. "*She* doesn't think it's a race thing."

"Oh thank god," I said involuntarily. Ultimately, I'm still just a white woman from the South, with the accompanying combination of hypersensitivity and total obliviousness. "What does she think it is?"

"She doesn't know. But she broke her foot last time we went out there—did you hear about that? One of those big glass-fronted cabinets, you know? The hinges went loose on one and fell down and landed on her foot. Broke it in three places, total mess."

I winced. "Yeesh. Is it better now?"

"Yeah, they took the pins out a couple months ago. She says she can feel when there's a rainstorm coming now, but fortunately that only happens a couple times a year out here."

"Heh." I missed the dry heat. In another month or two, the humidity would be high enough here that the state would feel like a giant armpit.

"Right. Anyway, after that happened, right before we left, Mom hugged her really hard and told her not to come back. Said it wasn't safe. Maria said she seemed genuinely scared for her."

The vulture was joined by another one, still circling overhead. They had big pale semicircles at the tips of their wings.

I didn't know how to deal with the idea of Mom being threatened, so I picked a different topic entirely. "Do you remember when we were little kids and Gran Mae would threaten us with the underground children?"

"The underground . . . Oh lord." His snort made the line crackle with static. "I'd forgotten about that. *Brad, eat your carrots or the underground children will come for you.*"

"That's the one, yep." The vultures swung in their low circle. "Where did she get that, anyway?"

"No idea. People from that generation have all kinds of weird stories, don't they? Like if you wank, you get hair on your palms, and if you swallow chewing gum, it'll clog up your stomach until you die. And you don't even want to know the stuff Maria's grandmother told her about La Llorona coming for you if you're near water. She still crosses herself when she sees an owl."

I wondered what Maria would think of our resident vultures. "That's probably more like the underground children than the one about swallowing chewing gum."

"I always got them mixed up with the starving children, you know? *Clean your plate, there's starving children in . . .* I dunno, wherever they were having a famine at the time. Like if we left food on our plates, these children would come out of the ground and take it and then they'd want drinks to go with it and a straw for the drinks and . . ."

"Brad, that's the plot of *If You Give a Mouse a Cookie.*"

He was silent for a moment, then said, "Son of a bitch. So it is. Another childhood trauma vanquished by science."

It was my turn to snort. "I just thought they were like the boogeyman. They lived underground and would come up and get you if you were bad."

"That's a lot more logical. I used to have nightmares about them."

"You did?"

"Yeah." He sounded embarrassed. "You were probably too little to remember. I really did think they'd come out of the ground. I just remember dreaming about these weird pale children, all white and twiggy, reaching for me."

"Gah. That sounds awful."

"Yeah, well. I was only six or seven, and you were a baby. I think Mom yelled at Gran Mae about filling my head with scary stories and she stopped for a bit, though."

I nodded, forgetting he couldn't see me. She obviously hadn't stopped completely, because I remembered the underground children too.

"I used to have nightmares about her," I offered. "That she was grabbing my hand and stabbing it with rose thorns, and telling me to let them taste me." I snorted. "Can you imagine?"

"Uh," said Brad. "Sam."

His voice had gone very odd suddenly. "What?" I said. "It was just a dream."

"No, it wasn't. That happened. When you were about five, I think."

"*What?*"

"I don't know what she said to you," said Brad. "I was watching from upstairs. I must have been eleven or twelve, and the window overlooks the garden. I saw her grab your hand and squeeze it around a rose stem. Then you started screaming and she let go and Mom came running."

"That sadistic old *cow*." My chest felt tight. I'd had nightmares about that for years.

"I tried to say something," said Brad, "but she'd already told Mom that you grabbed the rose yourself. You know how it is when you're a kid—you can't argue with an adult. You're always wrong and you end up having to apologize, no matter what. And you were five, so it wasn't like it was strange that you'd forget the thorns."

"Fuck."

"I'm sorry, Sam." He sounded genuinely miserable. "I didn't let you out of my sight for years after that when we were at her house. You were my baby sister and I should have protected you."

"I don't care about that." Any outrage I felt on behalf of child-me was swamped in the wrath that Brad, at eleven, was running himself ragged having to protect me from adults. "I don't remember it happening. She was always so careful about snapping the thorns off for bouquets, I never imagined . . . Christ, no *wonder* you hated her."

"So much. Living with her after Dad died . . . God. I was counting down the days until I could get out and enlist, but I couldn't until you and Mom were out too."

"I remember the screaming fights you'd have," I said dully. "But you never told Mom."

"How could I? She was working around the clock trying to get enough money that we could get out. And it wasn't like she could fix Gran Mae."

He'd never told me any of this. Then again, I suppose when you're sixteen, you don't tell your ten-year-old sister about your emotional struggles.

Of course, this brought us back to Mom. I took a deep breath and went for the question I'd been trying to avoid. "Do you think Mom's . . . do you think it might be in her head? Maybe an early symptom of something?" Words like *dementia* floated through my head but I didn't have the courage to say them out loud.

Brad was silent for a bit, then said, "I don't know. That's what I'm afraid of."

"Right." I nodded again. "Right, okay."

"Is it anything other than being jumpy?"

"Well . . . we were talking about Gran Mae, and she claimed she didn't remember her calling the woman at the end of the road the old witch."

Brad snorted explosively again. "She did that all the time! I don't even know that poor woman's real name!"

"Thank god you remember it too. I was starting to think I was . . ." I almost said *going crazy* and then it seemed like it would be in really poor taste, so I didn't.

"She bitched about it constantly. It was one of her favorite topics. Mom doesn't remember?"

"She says she doesn't. But I think it might be more rose-tinted glasses than actually forgetting." I told him my half-baked theory about her age and Gran Mae's death and Mom being in delayed mourning.

"I guess that's possible," he said, sounding doubtful. "I can't believe she's mourning that awful bitch, but brains are weird sometimes. What do we do about that?"

"Jesus, I dunno. I got into archaeology because live people were too much trouble."

"Maria says gringos are shit at mourning."

"She's not wrong there."

"Can you talk to Mom about Gran Mae? Maybe see if she wants to talk about it?"

I opened my mouth to say that I had tried to talk about Gran Mae and Mom hadn't seemed pleased, but I realized nearly everything I'd said had been critical. If Mom was genuinely missing her mother, then I should be sharing positive memories, right? Nobody responds well, when grieving, to, "Don't be sad, they were freaky and a little scary and had a Southern nostalgic racism thing going on and also I just found out they once impaled my hand for fun when I was a toddler."

"I guess I'll . . . see what I can do," I said. Positive memories. Right. Gran Mae hadn't exactly been an easy woman to live with, but surely I could think of something. Probably. If I had a few minutes.

"Call me any time," said Brad. "If you need money, tell me. I'll do anything I can. Hell, she could move in with us, if she needed to. Maria said she wouldn't mind."

"You live in a *shoebox*, Brad."

"Yeah. That's what Mom said too." He sighed.

"Well, at least she's not delusional about that," I said tartly. My brother made a sound that might have been a laugh or a protest, but he didn't argue, and I stared at the vultures circling until we said goodbye.

I didn't want to deal with this. I didn't want to be wondering if maybe Mom had a stalker or maybe she was depressed or maybe she was losing her marbles. I wanted to sit on the couch and classify bugs and watch vaguely rumpled British inspectors solve crimes based on the way that someone had parted their hair in a photo taken twenty years ago. I wanted this, very much, to *not be happening.*

But that's life for you. Hate it, complain about it, it's still happening.

Eventually I went back in, reclaimed my laptop, and got a refill on my floofy extravagant latte. I reassured Mom for the tenth time that I was okay and didn't need to come stay with her in the hotel, and drove home wondering what the hell to do next.

❧

The vulture was back on the mailbox. I detoured around it, went in, sat on the couch, and made a list on my phone. It didn't actually accomplish anything, but at least I had a list at the end of it.

> *Possibilities:*
> 1. *Mom has a stalker*
> 2. *Mom is depressed (maybe missing Gran Mae?)*
> 3. *Mom has dementia or similar*

I stared at the list for a bit. The scientific method dictates that one form a hypothesis, determine how to test it, then discard or amend it in the light of the new data. I had three possible hypotheses, and now I had to figure out how to test them. And also determine what to do if any given one was true.

Well, the stalker one was easy, anyway. I would tear off his head and shit down the stump for daring to mess with my mother. (I considered writing this on the list, but decided that might be used against me at the eventual murder trial.)

(Probably this was bravado and I wouldn't actually do it. I'm a very peaceful person.)

(Usually.)

(Hypothetical fucker *scared my mom.*)

(Anyway.)

Number two was . . . well, not easy, but at least I had a road map for
it. Talk to her about therapy or medication or other things that might
help. And if it was belated grief, caused by reaching the same age as
Gran Mae or what have you, try to help her work through that.

Number three was terrible and I didn't know what to do about it
if it was true, but it's fundamentally medical and a doctor could either
help or confirm or . . . something. I'd still have to get Mom in for tests.
Maybe I could call her current doctor and ask if he could run them?
Although doing that behind Mom's back seemed really sleazy, but I
suppose the families of people who slowly lose their minds have to do
it all the time. Probably there were online forums and support groups,
something like that. There were probably lists of symptoms to watch
for too. I could research it. I am a champion researcher. It's why they
pay me the meager academic bucks.

So, with that in mind, I spent an incredibly depressing hour on my
laptop looking up the symptoms of dementia. By the end of it, I was
ready to weep for humanity, and also to check myself into a home the
next time I lost my car keys.

Mom was out of the normal age range for the onset of schizophre-
nia. (I myself was in the prime age for onset in women. Yay, me. The
internet reassured me that it was treatable and that there was no reason
I couldn't live a perfectly fine life, but also that it involved a lifetime of
treatment and something called "psychosocial therapy." This did not
bode well for someone who had successfully stonewalled the school
counselor.) She wasn't old enough for normal Alzheimer's, but early
onset was definitely possible.

Anxiety was indeed a symptom, but I don't know if it was diagnostic,
given that anxiety is a symptom of nearly everything, notably including
having just spent an hour reading lists of symptoms of early onset Alz-

heimer's. Mom forgot things, sure, but she'd been doing that her whole life; witness the notes. There were not significantly more notes than usual, as far as I could tell, and she wasn't losing words and she could keep track of who the suspects were in any given mystery better than I could.

I decided that this was enough research for one night and that it was time for me to renew my acquaintance with Mr. Boxed Wine.

It was almost midnight when I heard a key in the lock and sat bolt upright on the couch. I'd been watching Inspector Lowell solve a series of clues hidden in Bible verses that led to the location of the ruined barn where the murderer was keeping his latest victim.

I'd only just had time to think, *Oh god serial killer—no, don't be ridiculous, where would a serial killer get the key to the front door—it's got to be Mom—unless the serial killer killed Mom and took her keys,* when the door opened and Mom walked in. (Look, I said that Mom is more anxious than I am, not that I'm immune to it.) She looked surprised to see me. "I thought you'd be in bed already, hon."

"Eh, couldn't sleep. I think my sleep schedule is still messed up. I thought you were going to spend another night at the hotel. Did the tour wrap early?"

"No, it was after ten by the time I got him back to his hotel." She stifled a yawn against the back of her hand. "But getting him to the airport is the hotel's problem, not mine."

"And you drove an hour home?"

Mom shrugged. "I didn't like the thought of you having to be here all by yourself."

"Mom, I'm thirty-two." I tried to soften it with a smile. "I can stay home alone. It's okay. Really."

"Oh, I know . . ." She dropped her purse. "Everything fine here?"

"Nice and n . . . quiet." *Nice and normal* had been on my lips, but I managed to change it at the last second. I hefted my wineglass. "You want any?"

"No, I'm going to go straight up to bed, I think." She yawned again, which had the knock-on effect of making me feel sleepier. "Sleep tight, hon."

I listened to the sound of her footsteps going upstairs, the door shutting, and the rumble of water in the pipes. On the screen, Inspector Lowell arrived at the last moment and managed to save the victim from falling into the running harvest combine. I finished off my wine and consoled myself that whatever was going on with Mom, it was unlikely to end in a combine accident, then took myself off to bed as well.

CHAPTER 6

I woke up in the night—too much wine, too small a bladder, the drinking woman's lament—and swung my feet over the side of the bed and onto the floor.

Something went *crunch.*

A lot of something, actually. My sleep-addled mind went to cereal for some reason. It had that sort of fragile crunchiness about it.

Gran Mae will be so mad that I was eating cereal in bed . . .

Wait, was I eating cereal in bed?

Why is there cereal on my bedroom floor?

Is there cereal on my bedroom floor?

The soles of my feet, which had been waiting politely for my brain to sort through this, delivered the message that something was tickling them, in addition to the crunch problem.

I groped for my phone on the nightstand, got the screen lit up, and held it up for light.

The floor was dark and seemed to be moving.

I still wasn't scared. I should probably have been scared, but I really had to pee and the part of my brain that processes fear had only just figured out that Gran Mae was not alive to yell at me about eating cereal in bed. The relief from that carried me long enough to reach over and turn on the bedroom lamp, whereupon I discovered that the floor was covered in ladybugs.

"Oh Jesus," I said.

There were thousands of them, a writhing scarlet stain. They covered the carpet and were starting to go up the walls. They crawled over and under one another and sometimes they lifted their shells and flew. There were individual ladybugs scattered across the bed, getting lost in the blanket and wandering around the nightstand.

I'm an entomologist. I don't think bugs are gross. But I generally don't sleep with them crawling on me, unless you count my eyebrow mites, which are arachnids, not insects, and anyway have the decency to keep to themselves. And I certainly don't like stepping on them barefoot, which is even less fun for the insect than for me. I pulled my feet up and brushed at them, already smelling the green-pepper-and-mold smell of crushed lady beetle. Live ladybugs and squashed dead ones tumbled to the floor.

(Okay, I admit it, even as a dedicated insect aficionado, this was wavering between *alarming* and *gross*.)

Once I was over the initial shock, it was all perfectly understandable. Ladybugs do swarm, like I said. Seven-spotted ladybugs swarmed in Britain in 1976. One of my professors was from Kent and said it was like a Biblical plague. "They covered everything. The ground crunched when you walked on it, and you couldn't *not* step on them. And they kept crawling into your hair to try and drink your sweat. It was dreadful."

Dreadful. Yes. I could agree with *dreadful*. I checked my hair involuntarily, and a ladybug climbed onto the back of my hand. As plagues go, this one might be localized to my bedroom instead of the entire southern British coastline, but it was still pretty Biblical. I couldn't even see the floor.

And to think I'd been upset that there was only one in the garden!

I looked carefully at the one on my hand and it was a two-spotter, but the ones on the nightstand were all Asian lady beetles like the one in the garden earlier. Well, presumably whatever conditions drove them indoors affected both varieties equally. A cold snap, maybe? Sudden intense rains?

I could worry about that later. At the moment, I had to get out of bed, preferably crushing as few ladybugs as possible.

I leaned over far enough to reach the doorknob and yanked the bedroom door open. Ladybugs spilled into the hall, but they looked much less concentrated, as far as I could see. I took a deep breath, stretched my right leg out as far as it could possibly go—*Oh god, why did I ever give up yoga, I know there were schedule problems but I really should have made time*—and stepped onto my toes.

I couldn't *hear* the crunch, but I could definitely *feel* it.

I launched myself out of the bedroom, one foot on ladybugs, one on, god willing, carpet, and charged down the hallway. "Mom! *Mom!*" (Jesus, it really was like being ten years old again.) "Mom! *Problem!*"

I banged on the door to her bedroom. "Mom, I really, really need a shop vac!"

"Whuh . . . ?" Mom pulled the door open, bleary-eyed. "Sam? What's wrong?"

"Ladybugs have swarmed in my bedroom."

She blinked at me.

"I think they're a mix of Asian lady beetles and two-spotted ladybugs," I added, in case that helped her to process faster.

"You're having a dream," she said.

"No, I'm really not. I need a shop vac, or at least one of those little handheld ones."

She leaned against the doorframe. She was wearing a dark blue bathrobe with frayed hems that hung on her like a sack. "What time is it?"

"Quarter to three."

"Right. Okay." She rubbed her face. "Let's go take a look . . ."

We went and took a look. Mom woke up very, very quickly after that. "Holy sh . . . *sugar!*"

"You see the problem," I said, while thinking, *Sugar? Mom has never had a problem saying* shit. *She says it frequently and with great passion. Or used to, anyway.*

"Where did they all come from?"

"That's a great question."

"Do we call the exterminator?"

"No!" The thought horrified me. The last thing I wanted to do was hose the place down with poison. It wasn't the ladybugs' fault that they were trying to get warm or dry or whatever and picked my bedroom. I wanted to sleep there too. "I just need a vacuum. Or at least a piece of cardboard and a garbage bag."

We ended up using both. I pushed the cardboard under swaths of ladybugs, then dumped it into the garbage bag before the majority could fly away. (Mom held the bag.) The carpet slowly began to reappear. After about an hour, I switched to the little vacuum cleaner and went around sucking up stray ladybugs. Some of them were probably injured by it, but the majority would be no worse for wear from their brief trip through the Wind Tunnel of Doom. I kept filling up the little vacuum reservoir and having to dump it into the big garbage bag, though. There were a *lot* of ladybugs.

"This," said Mom, holding up the gently rustling garbage bag, "is really unsettling."

"We'll go dump them out in the field in a minute," I said, sucking up the stragglers who had climbed into my shoes. "I'm gonna release some in the backyard first, though."

"Then I'm going to need coffee."

"Coffee sounds great."

"Maybe we could go to Waffle House."

"Waffle House sounds *amazing*."

"We can drop the rest of the ladybugs on the way?"

"Works for me. Just not too far off, I don't want to introduce diseases . . ." I looked around the bedroom. It was no longer a seething sea of scarlet. I'd probably be chasing stray ladybugs for days, mind you, but this was a definite improvement. "Right. Next stop, Waffle House."

⌒⊃

Waffle House at four in the morning is a liminal space occupied by long-haul truckers, bleary-eyed shift workers, and teenagers so high they can smell God's breath. Mom and I took a booth and she apologized for the sixth time.

"I'm so sorry, Sam. I've never had bugs in the house before. Not like that."

"Mom, it's not your fault. Bugs swarm when they swarm. And really, truly, other than both of us having to wake up in the middle of the night, it's not a big deal." I mustered a grin. "Hey, it's me. I was too busy identifying the species to be horrified."

She held out her mug as the waitress came around with refills. "Well, I suppose there's that. God, there were so *many* of them."

"It *was* pretty impressive . . ." I had signal on my phone and tried to scroll around for recent ladybug swarms in the area, but didn't get anything other than the usual run of news articles about ladybugs trying to get in the house, Japanese millipedes trying to get in the house, and of course ants trying to get in the house. Plus a load of ads for exterminators who would like you to believe that the entire insect world wakes up every morning with the sole goal of getting into your house, flying into your face, and eating your cat. I put my phone away in disgust. "Really, though, ladybugs try to get into the house sometimes. It's just a thing that happens. This was a really spectacular example, but it's absolutely not something you did."

"It just feels so dirty," muttered Mom. "Bugs in the house like that. Like I left out food or something."

"Unless you were leaving out bags of aphids, I promise it was nothing you did. I swear it on my honor as an entomologist."

She laughed finally. "Okay. If you *swear.*"

"Cross my heart and hope to die."

Our hashbrowns arrived. (Going to Waffle House for the waffles seems very weird to me. The hashbrowns are where it's at.) I dug in. Mom poked hers with her fork. "How do you think they got in?"

"That I don't know." I had checked the usual spots—vents and windows—and hadn't found any obvious lines of ladybugs. "We'll figure it out, though. A little caulk will fix it right up." (I was not actually quite as confident as all that, but soothing Mom was more important than accuracy right now. Also I've never seen that many arrive that *fast.*)

"Do you think there will be more when we get back?"

"It's possible," I admitted. "But I don't know where they'd come from. I only saw one in the yard yesterday, and no other insects at all. That's why I called you about spray."

I remembered standing in the garden, staring at the lady beetle and saying, *There should be a lot more of you!* Be careful what you wish for, I guess. Although even if it meant a late-night ladybug shoveling, I'd rather have insects than not.

We finished up our hashbrowns and left the alternate world of Waffle House. Three teenagers with pupils the size of pancakes slid into our booth before we were even out the door. We drove home, and to Mom's great relief, there was no renewed ladybug incursion. I took a blanket and a pillow down to the couch until we could wash the sheets anyway. Mom fussed a bit, but she was clearly flagging, so it didn't take her long to go to bed. I thought about getting out my laptop to check if there were any recent papers on ladybug swarms, but I was also tired and the coffee didn't seem to be doing much. I stretched out on the couch and closed my eyes to see if sleep would come.

It was probably no surprise, given my talk with Brad, but I dreamed about Gran Mae and the roses again. It wasn't a long dream. Just her hand closing over mine and a whisper in my ear, *"Let the roses taste you."* Then a flash of pain, except that pain in dreams is always strange, so it felt more like heat being pulled out of my hand into the roses and I struggled and tried to scream but she put her hand over my mouth and on the far side of the roses, something white squirmed and I woke up with a gasp.

I admit, it took me a minute to swing my legs over the side of the couch. But I did it, and nothing grabbed my legs, because monsters aren't real. I staggered into the bathroom. Real or not, monsters don't bother you while you're peeing. (This is one of the lesser-known laws.) I sat there until my heart slowed down, then washed my hands and went back to bed.

Something crunched under my foot. Oh god, had I squished another ladybug? I did the awkward wiggle that not-very-flexible people do when they're trying to see their own feet, looking over my shoulder, and relaxed. Just a leaf. I peeled it off my heel. It looked like a rose leaf, probably something I'd tracked in on my shoes from the garden. I tossed it into the trash can and fell back onto the couch. *Now let's not do that again, shall we?*

Whether or not my brain listened to me, I couldn't say, but I slept the rest of the morning without even a dream.

The Fourth Day

Peace: Most famous of the hybrid tea roses, developed by the French gardener Francis Meilland, on the eve of war with Germany. Large primrose-yellow blooms edged with pink bloom all summer on bushy upright shrubs. Mildly scented.

CHAPTER 7

A few hours later, I woke up because the front door had opened.

The couch is positioned so that you can see down the entry hallway, so my first groggy impression was of bright light filling the doorway and a figure silhouetted against it. A tall figure, holding something in one hand. A man's figure.

I wasted precious seconds wondering if I was dreaming the whole thing. Then it occurred to me to try to move.

I could move.

Therefore the man was really there.

Mom lived alone.

Therefore we were being burgled.

I was on the couch under a blanket and he was going to see me at any second so I did the only thing I could think of, which was to sit bolt upright and roar, "*I have a gun and I'm not afraid to use it!*" (Actually I had my laptop, my phone, which couldn't currently call 911, and an empty wineglass from last night, but he didn't need to know that.)

The burglar yelped and dropped what he was carrying. It made a metallic crash as it hit the floor. Nails and screws skittered across the floor. He flung his hands over his head. "Don't shoot! It's just me!"

"Who the hell is *just you?*"

"Me! Phil! I do the lawn!" He slowly lowered his hands. "Where's Mrs. Montgomery? And who the hell are you?"

Well, this was awkward.

Mom came tearing down the steps in a bathrobe. "Is everyone okay? I heard a crash. Oh, hello, Phil . . ."

"Hi, Mrs. M." He was still in a bit of a defensive crouch, but he straightened up once Mom was between the two of us. Possibly he thought I wouldn't shoot with Mom in the way.

"Um," I said. "I . . . uh . . . I thought you were a burglar. I wasn't expecting anybody."

Mom looked from me to Phil and back again. "This is Phil," she said. "He's Mr. Pressley's grandson."

"Poor bastard!" I said involuntarily, thinking of our one-man neighborhood watch. And then, "Oh boy, that didn't come out right at all. Sorry."

"Don't be," said Phil. He was a tall, lantern-jawed man with short blond hair and a hawklike nose. Attractive enough if you have a thing for old-time Puritan preachers, but looking somewhat incongruous in jeans and a T-shirt advertising a local feed store. "I know." He waved his hand over his shoulder, in the vague direction of Mr. Pressley's house. "Believe me, I know."

"He's the one who takes care of the yard for me, and he's the best handyman," said Mom.

"Do you live with your grandfather?" I asked, mostly because the more conversation that we got between us and the bit where I'd threatened to shoot him, the better. I really didn't want to drive Mom's handyman away.

"Lord, no. I come out three times a week to make sure he hasn't holed himself up in the attic with a video camera and a gun." He looked over his shoulder. "So far, so good."

"I'm sorry," said Mom. "I should have warned you that Phil was coming over. But it was late and I didn't even think about it."

"No, it's fine," I said. I wrapped the blanket around myself. I was wearing an oversized T-shirt with Eeyore on it and no pants. I was also not wearing a bra and I had probably drooled on the pillow. Lovely. Good first impressions are so important, don't you think? "I'm sorry, Phil, I panicked. I'm not good in the mornings."

"It's fine."

"I wouldn't really have shot you."

"That's good."

"I don't actually have a gun. I just thought it would scare you."

"Mission accomplished there." He gazed sadly down at the wreckage of his toolbox. In addition to what looked like a full box of nails, apparently a box of drill bits had come loose.

I said the first thing that came to mind, which unfortunately was, "I would help you pick that up, but I'm not wearing pants."

Mom made a small, pained sound. Phil looked up, probably involuntarily, looked at my bare calves, and immediately looked back down at the floor. I had not shaved my legs for weeks, because I had planned to do fieldwork and showers might be a rare commodity. There was no point in going through the whole dig with my legs feeling like sharkskin and itching madly. Unfortunately this entirely logical chain of thought meant that from the knee down, I currently resembled a hobbit. (Which I don't care about, dammit, down with the patriarchy, women shouldn't have to shave their legs. It was just one more damn thing on top of all the other damn things.)

"... I'm going to go take a shower." I looked at Mom hopefully. "Could I beg you to make coffee? Then we can do the introductions a second time and pretend I didn't threaten to murder anyone."

I limped upstairs, wearing the blanket as a makeshift bathrobe. I could hear the metallic clatter of Phil picking up his tools.

By the time I came downstairs again, I could hear the lawn mower going out front. It was probably for the best. The air outside was barely less humid than the air in the shower and my hair was curling like a kraken. I felt soggy. I missed Arizona, where you got out of the shower, looked at the towel, and then ignored it because you were already dry.

Mom handed me coffee. I drank three sips, closed my eyes, and said, "I'm sorry I threatened to murder your handyman."

There was a long silence and then I opened my eyes again because I could hear her muffling giggles.

"Oh god," she said as I glared at her. "Your face . . . And his . . . If you could have *seen* it."

I felt a smile pulling at my lips. Here I was worried about Mom, but it appeared that I was the one acting erratically. "I was a little surprised," I admitted.

"Not as surprised as he was."

I groaned. "Do you think he'll ever forgive me?"

"He's bound to," said Mom. "After all, he's Pressley's grandson. He probably gets threatened with murder every day."

"Mom . . ."

"Don't shoot me!"

"*Mom—!*"

<hr>

"The Goldbergs are having a cookout tonight," Mom said a few hours later. She was looking tired again, though that was probably from a long day of client herding followed by a late night of ladybug herding, followed by the Phil Incident. "Would you like to go?"

I closed my laptop. "Is that an 'I'd like to go, but I don't want to pressure you,' or an 'I don't want to go and I'm looking for an excuse'?"

That got a smile out of her. "I'd like to go," she admitted. "The Goldbergs are very sweet. And I don't get out too much, except for work, so I start to feel like a hermit."

"Then let's go." I put my computer aside, aware of a feeling of intense relief. "Withdrawing from friendships and social events" was an Alzheimer's symptom. "Is this a formal cookout? Should I put on a dress?"

She threw a dish towel at me. I ducked and went back to my laptop.

"You sure you don't mind?" she asked later, as we walked down the street toward the Goldbergs'. "I know you're probably still tired after your drive . . ."

"Mom, it's free food. Once a grad student, always a grad student." She laughed.

Gran Mae would have approved of the décor in the Goldberg house.

It was the sort of beige with pink accents that makes you think the word *gingham*, even if, like me, you have no real idea what *gingham* is. (Some kind of fabric, I think? Something very country kitsch, anyway.)

Mom introduced me to the Goldbergs. I immediately forgot their first names. "You must be Samantha!" said Mrs. Goldberg. She beamed at me. "The doctor!"

"Well, yes, but not the medical kind."

"Edith says you do very important archaeology work out in Arizona."

"Oh, well . . . it keeps me out of trouble." I hoped they wouldn't ask any follow-up questions. It's not that I don't want to talk about it, it's that I get very excited about what I do, and if people ask, I want to answer at length and then I look up and realize that everyone else is glassy-eyed and probably did not actually want to know quite that much about grain moths. These days I just deflect.

"It must be so fascinating. Like a treasure hunt."

"I spend a lot of time looking at dirt," I admitted. "I enjoy it, but . . . it's a lot of dirt." I looked around the backyard. "You have a lovely yard back here."

Mrs. Goldberg was no stranger to deflection herself. "You're kind to say it, but I've seen Edith's garden. I don't know how she keeps those roses looking so spectacular." She waved at her own yard, which was mostly taken up by an enormous deck with plenty of seating. Camellias and azaleas lined the perimeter and she had a small, tasteful arrangement of containers, with the obligatory potted tomato.

"I don't do anything," said Mom, drifting in the direction of the food. "Really, they basically grow themselves. Phil does all the real work in the yard."

"He's so handy," said Mrs. Goldberg enthusiastically, accompanying us to the stacks of burgers. "He's here too."

"Oh, I see him!" Mom waved across the yard. I attempted to hide behind a knee-high potted plant. It didn't work well.

Mom excused herself to chat with someone else, and Mrs. Goldberg, being a good hostess, embarked on the usual Southern call-and-response about the weather. "It's been so nice out." "Oh, yes. Of course it'll get hot later." "Oh, I know. And the *humidity* . . ." etc., etc., until either winter comes or you die of old age.

"You haven't seen any ladybugs in the house, have you?" I asked, which broke the call-and-response script and left her puzzled.

"Ladybugs?" She blinked at me. "We do get them in fall, and those awful little millipedes whenever it gets too wet, but no, not recently."

"We had a horde break into the house last night," I said. "You know how they can be."

"Oh yes. So nasty. And I always feel bad for the ladybugs, though not the millipedes."

I had no particular opinion on the merits of invasive millipedes vs. invasive lady beetles. I did know a fascinating fact about Japanese millipedes being on a multi-year cycle like cicadas and emerging in massive swarms that can coat train tracks and cause derailments, but long years of experience have taught me that very few people want to hear about this while they're eating. (I am an endless font of horrible knowledge at parties, but I try to wait until after the food has been cleared away.)

Mom returned with Phil. Mrs. Goldberg turned from him to me. "Have you two met?"

Phil gave a strangled cough. I felt myself turning beet red. Mrs. Goldberg looked between the two of us, probably wondering from our reactions if we were childhood sweethearts or members of the same gang.

"We've met," I said. "About eight hours ago, in fact. Phil, I really am sorry I thought you were a burglar."

"It's fine," said Phil. "No harm done. Grandad thinks I'm a burglar here to kill him about once a month, so it's not the first time."

"Oh lord." Being compared to Mr. Pressley did not make me feel any better, and moreso because Mom had predicted it. "I promise that the next time you come to mow the lawn, I won't threaten your life."

Mrs. Goldberg had an increasingly glassy smile on her face and excused herself to go tend the beagle.

"I was not at my best," I said. "We'd had a ladybug incursion the night before."

He raised his eyebrows. I explained as best I could, with Mom jumping in occasionally. "I know that people say there's hordes of bugs when there's more than a dozen," I said, "but I'm actually an entomologist. There really was a horde. I could barely see the carpet. Just in that one room, though."

"Now that *is* weird." He rubbed his chin. "And at this time of year?"

"That's what I said!" My estimate of Phil went up several notches.

"I know people release ladybugs as pest control. Maybe somebody in the neighborhood went a little nuts." He glanced over at Mom. "I can check the window frames and the siding if you like, Mrs. M. See if there's some way they're getting in."

"I'd appreciate that," said Mom. "Believe me, vacuuming up ladybugs in the middle of the night is not my idea of a good time."

I snorted. Mom went off to talk to someone else, leaving Phil and me standing next to the drinks. I fished out a hard cider and Phil located the bottle opener and gallantly cracked it open for me.

"So you're a bug person? For some reason I thought you were an archaeologist."

"Both."

"Huh. So what exactly do you do?"

I told him.

He looked puzzled for a moment, then broke into a wide grin. "What, like in *Jurassic Park*, where they find the mosquitoes in amber?"

I kid you not, everyone says this. *Everyone.* Or at least enough people that I have developed a script to handle it. "Heh, no, I wish. That would be awesome. But I'm working with much more recent stuff, so no dinosaur blood. And mosquitoes don't last very long outside of amber. Lots of weevils, I'm afraid. On the bright side, I'm not going to be eaten by velociraptors at work, so that's something, right?"

And then they agree that this is definitely positive and then they never ask any follow-up questions and we talk about something easier, like the weather.

"What kind of weevils?" Phil asked, going off script.

"Anything that gets into food storage," I said. "You can tell a lot about what food somebody stored by what bugs they're dealing with. Sunflower seed weevils." I waited for him to make a lesser-of-two-weevils joke, which is another thing that everyone does. After basing my entire thesis on them, I believe I am entitled to freely murder anyone making this joke, but for some reason the courts disagree.

He did not make the joke. Phil was rising in my estimation by the moment. "We learned a little bit about them in my master gardener classes," he said. "Fuller rose beetles. They can be a real problem."

A master gardener? Interesting. But that brought me back to my grandmother's roses and the strange lack of insects. I took a sip of my cider and wondered how to accuse him of poisoning the entire garden in a nonhostile fashion. "There aren't any on the roses at Mom's house. I understand you're the one taking care of them?"

To my surprise, he shook his head. "Oh no. I just cut the grass. I don't do anything with the roses. Mrs. M handles all that herself."

"She says she doesn't do anything."

He snorted. "She's being modest. Those roses are in fantastic shape. They're healthier than the ones at the botanical garden. I've never even seen a Japanese beetle on them, and that's practically black magic."

As if the mention of garden black magic had been a summoning spell, the house door opened. "Gail!" Mrs. Goldberg set up a cry like a one-woman cast of *Cheers*. "You made it!"

"Of course I did," said the newcomer. "You know I never turn down free food."

So I finally meet the old witch, I thought. Gail stepped out of the house and down onto the deck, and I felt my eyebrows shoot up.

Gran Mae . . . well, I couldn't speak to the *witch* part, but apparently Gran Mae had been lying about the *old* part. Gail looked to be in her mid-sixties, with gray hair cut in a short bob. She couldn't be more than a decade and change older than Mom, which meant she would have been considerably younger than my grandmother.

She was dressed in that style I associated with aging hippies with money, Berkeley moms and art therapists—layered, flowing linen with asymmetric hems and a chunky necklace. My eyes dropped automatically to her feet to see if she had on Birkenstocks, but instead she was wearing gigantic shit-kicker boots that had clearly seen a lot of wear and tear in their life.

When I looked up from her feet, she had spotted Mom and was making her way toward her. "Edith! Long time no see." They hugged, and then Mom began to steer her back toward me. "And you must be Samantha."

"Sam," I said, extending my hand automatically. Her fingers were dry and callused and she had a solid grip. "And you're . . . Gail?"

"That I am." She looked me over in a friendly fashion. "The archaeologist daughter, right?"

"Some archaeology. Mostly entomology. I study bugs in archaeology digs." I decided to head off the *Jurassic Park* joke. "And Mom said you were a wildlife rehabilitator?"

"For my sins," she said, laughing. "Mostly a retired one now. They still sucker me into the occasional turtle, but I flatly refuse to bottle-feed fawns anymore." She helped herself to a bottle of cider. "Phil, how are you doing? And do you still have eggs?"

"The girls keep laying," said Phil solemnly.

"Then sign me up for a dozen."

They talked chickens and I sipped my drink and plastered a vague, pleasant expression on my face, like every outsider at a party where everyone else knows one another. After a few moments, when conversation had lulled, I ventured, "Mom says you have vultures."

Gail laughed. "I don't know if I have them or if they have me. Yes, there's a roost in the back of the garden. And I have Hermes."

"Hermes?"

"My house vulture. He's a rescue. Hit by a car, lost a wing. It happens to a lot of young birds when they're eating roadkill, before they figure out cars." She grinned. "You should come over sometime and I'll introduce you. He likes meeting people."

"Is he housebroken?" I pictured a vulture perched on the back of a chair. There weren't enough antimacassars in the world.

"Not in the slightest." Gail grinned. "Screened-in porch and a lot of closed doors. I love him, but vulture shit is nasty."

"There was a vulture on our mailbox when I drove up the other day," I said. "I'm guessing that wasn't him."

"No, it would have been one of the wild ones. I'm not surprised, though. They like to keep an eye on that house." She took a sip of cider, but she was watching my mother's face, not mine.

My eyebrows shot up. Mom got that worried expression again and looked over her shoulder toward my grandmother's house.

Good lord, what is going on here? I'd been thinking that Mom was acting oddly, but maybe she wasn't the only one. "Why would they want to keep an eye on Mom's house?" I asked, aware that I sounded defensive and not bothering to hide it.

"It's not the current owner they're worried about," said Gail. "They're very intelligent birds, and they have long memories."

"Are you saying my grandmother was unkind to *vultures*?" The conversation had skidded wildly out of control, and I wasn't sure whether to laugh or back away slowly. I looked to Phil, hoping for some kind of social second opinion. He looked bewildered, which didn't help.

"Gail . . ." said my mother.

Gail shrugged. "It's not for me to say. I just know that they like to post a sentry to watch it." She grinned abruptly. "Relax, Edith. I'm not about to drag up all the old gardening rivalries at a cookout."

Despite my confusion, I felt a burst of smugness. Dammit, there *had* been a rivalry. I knew I hadn't been imagining it. Mom may have claimed to forget, but Gran Mae had loathed the other woman's garden and would say so at the drop of a hat. Hell, even on her deathbed, she'd been complaining to a nurse about "the old witch's weeds." I *knew* it.

"I'm sure Gran Mae never meant any of it," mumbled Mom into her drink, which was absolutely a lie. Gran Mae had meant every word.

"Mmm." Gail turned to Phil. "You know how it is, Phil. Someone grows a better tomato than their neighbor, and they're at daggers drawn for the next twenty years. How is the extension office treating you?"

"It's fine," said Phil, and to my relief, he went into a discussion of county extension programs, which wasn't interesting but also didn't make my mother look like a deer caught in the headlights. I gazed vaguely into the distance again, noting that the spring webworms were hard at work on one of Mrs. Goldberg's shrubs. (Better known as Eastern tent caterpillars, *Malacosoma americanum*, in case you're curious. Not to be confused with the fall webworm, which forms a much larger nest and turns into a handsome white moth, and if I stared at the shrub long enough, I could probably remember the Latin.) Well, at least I had proof there were bugs in other people's gardens on Lammergeier Lane.

"Phil," I said, during a pause in the conversation, "do you remember the Latin name for fall webworms?"

He grimaced. "*H*-something, isn't it? Mostly I call them 'squish the nasty little buggers.'"

"Sorry," I said, waving a hand toward the tent caterpillars. "I had noticed those over there and then I was thinking of caterpillars and . . . ah . . . sorry."

"*Hyphantria cunea*," said Gail, winning my heart forever.

"That's the one!" I raised my cider in salute. So did Phil.

Mom smiled into her drink, shaking her head. "She hasn't changed a bit," she said to Gail. "She was like that as a child too. She'd find a bug and come charging home to look it up. Or to demand that we go to the library and look it up there."

"Seems to have worked out well for you," said Gail, nodding to me. "Raking in the big academic bucks now, right?"

"Oh yes, rolling in it," I said. "My last raise was five whole cents."

"Good heavens! A fortune." Gail grinned. "Sorry, my stepdaughter's a medieval historian. I know how it goes."

I nodded in sympathy to a fellow laborer in the academia mines, then discovered my bottle was empty. I excused myself to get another one, checked my phone fruitlessly for signal—no luck—and ambled back.

The knot of people had dispersed. Phil was over by the grill and Gail and my mom had vanished. I found myself standing at a corner of the house, drinking my cider and idly checking the plants for insect life. (I am so much fun at parties.)

I had just about decided to go bother Phil, who was probably sick of me but was also a master gardener and could perhaps have a nice conversation about pollinator-friendly plantings, when I heard Mom around the corner. Her voice was muffled and I could only pick out a couple of words.

"... want to upset her," she said. "You know ..."

I strained my ears and was startled when Gail spoke up, rather louder. "You already know how I feel about it, Edith. I'm not here to browbeat you. I just worry."

Worry? About what?

"... be fine ..."

"You know best. But you know if it ever gets too bad, you can come stay with me."

"... into it ..."

"You aren't dragging me into it, I'm offering. Look, I didn't mean to ruin your evening. Just promise you'll come get me if it gets too bad."

If what *gets too bad? And who does Mom not want to upset?* I really hoped she didn't mean me. Then again, Mom lived in absolute terror of upsetting people, so it could be anyone.

The way that Gail was talking made it sound like Mom was in an abusive relationship, but with who? She lived alone—not that living together was the only way to have an abusive relationship, of course, but how was I going to find out who to threaten with unspecified doom if I didn't know who it was?

"Hi again," said Phil behind me.

I yelped and nearly dropped my cider. That's the problem with eavesdropping, you know you're doing something wrong. I spun around and Phil had both his hands up, probably expecting me to try to kill him. Again.

"Sorry," I said. "Sorry, I . . . uh . . . I was looking at a mantis."

"Oh, what kind?"

Dammit, this is why you don't start lying to begin with. "One of the big Chinese ones, unfortunately," I said, consigning the fictional mantis to perdition.

Phil smiled. "I know they're invasive, but I kind of love those. They always look at you so intelligently, like they're actually thinking about what to do next. But I know, I know, they crowd out the little brown ones."

"Don't worry, I won't report you to the secret entomology council for liking the wrong mantids."

"You're too kind."

Mom and Gail came around the corner. Gail still looked serene, in a hippie kind of way. Mom had lines at the corners of her eyes, but she always did, so it wasn't as if that was a change. "Oh there you are," she said, hooking her arm through mine. "What's up?"

"Not much. Admiring the local insect life."

We stayed for another few hours, chatting with various neighbors. Phil excused himself with a promise to come over and check the siding for ladybug access points. Gail told amusing stories about wildlife rescue and trying to bandage up an injured great blue heron. "I had to wear a welding face mask," she said. "And if I'd had a riot shield, I'd have used it. Those beaks are like a spring-loaded javelin, and they're never grateful." She smiled fondly at the memory of a bird trying to put its beak through her eye. Wildlife rehabbers are special people. Everybody hung on her every word, though. If Gail was the local eccentric, she was a popular one.

Afterward, as we headed home, Mom gave me a sidelong look. "You and Phil seem to be getting along better."

"He seems nice enough."

"He's single."

"Oh god, Mom, don't start." I stifled a groan. "I'm only here for a month or two."

"What, that means you can't have a fling?"

"Mom. I am not going to have a fling with your handyman."

"I'm just saying, never say never."

I did not dignify this with a response. While I did have the occasional fling, it increasingly just seemed like so much *work*. You had to meet people and figure out if you liked them and if they liked you and if they were actually single or if things were "complicated." I had had my share of complicated already, thank you very much. Also I had three roommates, which made date night difficult, although probably not as difficult as having wild sex with the handyman in my childhood bedroom, two doors down the hall from my mother.

"Why don't *you* date him?" I asked.

Mom swatted my shoulder. "He's twenty years younger than me."

"So was Bondage Guy. I'm telling you, you need to start looking at these younger men."

"Maybe I should give Bondage Guy *your* number."

"Nah, it'd be weird at Sunday dinner when he was obviously pining for you."

We both dissolved into alcohol-assisted giggles. I looked around, wiping my eyes, wondering if anybody was noticing the two tipsy women meandering up the street. Nobody was in view. Even the vulture on the mailbox had abandoned its post for the evening, but there was a hulking silhouette on a neighbor's roof that made me think it hadn't gone far.

Mr. Pressley was probably still watching, of course. ("That's them, Officers! Those two women! They were giggling! *Giggling with intent!*")

Mom's laughter cut off as she opened the front door and looked around the entryway for a moment, then stepped inside. I probably wouldn't have noticed if I hadn't been watching her. It was an odd gesture. She didn't look as if she expected anyone to be lurking. Instead, it seemed almost as if she was looking to see if anything had changed.

I looked around myself, but everything seemed the same as it always was, ecru paint and all. I wondered what she'd been looking for, and why the thought made me inexplicably afraid.

CHAPTER 8

Much later that night, I woke from a deep sleep because my roommate's cat was walking on my head.

I burrowed farther into the pillow, muttering, "Salem, go bother your person. I'm not the food monkey." Salem patted the back of my head. I felt a claw graze my ear. "Dammit, cat..." I mumbled, dragging the blankets up higher.

Slowly—very slowly—it percolated through my sleep-sodden brain that I was several states and the length of Texas away from my apartment, I was still sleeping on the couch, and my mom didn't own a cat.

There was something touching my arm. It wasn't a hand. It didn't feel like flesh at all. It was cool and slick and very thin, and scratchy—like a twig? And it was moving.

In fact, it was stroking my bare arm.

It wasn't an insect. I have been climbed on by any number of insects. This had weight and pressure. The largest Hercules beetle in the world would not have felt like this.

Dread rose up and took me by the throat. Oh god, what was happening? I pictured a skeletal hand—a rake—claws. I couldn't move. I couldn't think. I could barely breathe. All I knew was that I could not move. If I moved, if I acknowledged it in any way, then it could get me. (No, it wasn't scientific, or even sane. We were way past either of those things.)

The thing moved up my shoulder. It couldn't be a hand. Even though it seemed to have multiple fingers, it was too thin to be bone. My heart hammered against my ribs.

From my shoulder, it traced the side of my face and went into my hair. I could feel it sliding through like the teeth of a comb, catching on the curls. It came loose for an instant then slid back in. Then again.

I was lying on the couch pretending to be asleep and a monster was combing my hair.

People say, when they hear about a terrifying event, that they would just drop dead of fear. I've said it myself. "I'd just die." Or "I'd just pass out." But nobody ever tells you what to do when you don't die, when you're lying there and something is touching you and you're pretending to be asleep because everybody knows that monsters can't get you as long as you're asleep and your heart pounds but you keep not dying and you stubbornly remain conscious and it keeps happening.

"The roses say to say your prayers," whispered a voice in my ear.

My breath came in short, miserable gasps. *It has to know I'm awake,* I thought. *It has to be able to tell by my breathing.* This was bad, because if it knew I was awake, it could do . . . something.

If it saw through my pretense, it gave no sign. The thin, twiglike touch continued raking through my hair and I was completely paralyzed.

Paralyzed.

Paralysis.

Oh sweet Jesus, I thought, with unutterable relief, *this is sleep paralysis.*

It's never happened to me before, but I've read about it. It happens to a lot of people. One of my roommates used to get it all the time. You can't move, and you have a dream—somewhere between a nightmare and a hallucination—about an intruder in the room. Alien abduction experiences are usually sleep paralysis. It doesn't feel like a dream, it feels real. *This* felt real. But it wasn't. It couldn't be. There were no monsters, just a glitch in my brain chemistry.

I sagged with relief. My muscles unlocked and I sat up.

I caught a glimpse—just a glimpse—of something vanishing below my eye level. I jerked back, even though I knew it had to be part of the hallucination. *It's not real, it's not real, your brain is just catching up to the rest of you . . .*

I laughed shakily and looked around the room. Nothing there. Of course. There wouldn't be. "Right," I said out loud. "Just my brain." Shit, though, that packed a wallop. No wonder people believed in UFOs afterward. If I had a brain that saw little bug-eyed gray dudes instead of unknown monsters combing my hair, I'd probably believe in them too.

I got to my feet. My bladder had strong opinions about the four bottles of cider. It was probably still pissed—ha ha—at me about the drive across Texas. You have to drink a lot of coffee to cross Texas, but there are not rest stops nearly as often as there should be. Somewhere in West Texas, at the bottom of an off-ramp, a coyote is probably still wondering who left the strange mark in his territory.

I padded down the hall to the downstairs bathroom, not bothering with the light. Even now, the route was basically muscle memory. The moonlight streamed through the sliding glass doors. The yard was blue and white, with sharp-edged shadows. The rosebushes made a complicated topography, and I could make out at least one bloom that practically glowed in the moonlight. Pretty, in a gothic sort of way. I'd have been more impressed if I didn't have a sinking feeling that the garden was as devoid of moths as it had been of bugs.

Still, there had been ladybugs. Weird, erratic ladybugs, sure, but they'd been there. That was positive? Maybe? *Unless they were trying to get away from some kind of pesticide residue . . . but that doesn't make sense, they'd just fly next door. There's plenty of bugs everywhere else on the street. No, there's got to be something on the roses . . .*

Whether thinking about the roses distracted me, or the limit on sleep paralysis is one per customer, I slept through 'til morning without so much as a dream.

The Fifth Day

Angel of Sleep: Flawless yellow blossoms are blushed with red at the tips, on matte green stems. A vigorous grandiflora rose, this spring bloomer produces long-stemmed blooms perfect for cutting. Mild fragrance is spicy and sweet.

CHAPTER 9

Mom slept late again. I think the lady beetles took a lot more out of her than they had out of me. We can't all be trained entomologists, I suppose. (Well, actually we could be, and in a perfect world we would be, which might provide just about enough manpower to finish The Project and maybe make some inroads on beetle taxonomy.)

I made coffee, then sat down with The Project, only to find that the next section was all scale insects. Trying to ID scale insects down to the species level is one of those jobs that makes entomologists old before their time. Is that a quinquelocular pore or just a cerarius? *Who can say?* (Never mind the beetles. We're putting humanity to work on the damn scale insects.)

Not feeling up to scale insect identification on my current level of caffeine, I stepped out into the garden instead. Still no insects, though I did see a tiger swallowtail pass overhead at treetop height. Butterfly ID is easy. The scale insects could learn from them. I checked for the lady beetles that I had released from the invasion, but they were long gone.

The roses smelled like . . . well, like roses. It was still early enough in the day that they hadn't filled the garden with musk. I remembered the way that the house used to smell, how Gran Mae would cut armloads of tightly furled rosebuds, nipping the thorns off with her little pink pliers, and put them in vases, where they would open up over the course of days.

A thought occurred to me. I was trying to bring up positive memories of Gran Mae, right? In case Mom was in mourning? Why not cut some rosebuds and put them in vases for her? I could get one from each bush, make a nice arrangement of pinks and reds and whites.

I went back inside and found a pair of vases in the cabinet over the sink where random glassware goes to die. Was I supposed to add something to the water? I couldn't remember. There were shears in the shed, at least, and the pink pliers for removing thorns. The shears had a patina of rust and didn't want to open, but the pliers looked just like they had when I was ten years old.

I wasn't sure how much stem you left on a cut rose, so I erred on the side of length and ended up stabbing myself with a thorn. I jerked my hand back, sucking on my fingertip. How had Gran Mae done this every day?

Let the roses taste you.

I believed that Brad believed what he had seen, but it occurred to me that maybe the adults had been right after all. Maybe he hadn't seen what he thought he had. Maybe I'd grabbed for a stem and Gran Mae really had tried to stop me. I was thirty-two now and couldn't touch these plants without stabbing myself. God only knows what I would have been like as a small child. Gran Mae had been an awful person, but in retrospect, the fact that I hadn't come into the house dripping blood every day might prove that she'd been looking out for me. Or maybe just that she didn't want to deal with a little kid screaming and bleeding everywhere, take your pick.

Five more roses entailed five more blood offerings to the rosebushes. I'm not sure why, but being stabbed with a rose thorn hurts more than it has any right to, given the relatively small size of the stabby bit. Maybe it was like caterpillars. The hairy ones often have what are called "urticating hairs," which aren't actually venomous, but have little barbs that work their way into your skin so they're far more painful than just getting poked with a comparably sized needle.

Maybe I'd just do one bud vase.

Still, I was determined to get a rosebud from every bush, dammit. I was a tool-using mammal. (A tool-using mammal who should have been wearing gloves.) I was not going to be outsmarted by shrubbery.

I ended up with thirteen buds, one for each of the thirteen rose-bushes. My left hand looked like I had tried to wrestle a feral cat. I snapped a couple of thorns off with the pliers, acquired a fourteenth wound, told myself that it was silly to worry about thorns for a plant that was going directly into a vase, and came inside feeling vaguely martyred about the whole thing.

Roses went in vase. I tried to arrange them attractively and immediately realized why Gran Mae had taken off the thorns. Fifteen. The results looked exactly like someone had cut some roses and then jammed them into a vase with no idea what they were doing. I decided that *awkwardly charming* was the best I could aspire to and went to bandage up my hand.

I looked up rose thorns on the internet to see if they had some kind of extra barb, and discovered that there was something called "rose picker's disease" caused by a fungus growing on rose thorns, which manifested in small bumps under the skin, which then spread and became ulcers. Jesus Christ. I have *got* to stop looking up medical things on the internet.

There was a knock on the front door and Phil cautiously poked his head through. "I'm here to check for ladybugs."

"Go on up," I said absently. "Did you know that there's a fungus spread by stabbing yourself on rose thorns?"

"Rose picker's disease," he said. "Yeah?"

"Does everyone know about this but me?"

"Probably only the gardeners. Why?"

"I tried to pick some roses." I held up my battle-scarred hand. He winced.

"Yeah, you probably want gloves for that. Heavy-duty ones, not the little wimpy gardening gloves they sell you at the hardware store."

"That's okay. I am retiring from the field of botany." I got another cup of coffee and settled down to work on The Project. Phil came downstairs after a few minutes and said he had to go get a ladder to check the outside wall.

"I won't panic if I hear thumping."

"No, but if you hear a scream and a thud, I'd appreciate it if you called 911."

"Heh." I dumped all the scale insect photos into one directory called "Scale insect spp." for some other poor bastard to go through and went on to the next bit, only to discover that some asshole had dumped all the termites into a single directory for some other poor bastard to go through, and that poor bastard was me. Soldier termites have distinctive head shapes, but the workers—and they're mostly workers—all look alike. You tell the difference by doing measurements of the relative length of their antennal segments. After the first dozen or so, you start to wonder why you didn't become a medical test subject instead. The pay is similar and it's much less painful.

I was just wondering how soon I could be injected with questionable drugs when Mom came down the stairs, made the groggy pre-coffee wave, and went into the kitchen. I heard the clatter of mugs and then she let out a gasp and glass shattered.

"Shit! Mom!" I jumped to my feet, dropping my laptop to the couch. "Are you okay?"

She did not look okay. She was standing in the remains of the coffeepot, surrounded by spilled coffee and shattered glass, staring straight ahead. Her skin had gone so white that I was afraid she was going to faint.

"Mom! Oh god, don't move . . ." I ran for the dustpan. "Mom, talk to me!"

"It's . . . I'm fine . . . I just . . ."

I returned and began frantically sweeping broken glass from around her feet. Thank god the coffee had started to get cold. There were a few drops of blood starting on her legs where splinters of glass had caught her. "Oh jeez, Mom."

She swallowed. "The roses," she said. "They startled me. I wasn't expecting to see them. You . . . ah . . . *you* picked them, right, Sam?"

"Yes." *Oh, great job, you wanted to start a positive conversation about Gran Mae and now she's got glass in her feet. A+ work. For your next trick, maybe you can just shove her down the stairs and be done with it.* "I'm sorry! I remembered that Gran Mae always had roses in vases and I thought . . . I'm so sorry. I shouldn't have done it without asking."

"No. No, it's fine. It's very sweet." Color seemed to be returning to Mom's face. "Gran Mae . . . Gran Mae would have loved them, I'm sure."

Say something positive. It was hard enough to think of positive things about my grandmother when I *wasn't* surrounded by broken glass. "Well, she always grew such beautiful roses."

"Yes. Yes, she did." Mom looked down at her legs and grimaced. "Oh, this'll be fun. I can't believe I was so clumsy."

"It's my fault."

"It's nobody's fault," said Mom firmly. She lifted one foot clear of the glass. "No harm done."

"You're *bleeding.*"

"Five minutes with the tweezers, it'll be fine." She patted my shoulder and went upstairs. I made another pass with the broom, wondering if the glass fragments could carry rose picker's disease and feeling like history's biggest fool.

When I brought the dustpan full of glass outside to the trash, there were two black vultures sitting on the neighbor's roof, watching me until I went back inside.

Mom had to go into town to mail some packages for a client. I waited until she left, then dumped the rest of the worker termites back into the directory for the next, next poor bastard and went to talk to Gail.

I had no idea how I was going to start the conversation, I admit. "Excuse me, but has my mother been losing her mind lately?" did not seem like the best opener. Still, I could hopefully fumble through something.

When I arrived at the garden at the end of the lane, though, the thought of my mother briefly went out of my head. So did everything else.

There were *insects* here. Gail's garden was tucked into a clearing in the pine trees and it glowed with flowers. All kinds, not Gran Mae's monotony of roses. I couldn't tell you what most of them were, I'm no botanist, but they were swarming with hoverflies and solitary wasps and big hefty carpenter bees and at least two varieties of bumblebee— probably American and black-and-gold, although I'd need to get closer, *Bombus* wasn't my specialty—and little iridescent sweat bees and skipper butterflies and all the other things that should have been in Mom's backyard and weren't.

"Hey there," called Gail. I blinked and pulled myself out of my reverie. She was dressed much more casually today, in jeans and a T-shirt that read I CAME HERE TO PULL WEEDS AND CHEW GUM AND I'M ALL OUT OF GUM.

"You have insects!" I blurted.

"I sure hope so," she said cheerfully, as if this was a normal replacement for "Hello" or "How are you?" "I planted the flowers for them. It'd be a shame if they didn't enjoy them."

"Sorry," I said, trying to focus. A dragonfly cruised by overhead. (Eastern pondhawk, female.) "I—ah—there's none in Mom's backyard. It's been bugging me."

"It'd bug me too," said Gail. She ambled toward me. Something followed her, and for a second I thought she had a cat or a very small dog, but it moved all wrong and then the shape resolved into a small vulture.

It didn't move at all like I had expected. You see little birds hopping around on the ground, and you don't think of them walking. This one walked, in a kind of bouncing gallop. Its wings were folded up and the longest feathers stuck out behind it, at least on one side, and it rocked from side to side as it galloped along. I'd never seen any animal that moved like that. It was unsettling and hilarious all at once.

"This is Hermes," said Gail. "He's friendly, but please don't try to pet him."

I eyed his hooked beak with respect. "He looks like he could take a finger off."

"Well, yes, but he'd be mortified afterward. Vultures use their beaks to interact with everything, and it makes people nervous if they aren't used to it. Then they jerk away and get hurt, and Hermes gets confused."

"Pleasure to meet you, Hermes," I said to him.

"Well, go on," said Gail, in the voice you'd use with a toddler. Hermes bounced up to me and made a careful circuit of my legs. I'd rolled up my jeans into cuffs—it's very hard to get pants that are both wide enough and short enough when you're my size—and he cautiously reached out and took the edge of the cuff in his beak. He nibbled it, very carefully, then Gail called him back and he bounced over to her. She tossed him something and he devoured it with one gulp.

"I take it he's not ever gonna be released," I said, eyeing his distinct lack of wing on one side.

"Nope. He's in training to be an ambassador bird. He's a sweet little guy, and people have a lot of hang-ups about vultures, so we're hoping he'll make friends."

"I promise I am very pro-vulture."

She grinned at me. "Glad to hear it. They're revered in many cultures, as I'm sure you know."

"Sure. Egypt went nuts for them."

"Yep. Powerful psychopomps. Like crows in *The Crow*."

I probably looked blank, because she sighed. "It was a movie . . . which probably came out right around the time you were born. Don't mind me, my bones are just crumbling to dust, that's all."

"Sorry?"

"Not your fault." She shook her head. "Anyway, vultures are supposed to escort the dead to the afterlife."

Hermes bounced back and forth, looking more like he would ask the dead to play fetch.

We chatted about vultures for a few minutes before I shook my head, realizing that I'd gotten distracted. "I'm sorry to drop in on you like this," I said, remembering why I had come. "I had a question for you, but if this is an inconvenient time . . ."

"Nah. Come on up to the house and I'll get Hermes settled." She led me to a screened-in porch. Hermes bounced up onto a stool and she gave him another chunk of something meaty. "Dead mouse," she said at my glance. "Hang tight and I'll get you something."

"Dead mice aren't really my thing . . ."

She cackled. "Have a seat, if you can find a spot that doesn't have vulture poop on it," she said and went inside.

This was not the most encouraging statement I'd ever heard, but I located a wicker chair that did not appear to have vulture poop on it, though the back bore the marks of grasping talons. I sat. I looked at Hermes, then at my phone. I had a smidgeon of signal, so I took a photo of Hermes and sent it to my coworkers with a text saying, "Made a new friend."

Gail came back, bearing lemonade and cookies. "Oh my," I said. "You didn't have to go to all this trouble."

"Bah. I'm an old lady and easily amused." She set the drinks down and handed me one. On his stool, Hermes sagged down into a pancake, which wasn't a position I associated with vultures.

Gail regarded me with eyes as sharp as her bird's. "Let me guess. It's about your mom."

"Are you a mind reader?"

"No, just a witch." She snorted at my look. "Nah, relax. You get the same expression Edith does when she's upset about something but trying not to bother anyone else. What's the problem?"

Now that I came to actually talk about it, I couldn't seem to form the words. I took a swallow of lemonade. "I'm worried about her," I said. "She's acting odd. I don't know how well you know her . . ."

"Well enough."

"She's changed a lot of things in the house," I said carefully. "Wildly different. And she seems scared of something. I'm afraid that something's wrong. I just don't know if it's something . . . ah . . . external, or if it's all in her head. I was wondering if you'd noticed any changes."

Gail continued to study me. Her eyes looked much older than the rest of her, but that didn't dull their gleam. Some knives stay sharp no matter how old they are.

"Have you ever read any Agatha Christie?" she asked abruptly.

"Uh . . ." I was startled by the sudden change of topic. "I think I read *Murder on the Orient Express.*"

"Any Miss Marple?"

"I don't think so."

Gail shook her head. "That's a shame. Far superior to Poirot, in my opinion. Miss Marple is always saying that one sees so much evil in a small village. That's how she solves all the murders. They all remind her of things she saw in her village."

I raised my eyebrows. Hermes flipped his wing and continued to imitate a pancake. "You think there's evil here on Lammergeier Lane? In a subdivision?" It seemed so absurd to say it out loud that I had to make a joke. "If we had an HOA, I could maybe understand it."

She didn't smile. "Anywhere there's people, there's a possibility of evil, wouldn't you say?"

"I suppose in theory?" I rubbed the bridge of my nose. I could feel a headache coming on. I'd just wanted to ask if Mom had seemed odd, but I was getting more than I bargained for, none of which was particularly helpful. "But who do you think is evil here? Not Mom." That last didn't come out like a question. If Gail accused my mother of being evil, it didn't matter how cute her pet vulture was, I was going to call her a lot worse than an old witch.

"Oh lord, no!" Gail shook her head so hard that gray hair fell into her face. "Not Edith. If your mother was the worst humanity had to offer, we'd be living in a state of grace."

I relaxed. "Well, I agree. That's why I came to see if she's been acting odd, you see."

"Mmm. Miss Marple was also a gardener, you know."

My headache was definitely getting worse. "Mom isn't," I said.

"And yet there's a garden at her house, isn't there?"

"Well, yes, but . . ."

"Some things run in families," said Gail. "And other things skip generations. It's odd, isn't it?"

I was completely lost. Families? I suppose insomuch as Mom had inherited the garden from Gran Mae, but it's not like that was genetic. I had a brief flash of Great-Grandad Rasputin. Had he puttered around in a garden? Somehow it was hard to imagine. If he did, it would be one of those big Gothic numbers with poisonous plants twining up wrought iron fences, not pink hybrid tea roses.

Gail picked up a Tupperware container and began loading it up with chocolate chip cookies from the plate in front of us. "These are for your mother. And you, of course. I promise that Hermes didn't stick his beak in the batter."

"Uh . . ." Before I quite knew what was happening, she was very politely showing me the door. "But . . ."

Gail leaned against the doorframe, looking at me with an oddly sympathetic expression. "I know you're an archaeologist and it's in your nature to go digging around in the past. But it's best to let some things lie."

"But I'm worried about my mother," I said helplessly. "I can't just let that lie. What if she's got dementia?"

"Edith seems very sharp to me," said Gail. "Always has. Maybe she's acting completely rationally based on her experience."

I gaped at her. She smiled brightly. "Enjoy those cookies, dear. And tell your mother that if she needs anything, she knows where to find me."

CHAPTER 10

I went back home, feeling discouraged. I hadn't gotten anything out of the conversation with Gail, unless you counted the chocolate chip cookies. They were good cookies, at least, but I would have liked answers a lot more.

Mom's car was still gone. My headache wasn't going away. I went upstairs and got the aspirin. A ladybug strolled across the bathroom mirror. I swallowed the aspirin with a palmful of water from the tap, then caught the ladybug and took it out to the garden and put it on a rose. It wandered around, presumably confused by its sudden alien-abduction experience.

I lay down on the couch and put my arm over my eyes. Maybe a nap would help. Lord knows I hadn't slept well night before last. Maybe I still had some sleep debt to work off. And if nothing else, it might help ward off the headache.

I don't know how long I was asleep. Not long, I think. I had a brief, muddled dream about the roses, about plunging my hands into the rose-bushes and drawing them back covered in blood. The bushes leaned in closer, expectantly, as if they were waiting for me to speak. When I snapped awake, I wasn't groggy at all. I wish I had been.

It was touching me again.

I tried to move but my arms were frozen in place. I couldn't even turn my head. A shadow bent over me as the claws moved in my hair. They combed through the curls, my scalp stinging at the tug. I wanted to grab for it. I wanted to scream.

Sleep paralysis, I told myself frantically. *Sleep paralysis. That's all it is. It's your brain playing tricks.*

My conscious mind might know that, but the rest of me was not getting the memo. The claws moved and it felt real, as real as the realest thing I'd ever experienced, as real as my heart hammering in my chest.

The shadow bent lower. I couldn't see anything but a dark blur at the very edge of my vision. *Wake up wake up wake up this isn't real wake up!*

"The roses say . . . say your prayers . . ." whispered the voice.

My ear stung suddenly and I jerked free of the paralysis. I sat bolt upright, slapping at my ear with a yelp, and then collapsed backward, shaky with adrenaline and relief. For a long minute, all I could do was drag air into my lungs and wait for the shaking to pass. I rubbed my stinging ear. It still hurt.

Sleep paralysis, as my old advisor would have said, was a helluva thing. I could see why my old roommate had hated it so much. I'd always thought it sounded interesting, but I could have done without this much interest.

I swung my feet over the side of the couch and rose petals fell off my shirt to the floor.

. . . what the hell?

I reached down to pick one up. Pink rose petals. For a moment I thought they had red stripes, and then I realized that my fingertips were bloody.

No, really, what the hell*?!*

I staggered into the downstairs bathroom, baffled and annoyed. There were two more rose petals stuck to my shirt and when I touched my ear, it was bleeding.

"Son of a bitch," I growled, turning my head. (It's very hard to get a good look at the back of your ear in a mirror, have you ever noticed that?) Near as I could tell, I had stabbed it somehow. Maybe a shard of glass from the vase had somehow gotten into the couch cushions? "Okay," I muttered. I washed it as best I could. Had the dream been my sleeping mind's attempt to make sense of the pain? Dreams happen fast and rewrite themselves. Maybe what I thought I'd been experiencing had all happened in a heartbeat, like a dream of falling that jerks you awake.

I tried to put a Band-Aid on my ear. It could have gone better. Ears are not ideal surfaces for that. This did nothing to improve my mood. I stalked back out to the couch.

And stopped.

And stared.

There were at least a dozen rose petals on the ground, leading in a trail to the sliding glass door. How did they get there? The roses had been in the kitchen. I stared at the glass door for entirely too long, wondering if they had somehow blown into the house . . . through . . . a closed door . . . ?

Wait, had someone come into the house and dropped rose petals on me while I slept?

What the hell was going on?

Why would you drop a handful of rose petals on someone, anyway?

My brain, always a font of useless knowledge, skipped to the Roman emperor Heliogabalus, who once (apocryphally) dropped tons of rose petals on guests at a feast, smothering them. I could probably rule out either Roman emperors or murder attempts.

Had this been intended as some kind of romantic gesture?

I heard the thump of a ladder against the side of the house and saw red.

⌒

"Phil! Did *you* do this?"

"Hold the ladder, will you?" said Phil.

I didn't want to hold the ladder, I wanted to yell. But when people ask you to hold a ladder, you do it. It's reflexive. I grabbed the ladder and glared up at him as he descended.

"Sorry," he said, "the ground's a bit soft there. What's up?"

I waved a rose petal in his face. "Is this your idea of a joke?"

He took the petal, turned it over, then looked at me with the air of a man who is being polite in the face of adversity. "Is what my idea of a joke?"

"I . . ." What had felt like *righteous wrath* when I stormed out of the house suddenly felt a lot more like *jumping to conclusions.* "There were rose petals on me," I said. "When I woke up."

"There's one on you now," he said. "Also you've got a Band-Aid in your hair."

I picked the rose petal off the front of my shirt. So there was.

Phil's look of polite tolerance didn't change. It was not the look of a man who had dumped rose petals on me in my sleep in the name of flirtation. It was the look of a man who had a strange woman yelling and waving floral bits at him.

"Were you working with roses earlier?" he asked. "They get everywhere, I swear."

I had been. I'd had a whole bouquet. But surely if I'd tracked all the petals in myself, I'd have noticed when . . . when . . . *When you immediately went looking for a Band-Aid for your scratches, then went to work on The Project, then looked up rose picker's disease, then traumatized your mother and went rushing to clean up broken glass. Which involved bending over more roses, so that the petals could also have gotten stuck to you. And you took the trash out by the back door, so you could have scattered even more then.*

And while I'd like to say that I would have noticed if there were petals stuck to me, I had once gone to work with a sock clinging to my sweater and hadn't noticed until lunch. (The *front* of the sweater, no less.)

I am an asshole. Yup.

"I'm sorry," I said. I seemed to be apologizing to Phil a lot. Possibly because I kept acting like a dick to Phil. "I . . . uh . . . yeah. I was. I don't know why I thought . . ." I rubbed my face. "I'm sorry. I've been worried about Mom, and I'm obviously not acting rationally. Sorry." I didn't feel like explaining about the sleep paralysis and the feeling of an intruder. Phil must already think I was a few eggs short of an omelet.

"It's fine," said Phil. We stood awkwardly for a minute, and then he added, "I caulked up a hole by your windowsill. I don't know if that's where the ladybugs got in, but it can't hurt."

"Thanks." I mumbled something about letting him know if any others got in, then beat a hasty retreat back into the house with what shreds remained of my dignity. One thing was sure, I wasn't sleeping on the damn couch anymore. If that meant sharing the bed with a few stray ladybugs then so be it. Better that than making a fool of myself thinking the handyman was dropping rose petals on me in my sleep.

It was too early to have wine, but I milked the box for the last half glass anyway. *Squeezing the wine udder* my roommate called it, when you open the box and pull out the little bag and squish it to try to squirt out the last bit. Then I went back online to look up sleep paralysis. (I swear, I am not usually a person who looks up medical conditions online. I lived without health insurance long enough that I am far more likely to try to sleep off anything short of decapitation. This was just an extraordinary few days.)

Yup, it was sleep paralysis. I found out that what I'd had was called a "hypnopompic hallucination," the kind that accompanies waking, as opposed to "hypnagogic," which is what you get when you're falling asleep, except that all sleep hallucinations are lumped together under *hypnagogia*, because why should sleep research be any more logical than any other science?

Rarely linked to underlying psychological conditions. *Well, at least I've got that going for me.* No, they didn't know what causes it, except maybe stress. *Not that I have any sources of stress in my life at the moment. Ha.* May also be linked to sleep apnea, and narcolepsy. *Oh, joy.* Often accompanied by an illusion of an intruder or difficulty breathing. *Check and check.* The exact nature of the hallucination is strongly influenced by cultural context. In the old days, it was referred to as being *hagridden,* but now often manifests as an alien-abduction experience. *Oh, now that's interesting . . .*

I spent two hours down this particular rabbit hole, reading a paper about sleep paralysis in Brazilian folklore, and only surfaced when Mom came home.

"You're sitting here in the dark," she said. "You're gonna ruin your eyes."

It was such a normal Mom thing to say that I started laughing, partly from relief. Some things didn't change. I flipped on the lamp. "I got distracted and didn't realize how late it got."

"So you haven't eaten?"

"No worries. I'll nuke something." I microwaved a frozen potpie and munched it while Mom consulted her planner, muttering to herself about schedules.

I was halfway through the pie when she looked up sharply. "Did you say grace?"

"Uh . . ." I looked down at the remains of Swanson's finest. "No, sorry."

Her gaze was less stern than alarmed. I could have held out against disappointment, but she seemed actually worried that something would happen. I folded my hands, feeling ridiculous, and mumbled, "Thank you, Father, for the food we . . . um . . . have already received . . . from your bounty." I couldn't remember the rest, but apparently that was enough.

Mom nodded to me. "It's important."

"Okay." I found I wasn't particularly interested in the rest of it. I put it in the fridge for later and had a chocolate chip cookie instead. "Oh— Gail sent these for you."

"She came over here?"

"No, I went to go"—see if she'd noticed you acting strangely— "meet her pet vulture." I swallowed a mouthful of cookie. "She's an interesting person."

"She is," said Mom. "She's so funny. Always makes me laugh."

"Very nice garden too."

Mom stiffened. "Yes," she said slowly. "Though Gran Mae's was much nicer when she was alive." She went in search of wine herself and came out with a fresh box.

I did not think this was true, given the extraordinary insect life in Gail's and the ecological dead zone that was Gran Mae's rose garden, but I remembered my talk with Brad. If Mom was still mourning Gran Mae, I should talk to her about it. I tried to think of something positive to say, and came out with, "Gran Mae's was certainly much . . . tidier."

"She was a very tidy person," Mom agreed.

I flashed back to Gran Mae telling me to pick up my room. *You live like a little piggy, Samantha! Nobody wants to marry a little piggy!*

I'd said, "Pigs are one of the smartest animals on earth. Oink, oink." I was that kind of ten-year-old.

Gran Mae had pressed her lips together. "Always have an answer, don't you? No one can tell you anything." Then I think she'd threatened me with the underground children, but whether for sass or having a messy room, I don't know.

"She was always after Brad and I to clean our rooms," I said, trying not to sound aggrieved. "I know she was only trying to get us in the habit."

"Ye-e-e-s . . ." said Mom, drawing the word out and staring into her wine. "We used to butt heads about that when I was a kid too."

I felt stuck. Did I offer sympathy for young Mom or keep trying to say nice things about Gran Mae? "Um. Yes, she was definitely very into cleaning."

"Well, she was a hospice nurse, you know," said Mom. "Lots of nurses get like that, I think. And very brisk and efficient and rather exasperated with healthy people. They have to save their compassion for all the ones who are dying."

"I suppose that's true," I said, even though I had my doubts about Gran Mae being compassionate with anyone. She'd probably have fixed them with her gimlet eye and said, "Are you dead yet? Then make your bed and quit whining." "You've still got one lung, you know, some people would be grateful for any organs at all." "Life support? Nobody wants to marry someone on life support!"

I gulped wine to stifle this train of thought. "Remember how she loved all those old TV shows? *Leave It to Beaver* and *My Three Sons* and *The Patty Duke Show.*"

Mom chuckled. "I watched so many of those growing up. She always had them on. I thought they were still shooting them and kept wondering why they were black and white instead of in color."

That had gone pretty well. I tried to think of another good memory. "She always baked me a cake for my birthday with homemade frosting."

"She did. She loved you and Brad so much."

I had my doubts, remembering all those mornings with the power struggle over the eggs, and the arguments with Brad. Slammed doors, and her standing outside his room muttering, "Useless. Completely useless. I don't understand why men are so obsessed with sons." It didn't feel like love.

No. I was being positive, dammit. Something nice. Say something. *Nice and normal.* "She was always talking about me having a coming out."

"Oh, it was such a big thing for her generation. She hadn't had one and I think it really galled her." Mom shook her head. "She made sure I had one."

"That must have been a bit awkward."

"Well . . ." Mom stared into her wine. "She did an amazing job under the circumstances. It wasn't like there were dozens of debutantes when I had mine. But all her friends from work came, and I had an extremely fancy dress. And roses everywhere, of course."

"I'm sorry about the roses this morning," I said. I was starting to feel like a bull in a china shop, the way I kept having to apologize to everyone. Possibly the best thing I could do for Mom was to pack up and leave, preferably without threatening to murder anyone else or startling her out of her wits.

"It's all right, honey." She patted my arm. "I was just surprised, that's all. It was a nice thought."

"I could have planned better." I lifted my hand, raked by rose thorns. "I think I left a blood offering on every plant in the garden. I don't know how Gran Mae did it. Pact with the rose gods, maybe."

Mom didn't laugh at this. She picked up the remote and began to flip through until she found a mystery at random. "Have we seen this one?"

"I can't remember now."

"Good enough for me."

The Sixth Day

Loving Family: Porcelain-white double blooms on long, sturdy stems. Flowers large, with clean petals. Moderate fragrance with licorice notes. Excellent cut flower. Blooms in multiple flushes throughout the season. Extremely tall shrub, up to seven feet.

CHAPTER 11

Little piggy.

The thought was in my head as soon as I woke up, as clear as my grandmother's whisper. *Little piggy.*

I groped for my phone. Seven thirty in the morning. God, what an unholy hour. I had arranged my whole postdoc life to try to avoid getting up before nine.

This room is a sty. Oink, oink, little piggy.

"Christ," I muttered. I went to the bathroom. There was a ladybug on the mirror again. No, wait, the ladybug was on my forehead. Dammit. I removed it, opened the window, and bent out the corner of the screen to release it.

Padding back into my bedroom, I realized that the remembered whisper wasn't wrong. I'd been living out of my suitcase and a couple of bags of clothes. I'd meant to unpack, but then there had been the whole ladybug thing, and now it looked like a tornado had gone through. Probably I should at least put the clothes in drawers instead of heaping them on the chair.

Little piggy.

I shoved the voice aside and put my clothes into the drawers. I really would have liked to have coffee first, but the sooner I had everything put away, the sooner the memory of Gran Mae would stop yelling at me.

It didn't take long. I extricated a few stray ladybugs from the folds of my clothes and put my suitcases into the closet. I drew the line at making the bed. I was just going to sleep in it again anyway.

I was coming down the stairs when I heard Mom talking fairly loudly.

"Yes? This weekend? Saturday pickup from the hotel, you say?" She was clearly on the phone, so I halted halfway down the steps so as not to distract from what must be a business call.

"Oof. Clear to Southern Pines? Well, I've got my daughter visiting, so I don't know if I should . . ."

Do it, I urged her silently. Get out of the house and do normal things. I still didn't know if it was mourning or something more sinister, but if it was the former, a distraction was a good thing, and if it was the latter, being in a city around other people was undoubtedly a lot safer than a house in the country, even on Lammergeier Lane.

She fell silent while the person on the other end of the line talked. I could hear her pen scratching as she wrote herself a note.

I amused myself looking at the art on the staircase wall. It used to be a set of brightly colored paintings of sugar skulls that Mom had picked up on a visit to Arizona. Now it was framed photos of her family. *Nice and normal,* I thought grimly.

A wedding picture with my dad, a photo of Brad in his dress uniform. No Gran Mae. No Great-Grandad Rasputin, either, although I thought his sepia-tone glare would have made a hilarious contrast to all the carefully lit portraits. Maybe she could include him in a scrapbook. One of the ones where you put stickers with captions on things. FATHER SAYS: I WOULD NEVER HAVE ALLOWED GOSSIP. FATHER SAYS: I'M NOT ACTUALLY A WARLOCK, I JUST DRESS LIKE ONE. I stifled a giggle.

The best picture of me was a graduation photo taken in the backyard. I was grinning and brandishing my mortarboard, framed by roses. I stared at it. I looked so much younger then. Grad school with all its horrors was a distant cloud on the horizon. My gown was dark blue and I was wearing Doc Martens.

"Yes, I see that . . . two of them, huh? Have we worked with them before?"

Those had been good boots. I'd had them all through college and they'd seen me through multiple digs. I think they discontinued that style, which was a damn shame. I have wide feet and the newer ones pinch.

"I remember her but not him. Do you have a dossier?"

I was staring at Graduate Me's boots and eavesdropping shamelessly when I saw something odd in the roses.

What the hell is that? I bent forward, squinting. There was a shape in the shadow of the rosebush that I'd never noticed before. A very odd but very *distinct* shape.

It looked exactly like a human hand, and I mean *exactly*. Five pale fingers curving over the roots of the rosebush, the thumb dappled with a splash of light through the leaves. A long white wrist vanishing into shadow.

It had to be a trick of the light. Obviously there hadn't been a hand lying under the rosebush during my graduation photo. We'd have noticed something like that. Probably.

Actually we'd been a bit frantic as I recall, because the school had threatened death and doom and eternal suffering on any student who arrived even five minutes late. Everyone had to be in place fifteen minutes beforehand or we would not be allowed to get our diploma. I hadn't cared that much, but Mom had. But she'd also wanted to get a photo, presumably while the light was good, and I suddenly remembered her fluttering around the room, trying to find film for the camera, while I rolled my eyes.

Okay, maybe we *wouldn't* have noticed a hand. Possibly we wouldn't have noticed a live elephant. But it was still ridiculous. Trick of the light, definitely.

"I . . . well, yes, all right, all right, I can do that. And please tell Mark I hope he feels better soon." I cheered internally and abandoned Graduate Me and the optical illusion to continue down the stairs.

"Business?" I asked.

"Coworker's out sick and needs me to cover for him. I'm sorry, honey, I meant to spend this weekend here, but David's really been left in the lurch . . ."

"Go, go." I made shooing motions. "I'll be here for ages. You'll be sick of me in a week."

"I will *not*." She looked around the house with a worried air. "You're sure you'll be okay?"

"I survived the last time without being murdered in my bed."

"Yes, but then there were all those bugs . . ."

"If I'm murdered by ladybugs, I want you to tell everyone. Call my boss and tell her. She'll get a great paper out of it. 'First Documented Case of Successful Human Predation By *Harmonia axyridis*.' I'll be famous."

Mom rolled her eyes and swatted at me with her planner. I ducked out of the way, grabbed a can of fizzy water, and went to the backyard to see if I could spot any more insects.

The roses were still in full, dramatic bloom. I cracked open my can, scanning for movement, but didn't see any. In the photo, I'd been standing in front of the big white rosebush, which meant the hand would be about . . . there.

No hand. Obviously.

There isn't a hand. You're just picking out a random pattern and assigning meaning to it.

I almost believed myself. A large part of my job is picking out patterns in photos. I'd spent hours on The Project, matching diagnostic characters. Probably that made me more susceptible.

Or it means you're more likely to notice them.

Don't be ridiculous. There can't actually be a hand in that photo. That's just not a thing that happens.

I went over to the rosebush and crouched down, looking for something that might have made that shape. A particular tangle of roots, say. A pale rock and an arrangement of leaves. Something.

All I saw was brown bark mulch. The trunk and the thick line of roots looked like they had in the photo, although granted they'd been shadowed and barely visible. Nothing that even remotely resembled a hand.

I went back into the house and up the stairs. Mom was still scribbling on her planner, and I would have felt silly carrying a framed photo of myself around, so I snapped a quick shot of the bottom of the photo with my phone and went back down.

"You okay?" asked Mom, glancing up.

"Forgot something," I lied.

I am a skeptic. If you observe something that is impossible, odds are good the fault is with the observer. I pulled up the photo and zoomed in until the hand filled the screen.

Dammit, it still looked like a hand. In fact, it looked even more like a hand. I could see the dimpled knuckles and the soft lines of the wrist.

The screen was too small, that was the problem. If I could get it onto my laptop, I could blow it up and then I'd see that it was just a stray plastic bag or a white rock. I asked my phone if it was connected to the internet and it told me that it had a very close relationship with the internet. I attempted to pull up a web page and it informed me that it was not that kind of relationship.

"Something wrong?" asked Mom.

"My damn phone," I muttered, not wanting to get into the issue of hands in the roses. "Look, I'm going to run to town and get coffee and phone signal for a bit. Do you need me to pick anything up?"

"More wine, and maybe one of those rotisserie chickens for tonight."

I was so distracted that I was halfway down the walkway before I noticed the vulture on the mailbox. "Sorry," I told him, skirting his perch. "Busy. Gotta . . . figure out this thing . . ."

At the coffee shop, armed with an extremely froofy drink with extra whipped cream, I finally managed to get the photos sent over to my computer. The barista didn't comment as I hunched over the keyboard, muttering to myself. (Well, she was a barista. Baristas, like bartenders, have Seen Things.)

All those police-procedural shows gave the world a completely unrealistic view of how much detail you can pull from a photo. I blew the image up until I was staring at individual pixels, then slowly backed out. I fiddled with the brightness, hoping that it would resolve into mulch and shadow.

It resolved all right. It resolved into fingers and thumb and wrist. A child's hand, based on the proportions.

I slumped back in my chair and stared at the screen. I drank my coffee and licked whipped cream off my upper lip and the entire time, a pale hand reached for my ankles from the far side of the roses, as crisp and perfect as it had been when I graduated from high school fifteen years earlier.

CHAPTER 12

All right. I had seen a very strange thing. I had to think about this logically.

The most logical explanation, of course, was that I was hallucinating. The world continued to be the ordinary world, and the strangeness was all happening in the pink meat behind my eyeballs. Combined with my unsettling sleep paralysis the night before, there was definitely a possibility that things were going loopy in my brain. Before I did any other testing, I had to rule that out.

I was on a couple of medications—who isn't?—for acid reflux and birth control and my less-than-stellar thyroid, and I had a bottle of anxiety meds to be taken "as needed," which wasn't often because they put me to sleep. I hadn't taken any of those for months, and my prescriptions for the others hadn't changed in years. You can always develop new side effects, of course, so I couldn't rule that out completely.

I went to the internet, skipped past the first page of clickbait articles, and managed to pull up some literature. Hmm. Apparently psychosis and visual hallucinations *did* sometimes occur with unmanaged hypothyroidism.

"Oh goody," I muttered out loud. "It wasn't enough being fat and tired."

Still, there was usually a progression, wasn't there? You didn't just wake up one morning imagining hands in the bushes. Unless you had a psychotic break, and I'd expect to notice if I had one, right? (Come to think of it, what even *is* a psychotic break? We throw the phrase around but damned if I have any idea what it really means.)

Of course, I'd had that sleep paralysis, but that was just a thing that happened sometimes. Perfectly normal people got sleep paralysis. Really. Nice and normal people, even.

Ideally it would have been nice to go to the doctor and get it checked out, but my doctor was back in Arizona, and so I would have had to find a new doctor here. Which, let's face it, meant paying an exorbitant amount of money to be told that the problem was that I was fat and if I just dieted and exercised more, I wouldn't be seeing strange things in the backyard. Half the doctors on earth wouldn't even bother looking at my chart, they'd just see a fat person and conclude that any and all medical maladies were my own fault for being lazy and overeating. Never mind that I could probably out-hike most of them and my blood pressure is exquisite. I could hop into an ER carrying my severed leg and squirting blood from the stump and the doctor would congratulate me on having dropped all that leg weight and tell me to keep up the good work.

So, if you can't go to a doctor and you're probably not a reliable witness, what do you do then?

Obviously the only solution was to see if other people saw it too. Science hinges on repeatability. It's not enough that I observed something, you have to be able to observe it too, under the same conditions, before we can be sure it's a quantifiable phenomenon.

Right. I closed the laptop. I had seen something inexplicable. Now I just had to replicate the phenomenon and hopefully prove that I wasn't crazy.

"Phil," I said, "I need you to look at something."

Phil was trying to work the ice maker on the fridge, which was feeling finicky and making horrible noises. "Eh?" he called over the grinding. "What?" He frowned. "Is it your car? I can't do much with cars. They aren't anything like plants."

I reassured him that my car was in perfect health. "It's about this

photo." Mom had gone out, so I felt better about taking down the graduation photo.

He took the photo and looked at them closely. "Hybrid teas," he
said after a moment. "Don't ask me to identify the varieties. There's too
many."

"No, not that. Look right down here. By my feet."

"I don't see . . ."

"Keep looking."

Phil looked from the picture to me, then back again, but he kept
looking. I could tell the moment he saw it. He started, then gave me a
very suspicious look. "What the hell? Is that a hand?"

Oh thank god, he sees it too.

Oh shit, he sees it too.

"That's what it looks like." I set my laptop on the counter. "Here, I
took a photo and blew it up. Take a look."

Phil leaned over my shoulder, looking at the laptop. He smelled like
cut grass. He scowled at the screen. "Is this some kind of Photoshop
thing?"

"It's not. I spotted it this morning."

Another long look. "Are you messing with me?"

"I'm not. I swear I'm not." I could tell he didn't quite believe me.

He handed the photo back. "Look, if you're not messing with me . . ."

"I'm *really* not."

"Then somebody's messing with *you.*"

⌒

Phil's words stuck with me, because they couldn't possibly be true.

Yes, all right, it was *theoretically* possible that someone had snuck into
the house, scanned my graduation photo, digitally altered it to put a
child's hand in the background, printed it out, snuck back in, and hung
it up. But it didn't make sense. Why do it at all? You'd be relying on
either me or Mom—okay, most likely Mom—noticing a very subtle

change in the background of a photo, and that's an awful lot of effort to gaslight somebody when you could just mess with the hot-water heater or play creepy music through the wall.

Or . . . well, all right, fine, it was slightly more theoretically possible that Mom had done so, for some obscure reason of her own.

Yes, I could have asked her. But if I did, she would definitely say no, because obviously it was ridiculous, and then it would give her something else to worry about. So I didn't. Possibly this wasn't the right decision, but I didn't want to pile anything else on her. (And all right, *fine,* maybe I wanted to keep that as an option because otherwise I would rapidly run out of rational explanations.)

I rubbed my forehead. Did the fact that I didn't believe someone would go to all this trouble to mess with me or my mother mean that I wasn't paranoid? Paranoia is a symptom of something, isn't it? (Oh god, not another list of symptoms to look up. I still wasn't recovered from the Alzheimer's lists, or rose picker's disease.)

What was a better explanation—that someone was sneaking into the house to mess with my mother, or that there had been a hand under the bushes?

Could we really not have noticed the hand in the photo all these years?

How often do you actually look at these photos, though? Almost never. Everybody's got them and nobody notices them. And if anybody actually looks at the photo, they look at the face, not a shadow to the right of the boots.

First, however, it occurred to me that there was something else I could check. I'd seen the photo twice in recent days, and once it had been in the attic, in the stack of framed photos. Even if we accepted the completely bizarre idea that someone had snuck into the house to replace a photo in an effort to do . . . something . . . odds were they wouldn't even know about the photos in the attic. So if I was going to verify that the photo on the staircase wall was genuinely from my graduation, I could check it against the photo in the attic.

It was also a much larger photo, and I could get a better look at the supposed hand.

Right. Okay. Very logical. I jumped up and went to the attic stairs. There was some grumbling and stubbing of toes as I made my way to the pictures by phone-light, but I managed to locate the stack of pictures and began flipping through it.

I was halfway through the stack when I heard the front door open. Oh shit. Mom was home, and how was I going to explain this? "Sorry, Mom, I'm just afraid I've lost my damn mind, or that you have a really weird stalker . . ." No, that wasn't going to go over well. I flipped faster. *Great, trying to hide the evidence just as your parents come home. If you revert to childhood any faster, you'll be watching Saturday morning cartoons in footie pajamas.*

"Sam? Are you in the attic?"

"Yeah, hang on," I called back, since there was no point in denying it. I found my graduation photo just as I heard Mom starting up the steps.

By now I'd stared at that photo for so long that I could have recognized the hand in my sleep. It took a single glance to realize that yes, there it was, same position, same fingers, same shadow and light over the thumb. Well, that told me . . . something. I don't know what. I took a photo, hoping that the flash wasn't washing it out too much.

Mom poked her head over the level of the floor. "What are you doing?"

"I, uh . . ." I flipped another picture and hit my great-grandfather's photo. *Good enough.* "I was looking for this guy. I wanted to look him up online, but I couldn't remember how to spell his name."

"Oh," said Mom. "Elgar Mills."

"That's him." I made a show of turning the photo around to read the name. "Yup. All I could think was Rasputin." Mom snorted. "Is it okay if I bring this down?"

"Sure, honey." She sounded a trifle doubtful, probably afraid that I'd try to hang it up next to the hellgrammite.

"I'll put it back when I'm done, I promise." I came down, carrying

Elgar, and set him on the chair in my room. His eyes seemed to follow me as I changed out of my by-now dusty clothes and I left the room, mostly to get away from his expression.

I sat down on the couch and pulled up the photo I'd just taken on my phone.

A cold chill went through me. I didn't need the bigger screen. It was a hand, most definitely a hand. It couldn't be anything but a hand. I could see the shadows of nails, and the darker half-moons of dirt beneath them.

I would almost have preferred a stalker.

Maybe one of the neighbor kids snuck into the backyard and was lying under the rosebush. No, the angle doesn't work at all, the kid would have to have a broken arm or be . . . buried . . . under the roses . . .

Oh god.

"Finding anything?" asked Mom.

I gave a guilty start. Elgar. Right. Him.

Could I tell my mother that I thought there might have been a small child buried under the roses in my graduation photo? I tried to shape the words on my tongue and discovered that no, no I could not. I swallowed. Elgar Mills. Yes. Think about him. Don't think about the other thing. There's got to be a logical explanation. "Sorry, got distracted again. Let's see what we can find . . ."

I opened my laptop and punched in his name. The results began to scroll up on my screen, and that's when I got my second shock of the day.

MAD SORCEROR OF BOONE ARRESTED! trumpeted the headline of the *Siler Independent.* SO-CALLED "WIZARD OF BOONE" CHARGED WITH INDECENCY said the rather more sedate *Charlotte Observer,* who relegated it to the second page.

"I think he's from Boone," I said weakly.

"Really?" Mom looked up from her planner, interested. "I never knew that. Mother always said her family was from Gastonia. Maybe that was her mother."

"Mmm." Boone is a perfectly nice little college town in the Blue Ridge. I went to a concert there once. It is not really the sort of place that you expect to produce mad wizards, but that could be said of most places. (Okay, maybe not Florida.) "He, uh . . . you know how you said he was a bit of a character?"

"Yes?"

"A little more than a bit, I think." I turned the laptop screen to face her.

Mom's eyes went very wide. "Oh my."

"It appears he was into some very weird shit," I said.

"Language," said Mom. I let it go. She'd never minded my swearing before, but that was the least of my worries these days.

"Sorry. Very weird *stuff.*" I cleared my throat and read aloud. "'While the eyes of the nation turn to Tennessee and the trial of schoolteacher Scopes for the teaching of godless materials, a drama unfolds closer to home. Elgar Mills, 47, known among the more credulous as the Mad Wizard of Boone, was charged in court today with public indecency for acts befitting no good Christian. A crime carrying penalties up to a hundred dollar fine or thirty days in jail.

"'Far more than merely teaching the works of Darwin, the Mad Wizard has made claims better fitting to a lunatic than one who claims to have been educated among the finest universities, and went so far as to tell the assembled court that they would pay for their arrogance in thinking to bring their betters to task in such a craven fashion—'"

The hellgrammite print fell off the wall with a crash.

I let out a yelp like a small dog being stepped on and threw my computer mouse halfway across the room.

"I'm sure none of it was true," said my mother in careful, measured tones. "You know what these little local newspapers are like. No better than gossip rags."

This was a remarkably calm statement given that all the glass in the picture frame had shattered and the frame itself had turned into a rhombus. I clutched my chest. "I nearly jumped out of my skin!"

"Yes," said Mom, still sounding very calm. "Let me get the dustpan. Watch your feet."

I climbed over the back of the couch and went in pursuit of my mouse. My heart was still pounding. *Jesus.* And Mom hadn't reacted to the picture falling at all. What the *hell*?

I shoved my feet into my sandals by the door and came back to help clean up. Mom vanished outside with the glass and the broken frame.

The hellgrammite print had a scratch in it, which I found irrationally infuriating, but at least it was just over the riverbed, not anything important. "I'll get this reframed for you," I promised.

"You don't have to do that."

"No, I will. It's probably my fault for hanging it wrong or something. Can you drop it off at a frame shop when you're out this weekend? I'll give them my credit card."

She frowned. "Maybe I shouldn't take the job this weekend after all."

"You absolutely should," I said. "A picture fell, that's all. The house isn't about to come down."

Her gaze lingered on me for a moment, then she forced a smile. "Yes, of course. It's just that I have to stay at the hotel tonight, if I'm meeting them at the airport at six. Are you sure you don't want to come with me?"

"No, no." I waved my hands. "I'll watch TV and work. It'll be very boring."

"All right. I'll be back the day after tomorrow." She frowned. "Call Phil if anything happens, all right?"

"Sure," I agreed. It wasn't until she'd backed out of the driveway that I looked down at my phone, which barely had service anyway, and realized I didn't have Phil's phone number.

The silence in the house was suddenly very loud. I cleared my throat, just to have some kind of noise, and it was so small and feeble a sound that it only made the silence stronger.

I poured wine and sat down to think. My brain was full of hands under the shrubbery, the Mad Grandad of Boone, and Mom not even flinching at the picture falling. I took a few deep breaths to try to settle my thoughts, but the silence was still pressing down on me like a physical weight. I found a music playlist on my phone and turned it up to full volume. The speakers made it sound small and tinny, but it made a little clear space that wasn't smothered under the ecru-painted silence.

I couldn't do anything about the Mad Wizard. That was in the past. A weird past that I hadn't quite wrapped my head around, but it could certainly wait. And I couldn't do much about Mom right at the moment, unless I wanted to make myself nuts reading more lists of symptoms.

That left the hand in the rose garden.

All right. Now that I had a single target for my anxiety, I could turn all my analytic prowess to it. Let's suppose, worst-case scenario, that someone had buried a kid in the backyard, badly enough that an arm stuck out. Whoever this was would have had to come back and move the body in short order, or it would have started to smell, obviously. But this would have left a large hole, and they'd have to refill it. Was I a good enough archaeologist to tell the difference between fill dirt and native clay after fifteen years? You never knew unless you tried. And at least I'd know there wasn't anything buried behind the roses right *now*.

Which there definitely wouldn't be.

Well, probably wouldn't be.

. . . fuck.

It was still light out. I grabbed a trowel from the shed, got down on my belly, and wiggled under the roses. I felt ridiculous, but my only audience was the pair—no, it was a trio now—of black vultures on the neighboring roof.

"Don't judge me," I muttered to the birds. "This is perfectly normal. Ish." They watched me with interest, possibly hoping that I was about to die and leave a tasty carcass for them to eat.

There was almost no clearance between the ground and the rosebush. Thorns tangled in my hair and yanked at my scalp. There was also the not-so-small problem of my boobs, which were not made for lying facedown on any surface, let alone compacted ground and roots. I do not sleep on my stomach for a reason.

I stabbed the trowel into the ground, got about a quarter of an inch worth of dirt before I hit a tangle of roots, and cursed. I tried again, a little farther from the rosebush, and got the trowel almost an inch into the ground before I scraped the concrete foundation of the fence post. My left nipple encountered a piece of gravel and lodged a vociferous complaint.

"This is batshit," I said out loud. "This is ridiculous. I'm being ridiculous. There's got to be an explanation." I could feel the despair starting to pupate and erupt into anger. *Goddammit. There wasn't a hand under here. Nobody's buried here. You couldn't possibly bury someone back here. You couldn't even get behind the rosebush to start digging. If you were going to bury a body, you wouldn't put one here, you'd go on the other side of the fence where the woods start and drop it there. No witnesses.*

And who would bury a body in your yard anyway? Do you think your mother was killing children and shoving them under the roses?

No, obviously I didn't. Mom was the most unlikely serial killer in existence. Hell, even if she'd had the desire, she wouldn't have had the energy. She was still working two jobs then and she'd come home and fall asleep on the couch most days.

Now Gran Mae . . . okay, if it came to light that Gran Mae murdered someone and buried them at the base of her roses, I would be horrified, but maybe not completely shocked. I could see a certain someone, who kept a garden with "weeds everywhere, and no class at all," making Gran Mae's hit list. Still, small children? Not her speed. (What would Father have said?) Anyway, Gran Mae had been dead for years by the time the photo was taken.

I lay there covered in dirt—usually my happy place—and felt defeated. Was I obsessing over this because it was somehow better to think that there might have been a severed hand in the backyard than to think that something was wrong with Mom that I couldn't fix?

Yes. Yes, I was. I didn't need a school counselor to tell me that.

I started to wiggle back out, trying not to lose any more hair to the roses. The thorns yanked at my scalp like Gran Mae brushing my hair when I was little. I'd always shrieked and wiggled, and she'd huffed angrily. *I'm just brushing your hair so it isn't a rat's nest. You brush Barbie's hair, don't you?* (I did not in fact brush Barbie's hair. I did once attempt to mummify her, though. Mom convinced me that I did not actually have to remove Barbie's brains with a hook through her nose, but did allow me to wrap her in toilet paper and bury her in the sandbox. In retrospect, it's pretty obvious why I turned out the way I did.)

Doll parts, I thought suddenly. *What if it was doll parts?*

Relief flooded me. There. *That* was a logical explanation. There had been a severed doll arm under the roses. Granted, I'd never liked dolls myself—I had always been a stuffed animal person—but Gran Mae had had a couple creepy dolls in period costumes from the Franklin Mint. They were probably in the attic now. Maybe one had gotten damaged and thrown in the trash, then a raccoon had gotten into it and dragged a severed doll arm under the bushes.

Part of me knew that this was a terribly flimsy explanation, but it was the only one I had. Otherwise I'd have to worry about serial killers on Lammergeier Lane, and that really would be ridiculous. Serial killers didn't live in housing developments with white walls and builder-beige carpet and white picket fences and pictures of roses on the walls and . . .

Okay, now that I thought about it, they probably *did* live in houses like that. Stepford-style developments had to be a breeding ground for the darker side of humanity. But Lammergeier Lane wasn't Stepford. It wasn't neat enough. We didn't have an HOA. There were vultures on the roof and tangles of woodland pressing against the back fences. Our neighbors weren't painfully, terrifyingly nice; they were paranoid old men, like Mr. Pressley, or genuinely nice people with badly trained beagles, like the Goldbergs. Normal people.

Nice and normal.

And Stepford *definitely* didn't have a wild garden at the end of the road run by a woman who rehabilitated vultures. That wasn't normal at all. It was that lack of normalcy that must have stuck in Gran Mae's craw. She had wanted the fifties family so badly, my grandad coming home from his job at the office while she spent the day vacuuming the house in pearls and high heels, like June Cleaver in *Leave It to Beaver*.

Of course, by that measure we'd all failed. Grandad had done well enough, I think—at least, Gran Mae had seemed to think so—but there was no room in Gran Mae's perfect world for a fat granddaughter and a grandson who listened to heavy metal at top volume in his bedroom.

I dusted off my knees. My shirt was covered in mulch and there were dead leaves in my hair. The vultures on the roof next door croaked to one another solemnly. It sounded like commentary.

"Sorry to disappoint you, boys," I said. "I'm not dead yet."

Another croak came from across the yard. I looked over at the house opposite and saw that two more had settled on the roof there. They exchanged pleasantries over the top of our house, but none of them landed on our roof.

They like to keep an eye on that house, Gail had said, though she never said why.

Maybe someone was feeding them severed limbs and they're hoping it'll start up again.

Stop that, dammit. It was a doll arm.

Doll arms don't have dirt under their fingernails.

I took a deep breath and shoved the thought firmly out of my head and went inside to clean up.

❧

To top off an already rough day, I went to the bathroom to clean up my scratches and discovered that I'd started my period. (I know, I should have seen it coming, but I've had a few things on my mind, okay?) I groaned. Just what I needed. Did I have any tampons? No, of course I didn't. Great. Lovely.

I checked under the sink and located some scrubbing powder for the bathtub and an elderly loofah, neither of which would make an acceptable substitute. Did Mom have any?

Normally I wouldn't just wander into my mother's bedroom without permission, but this was an emergency and I knew Mom wouldn't mind. I kept my eyes down as I went through. (I didn't expect to see anything terribly illicit, mind you, but everybody's entitled to some amount of privacy, and if she happened to keep a vibrator out on the nightstand or something, I did *not* want to know about it.)

The master bathroom fixtures were all seafoam green, which I had thought was ridiculously cool at fourteen and still kinda do. Giant seafoam-green bathtub! What's not to love? The bathroom mirror was spangled with notes in my mother's handwriting. I checked under the sink, praying that menopause had not yet visited this house, and was rewarded with a familiar box. *Thank you, Jesus.*

I straightened, tampons in hand. I hadn't read the notes on the mirror—they were almost certainly all just reminders to refill the toilet paper or call the mechanic—but my own name jumped out at me from one at eye level.

she loves sam
she won't hurt her

I blinked. Underneath, in slightly larger letters, with three frantic exclamation points, was another note reading:

it will be okay!!!

"...um," I said. And as I slowly read the other notes on the mirror, my heart sank. "Oh, Mom..." I said, leaning on the sink. "Oh, Mom. Oh hell."

CHAPTER 13

There *was* something wrong with my mother. Hallucinations or paranoia or early onset of dementia. Thyroid condition. I was leaning toward that one. The sudden weight loss fit. And the notes. Oh god. The notes.

tell mother you love her every night
pray out loud before bed—important!!!
get new print of roses for kitchen

But most of all, the one on the back of the bathroom door, that said simply:

it's real you're not imagining things

Dear god, what was going through her head? Something terrible, clearly. Something she didn't want to talk to me about. (And who could blame her? If I was having problems, I'd have bent over backward not to inflict them on anyone else myself. Mom and I were too damn much alike, that was the problem.)

I left the bathroom, feeling desperately ashamed of myself. I'd been crawling around fretting about old phantom hands in the shrubbery, which was obviously ridiculous, and meanwhile Mom was in much worse shape than I'd thought.

Who could I talk to about it? I didn't know any of her coworkers. I sure as hell wasn't going to call her boss. Who did that leave? Phil? Gail?

Maybe Gail. Gail had said that she didn't think there was anything wrong with Mom. If she was covering for her out of friendship, maybe I could convince her to talk to me. And if she wasn't . . . well, I'd cross that bridge when I came to it.

It was too late tonight, of course. Too late for anything but wine and television and worrying. It seemed like that was all I did lately, but I couldn't think of anything else to do. I'd had too much wine to drive somewhere with signal and call Brad. I could text various friends of mine, who are generally lovely people, but what were they going to say? "Wow, that sucks. Tell me if there's anything I can do to help." And they'd mean every word, but they couldn't fix my mom's problem, and it wasn't like any of them had a spare fifty grand to move Mom into dedicated care, if that's what had to happen.

I felt suddenly desperately lonely. I don't, usually. When you grow up as the weird kid taking photos of bugs you get used to it, and when you later find that the world is full of other people who want to talk about bugs with you, it's a glorious revelation. But here I was, thirty-two, alone in my mom's house, and everything was terrible, and I couldn't fix *any* of it.

Fuck. I brought the box of wine into the living room, set it on the coffee table, and put on Inspector Lowell. Maybe I should get a Scottie dog. We could solve mysteries together. The Mystery of the Sudden Ladybugs. The Mystery of the Upsetting Notes. The Mystery of What Happened to All the Wine. The Mystery of What Is Going On With Mom.

Maybe all the beige had driven her bonkers. If so, I couldn't blame her. It was going to drive me bonkers soon. I wondered what Mom would say if she came home to discover that I'd painted the living room turquoise.

She'd be supportive, of course. Mom was always supportive. Dammit. That was the worst of this, that I didn't know how to be supportive in return. I was supposed to be helping, and all I was doing was upsetting her and bad-mouthing Gran Mae and breaking glass everywhere. And alienating Phil. "Can't forget about Phil," I muttered, raising my wine in a toast.

Maybe the best thing I could do was leave and tell my brother that he should come handle it, because I was making a god-awful mess.

On-screen, someone was murdered in their bedroom. The camera watched from outside as they collapsed against the window, hands clawing at the glass. Then the murderer finished up and the hands slid limply down the pane.

Disembodied hands was too much for me right now. I turned off Inspector Lowell, drained my wine in three gulps, and went upstairs. The clock ticked at my retreating back.

When I got up in the middle of the night for my usual trip to the toilet, the house was oppressively silent again. The air conditioner wasn't even on. Maybe this was the sound of beige paint, this fraught absence of sound. "I hear the souuuunds . . . of ecru," I sang, and began giggling. Christ, I must still be drunk. I shoved the bathroom door open.

Something moved in the bathroom sink.

A white hand reaching for me. I only caught a glimpse out of the corner of my eye, but for a horrifying instant, I *knew* that's what it was, coming out of the drain on an impossibly elongated wrist, and it was going to latch onto my face with its dirty nails and they'd find me in the morning dead and the hand would be gone, coiling bonelessly back down into the pipes, waiting . . .

I shrieked and flung myself backward. The towel bar struck me painfully in the back. The pain shocked me awake and I scrabbled for the wall and the light switch.

Fluorescent light blossomed overhead and chased away the vision of a hand. Something was moving in the sink, but it was a dark spreading stain.

Ladybugs.

"Goddammit." I leaned over the sink, my heart still pounding. They were pouring from out of the drain, spreading across the ceramic like blood. Hundreds of them, crawling on top of one another, sliding down the slick surface of the sink, with still more flooding out. Some had already reached the countertop and were scurrying across it, blood splatter from the open wound.

I hastily pulled the little metal knob that closed the drain, and the tide stopped. The green-pepper smell of crushed ladybugs hit my nose. Dammit. I hadn't meant to kill them.

"What are you doing in the drains?" I demanded. "Drain flies, sure. The occasional centipede, yeah, okay. But *ladybugs* do not swarm in *drains!*"

The ladybugs crawled around the sink, refusing to answer. My fingers itched. I held up a hand and ladybugs coated my fingers like a red glove, so densely I could barely see the skin.

"Jesus *Christ!*" I shook my hand wildly. Entomology brain thought this was all quite fascinating, but it was getting swamped under the sheer numbers of the invaders. Ladybugs flew in all directions, some of them actually flying, some of them hitting the wall or the mirror and raining down with tiny ticking sounds. A couple landed on my face and in my hair and I am embarrassed to say that I shrieked and slapped at them, and that didn't help at all and they were still on my hand and covering the counter now and I couldn't look in the mirror because they were on the mirror and I couldn't tell what was on me and what was on the surface of the glass and one was on my ear and in a minute it would crawl inside—

Get hold of yourself! You're a professional, dammit! They're not demons, they're not monsters, they're Harmonia axyridis *and maybe some* Hippodamia convergens *and they swarm sometimes and that's the reason they're here. Stop freaking out and think!*

I forced myself to stand still. I flicked the one on my ear away, took a deep breath, and looked in the mirror. There were two on my forehead and one meandering around my chin, like a giant mobile pimple. That thought made me snort and I felt a little bit calmer and picked them off and set them in the sink again, and brushed the last few off my hand. The webbing between my fingers was itching in earnest now, probably because they'd been trying to bite. (Yes, Asian lady beetles do bite, but they can't get through human skin, so it's just a small scratch. No matter how many there were, I wasn't going to get skeletonized by ladybugs. I was in more danger of rose picker's disease.)

It occurred to me suddenly that if the ladybugs were in this sink, they might be coming out of the other sinks as well. I had a horrible vision of all the drains in the house erupting with shiny red beetles, flooding our house like the elevator in *The Shining*. I took two steps to the bathtub, saw a single ladybug wandering around, possibly from being flung, and hastily closed the stopper.

Still wobbly from too much wine, I staggered around the house, closing all the drains. None of the others had ladybugs coming out, but you couldn't be too sure. The clock ticked at me from the mantelpiece. Mom's notes were dark squares and I avoided reading them.

Once again, I found myself vacuuming up bugs in the middle of the night and shaking them loose in the backyard. "That's enough of you in the house," I informed them. "Stay out here and take care of the roses."

I staggered back upstairs, grumpy and groggy. The shot of adrenaline had worn off while I was vacuuming. My hand still itched. I scratched it irritably and sat down on the bed.

I wanted to go back to sleep, but I had a nagging feeling that there was something I had forgotten to do. Something I'd dreamed about. Wasn't there?

The roses say . . . say your prayers.

Ridiculous. I didn't pray. I hadn't prayed in years. It's not a thing I did. I didn't know what was out there, but I was pretty sure it wasn't an interventionist god who cared whether or not I say grace over my pizza.

The roses say . . .

I stared at the ceiling, hearing the whisper in my head. It sounded just like the one that had whispered, *Little piggy.* Not a real voice. Somewhere between a thought and a memory.

I don't believe in God, but I do believe in ritual. I doubt you can be an archaeologist and not know that rituals have a powerful hold over human brains. I sighed and knelt down next to the bed.

I would have sworn that I didn't remember how to pray, but the words were right there on my tongue.

> *"Now I lay me down to sleep,*
> *I pray the Lord my soul to keep,*
> *If I should die before I wake,*
> *I pray the Lord my soul to take."*

Morbid damn prayer. I'd always thought so. Who wants little kids to fixate on dying? But I felt better after saying it, and I crawled into bed and didn't dream about ladybugs or hands or anything else.

The Seventh Day

Darkest Night: Velvety dark red petals on short, sturdy stems. Buds appear almost black. A beautiful, disease-resistant hybrid tea rose that performs well in high heat, blooming continuously throughout the season.

CHAPTER 14

Phil was in the kitchen when I went down for coffee. "Don't shoot," he said. "I'm just here to fix the ice maker."

"Ha." I told him about the previous night's ladybugs. His eyebrows shot up.

"I'll take a look," he promised. "I haven't seen any yet today."

"Thank goodness for small favors."

"None in the ice maker either."

"Oh good."

I sat down on the couch with my coffee. Phil did not immediately flee my presence, which was probably more than I deserved, given that I had so far threatened his life, brandished rose petals at him, and showed him ghostly hands in the shrubbery.

Opening my laptop, the first thing I saw was MAD WIZARD OF BOONE ARRESTED! I blinked a few times, and then decided that hell, I wasn't going to get anything else accomplished today, I might as well read about my infamous ancestor.

Finding information took longer than one might think. Outside of the coverage of his trial, where he did not exactly endear himself to the court, he seemed to have stayed out of the newspapers. But chasing Elgar Mills led me down another rabbit hole of frankly extraordinary proportions, and I have never been able to resist a good internet rabbit hole.

"The problem with the world," I informed Phil an hour later, "is that there's just so *much* of it."

"Is that from a Snapple bottle?"

"No."

He considered this at length, then said, "You should write Snapple bottles."

"It probably pays better." I waved at my laptop. "Look at this. I'm trying to find one d . . . darn sorcerer, and he leads to twenty others and a book on the history of Thelema in the United States."

"The what what?"

"Thelema. It's a religion, or a ritual magic system, or something like that. Aleister Crowley invented it."

Phil looked over my shoulder. "Oh, *him*. He was on a bunch of album covers in the nineties, wasn't he?"

"Also that, yes."

My great-grandfather, Elgar Mills, had not been an associate of Crowley's, so far as I could tell. Instead he'd hung out in the forties, briefly, with a man named Jack Parsons, who *was* an associate of Crowley's. Also a rocket scientist and also completely batshit. (I don't like to step on anyone's religion, but when you start mixing cocaine, free love, amphetamines, statutory rape, mescaline, and ritual black magic, you have crossed out of the religious-tolerance zone and into the perhaps-you-should-be-kept-away-from-other-people zone.) There was a lot written about Parsons and all of it was bizarre. Most of what I could find about Elgar that wasn't newspaper clippings about his trial lay in footnotes in books about Parsons. Fortunately large sections were available online.

Very . . . large . . . sections.

I'm a good researcher, in all modesty, but this was a lot to get through. While Phil probably didn't care much about my great-grandad, I kept reading bits aloud to him anyway. I'm not sure if I wanted someone else to witness the train wreck with me, or if, like the hand in the photograph, I wanted to make sure someone else saw it too. "Says here that Parsons wanted to fertilize a magic baby and have it born via immaculate conception, so it could be the new Thelemic messiah and bring about the Age of Horus."

"Is that like the Age of Aquarius?"

"I think it's the same principle." The authors of this particular book selection assumed that of course the reader knew what the Age of Horus was and also presumably why someone would want to bring it about. Parsons had consulted Elgar about this project, according to the footnotes, but it said that Elgar had been "dismissive of his plans" and "warned him against his stated goal of shattering the boundaries of space and time."

"Seems fair," said Phil. "I'd probably warn someone against shattering the boundaries of space and time too. You figure they're there for a reason, right?"

"What, like a big 'Do Not Enter' sign on the edges of reality?"

"Something like that."

"Phil?"

"Yeah?"

"What exactly *are* the boundaries of space and time?"

"No idea."

I kept reading. Then L. Ron Hubbard got involved and I had to go get another cup of coffee to fortify myself. By the time I picked up the thread again, Parsons was chasing his ex-wife over a failed yacht sale, was accused of espionage, and had decided that he, personally, was the Antichrist.

"That does seem like a lot," said Phil, when I relayed this last bit to him.

"Doesn't it, though?"

"And you say your grandad knew this guy?"

"Apparently Parsons liked him briefly." I flipped to the longest section about Elgar I'd found, where Parsons expressed his admiration for my great-grandfather's "innate skill at geomancy" and "proclaimed him the finest divinatory mind he had ever encountered." Elgar, the author informed us, did not return this regard, telling Parsons that he "risked awakening that which does not look kindly upon man's dominion." In return, Parsons called him a meddling old woman, which was apparently meant as a grave insult, and (the authors did not state, but heavily implied) went off on another mescaline binge.

Phil had stopped even pretending to work on the ice maker and was gazing off into the distance. "And you say this guy was from Pasadena?"

"Yup."

"My aunt lives in Pasadena."

I tried to think of something relevant to say. "I'm sure there's fewer sex cultists now?"

"I'm not," he said gloomily, and went back to work on the ice maker.

I tried to locate more information on Elgar that wasn't tied to Parsons, but it wasn't easy. Nobody'd written a book about him. I couldn't blame them, I suppose—what's the Mad Sorcerer of Boone compared to the Pasadena Antichrist?

Finally I found a blog that was devoted to Parsons and claimed to have reproduced the letters sent to him by Elgar and everybody else. (The letters from Crowley were particularly delightful. You ever wanted to read self-proclaimed Antichrists being catty at each other, this was the place.)

Elgar wrote in a distinctly nineteenth-century style, heavy on the adverbs and random capital letters. There were scans of the letters themselves on the blog, which had the cramped, heavily slanted handwriting that was the bane of entomologists when it appeared on labels. Fortunately the blogger had provided transcripts, which was above and beyond the call of duty.

Most of it was the sort of posturing that I usually associate with letters in academic journals, where the scholar stamps on their hill and bellows their credentials at the moon. Finally, about four paragraphs in, Elgar got around to his point.

Regarding your Stated Goal of conceiving a Magickal Childe, I must advise against it in the strongest terms, as one who knows What of he Speaks. In your quest to quicken new Life, you risk awakening that that do not look kindly upon Man's dominion. Is it achievable? In a word, Yes. But this Childe you seek to create merely by throwing your Substance into the Void and hoping for the Best may not be

what you *Imagine yourself to be Creating. The Seed you Sow may fall
on strange ground indeed. The Sleep of Reason may well breed Monsters, but the Sleep of the Sorcerer breeds Monsters made of the Flesh
of Men, and such a Thing made of Man's Substance is made to Rebel.*

*Be guided by the hard-won Wisdom of a Man who has made
the great Experiment to his Sorrow. You will find that this proposed
Childe will not Answer to your Hand, nor is there any Guarantee
given that the Childe will take after you and not the Other part
of Its Ancestry. All Golems and Homunculi must inevitably turn
against their Masters, as all Children must rebel against their Parents. The greater your initial Success, the more Terrible your eventual Enemy will be.*

*I say again, leave off this foolish Quest and follow Other Avenues
of Magick, equally fruitful, which leave less to Chance and Fate.*

*Yr Obedient Servant,
Elgar Mills*

Parsons, the blogger informed us, deadpan, did not take this well.
Whatever letter he sent in reply was lost, but Elgar's reply to that reply
was exceedingly terse and had even more capitals.

To the One Proclaiming Himself as the Aspect of the Risen Horus,

*Some Doors are Thrown Open at your Peril and do not Close as
you may Wish. It is my Devout Hope that you will Come to your
Senses in this Matter, but if Not, I find that I have No Time for those
who would abandon Scholarship for Hubris and who consider their
Great Mistakes to be Novel and Groundbreaking merely because
they are the ones Making Them.*

E. M.

I scrolled through a few more letters. Robert Heinlein showed up
briefly. God, this story had *everybody.* Maybe it was no wonder that Gran

Mae had been so obsessed with normalcy. If your dad was regularly corresponding with the Mescaline Antichrist of Pasadena, *Leave It to Beaver* probably seemed like a bastion of middle-class sanity. She probably couldn't wait to get out of the house, marry a respectable man, and live in a house with a white picket fence. Maybe Old Elgar had been right about children rebelling against their parents, at least in that regard.

Although Gran Mae had never had anything bad to say about "Father" at all. Quite the opposite. Then again, she'd also left off the Mad Wizard of Boone bits. I'd always been under the impression that "Father" was an old Southern gentleman, the sort who wear white suits and talk about carpetbaggers.

"Anything interesting?" asked Phil, emerging from the bowels of the ice maker.

"Old-timey sorcerers get really pissy about their hypothetical magical children."

"What, like the PTA?"

I had a sudden vision of Aleister Crowley at a PTA meeting and began giggling uncontrollably. There might have been some hysteria to it. (I don't know why, it's not as if I was under any stress or anything.)

Phil grinned at me. Dammit, I did like Phil. He was a good guy. He'd taken everything in stride, even when I was brandishing rose petals and imaginary weapons at him, and he was funny too. And he took care of Mom. And his T-shirt showed off pretty good biceps too.

No. Down, girl. I was absolutely not going to entertain thoughts like this about my mother's handyman.

The ice maker suddenly growled to life and dropped about five pounds worth of crushed ice on the kitchen floor. Phil cursed and snatched up a bucket. "Oh *no*," I said, and grabbed a towel to help him clean up.

"You don't have to . . ." he said as I got down on my hands and knees next to him, chasing ice across the linoleum.

"It's okay," I said.

"It's my mess."

"Against refrigerators, the gods themselves contend in vain, or something like that."

The ice maker spat out another half dozen ice cubes on Phil's head. He yelped. I tried not to laugh and did not entirely succeed.

"So what happened to your great-grandfather?" he asked as we mopped up the last of the ice.

"Good question." I dumped the wet towel into the sink and went to look up obituaries.

For once, there wasn't much to work with. One of the genealogy sites listed him dying in 1958, but the scholarship on those sites is, ah . . . I'll be tactful and call it *scattershot*. He hadn't had an obituary, and if he had a grave, it wasn't listed. (That struck me as odd. Southerners do love their graveyards.)

Finally I turned up a newspaper clipping from 1958, though it was in less than ideal shape. The printing had been poor, the paper thin, and words ran together into inky blobs. It said that Elgar Mills, notorious (something) had been found dead at his home (something something) following a long illness. An individual who (something something, a whole line was lost) as she was a minor, no (something) and she was remanded to custody of the state.

It seemed like an ignominious end for the Mad Sorcerer of Boone. I tried a few other searches, but nothing else came up. Apparently once he broke with Parsons, he ceased to be of interest. *Well, he outlived Parsons, anyway. That probably made him happy.*

I wondered about the minor who was remanded to custody of the state. Gran Mae? If my back-of-the-envelope math was correct, she'd have been about sixteen at the time. Then again, as weirdly obsessed as Elgar had apparently been with creating children, maybe he'd had others. Gran Mae might have had dozens of half-siblings.

She'd never mentioned any of them, though. Then again, she certainly hadn't mentioned free love or mescaline either. Gran Mae would not have considered those things classy *at all.*

I sighed and shut the laptop. A nice morning's diversion, but it hadn't gotten me any closer to figuring out Mom and the notes, and whatever I was going to do about those.

Maybe I could talk to Gail again. She hadn't been terribly forthcoming last time, but she was obviously Mom's friend. And I could ask her about the notes. If she wasn't worried once she heard about those, then she wasn't the friend that I thought she was.

I even had a good excuse. I took the plate that she'd sent along with the cookies and headed off to return it, leaving Phil to his heroic struggle against the ice maker.

⁓

"I've got a question for you," I said, coming up the steps to where Gail sat on the screened-in porch.

"Come on in," she said cheerfully. "If I don't know the answer, I can probably point you to someone who does."

"Thanks." I opened the porch door and settled in. Hermes stood up when I entered, but rapidly sank back down into a horizontal position rather like a meat loaf with a beak.

"I thought vultures perched," I said, looking over at him.

"When he's relaxed, he loafs." Gail accepted the returned plate. Southern etiquette demands that you never return an empty plate, but I don't cook, so was hopefully squeaking by on the "went to school elsewhere, forgot her manners, what can you do?" technicality. Anyway, she didn't seem to mind.

Gail leaned forward. "So what's your question?"

I plowed ahead. "I'm worried about Mom," I admitted. "I found these notes she wrote to herself—"

"Don't poke your nose in," she snapped, cutting me off immediately.

"You didn't see them. They're really upsetting. She thinks—I think she thinks she's being watched and she sounds paranoid—"

"Damn good sense being paranoid sometimes." She folded her arms, her eyes bright and hard as gemstone chips. "I know Edie. I don't know you, but I *do* know that if you start telling her she's going crazy, you're going to upset her. She needs support right now, not somebody picking away at her."

"But if there's something wrong—"

"There isn't a damn thing wrong with her that's not wrong with most of us. Maybe a bit less."

I lost my temper. She hadn't seen the notes. She clearly knew something was going on with Mom. "Why won't you tell me what's going on?" I yelled.

"Because I can't!" Gail yelled right back. "Don't you think I would if I could?"

We stared at each other. From the trees, I heard raspy hissing sounds. Alarm calls from the black vulture flock? Did they not like humans yelling? I certainly didn't like yelling. I had a raging headache again. It felt like someone was driving a railroad spike into my left eye.

"*Why* can't you?" I asked dully, pressing my fingers against my eyebrow where the pain was centered. "Do you think I won't believe you?"

"I'm too old to care if anyone believes me or not."

"Well, what then?"

"I don't *know!*" Gail folded her arms and glared at me. Hermes humped himself up and made a small, pathetic coughing sound.

"Oh." I ground the heel of my hand into my forehead, trying to find the source of the pain. "Have you got an aspirin?"

"Yeah." She went inside, leaving me with Hermes. He had clearly revised his opinion of me downward, and kept watching me as if I might murder an innocent vulture at any time.

She came back with a mug full of water and two aspirin. The mug said NC BOTANICAL GARDEN across it. I did not like being mad at people who supported botanical gardens. I swallowed the pills and drank down the water. Maybe I was dehydrated. I slumped back in the chair. There was a bumblebee on the flowers just outside the screen. I could hear it buzzing. I watched it moving from flower to flower, collecting pollen in little orange clumps on its legs. It was soothing to watch.

"What are you really afraid of?" asked Gail.

Her voice was gentle, given that we'd been yelling at each other moments earlier. I kept watching the bee. "I'm afraid that Mom will need some kind of care," I admitted. "I'm not good at taking care of people, and I can't afford much of anything. I'm afraid she'll be miserable and I don't know how to fix it."

Gail sighed, a long, drawn-out breath. "Well," she said, "your motives are pure, anyway. I think I can tell you that you don't need to be worried about that. She's not losing her mind."

"She isn't?"

"No. She's got perfectly good reasons to be scared. Hell, I'm scared too."

I finally looked away from the bee, baffled. Gail was scared? What on earth could Gail be scared of? I'd been thinking Mom was having delusions, but what if there was another explanation? *Oh please, God, let there be another explanation.*

"I won't tell anyone," I said. It sounded pathetic, even to me. "I mean, if you're scared of . . ." I trailed off, not sure how to end the sentence. Scared of what? A cult? The mob?

A cult sounded a lot more plausible than the mob. It would explain the note about saying your prayers. And anyway, the mob doesn't need to stalk little old ladies in Southern towns. We have the United Daughters of the Confederacy for that.

It was a flippant thought, but it struck me hard. Could this be some kind of white supremacist thing? Was that why Mom had told Maria it wasn't safe? Why she hung up an obvious Confederate painting? Was she afraid of some kind of racist group? Christ knows, we've got plenty of them, and they got really violent over the Confederate statues. Mom had protested to get the one removed. Could the two be related somehow?

"Is it white supremacists?" I asked, leaning closer. "Like . . . the League of the South and those people? Are they threatening Mom?"

Gail burst out laughing. "God, I wish! A garden-variety racist would be positively restful. You wave your shotgun at them and call their employer and they go away crying about free speech. No, it's nothing that straightforward or that . . . tangible."

"Tangible?" I snorted. "What, is the house haunted?"

Gail was silent.

"Oh come *on*." I set the mug down. "You can't be serious."

She shrugged. "Maybe. Would that be so impossible?"

"Haunted? How? It's what, thirty years old? And *don't* tell me that it's built on an ancient Indian burial ground, because that happens to be my specialty and it isn't."

"No, I'm pretty sure this is white-people foolishness, through and through. But I don't know what it is, all right? It might be a haunting but there's something else all tangled up in it, and I can't tell you what it is because I don't know. I know a lot about plants, a couple of things about vultures, and a little bit about uncanny things. Everything I know is telling me that something very bad is going on at your mother's house. That's all."

I swallowed. Did I believe her?

No, of course not. Ghosts aren't real, dammit!

(You saw that hand.)

It was a trick of the light.

(It was not a trick of the light.)

Fine, then it was a doll part or something like that.

(Dolls don't have dirt under their fingernails.)

Hell, maybe it wasn't a ghost. Maybe it was something much stranger than that. I'd just spent an hour reading about ritual magic-with-a-k and Thelemic children.

Hey, maybe Gran Mae was the Antichrist. That'd make as much sense as anything else, right? Elgar said he'd already made the experiment. Maybe he got Gran Mae, and we just got lucky that she was so busy loathing Gail and growing roses that she didn't bring about the end of days.

The Antichrist in Ecru. I made a noise that might have been mistaken for a laugh, and Hermes moved a little bit farther away.

"You're a scientist," said Gail, watching me. "I realize that makes this hard for you. I'm telling you, what's happening isn't something you're going to be able to put under a microscope. I'm hoping it'll go away on its own."

"Does anything ever go away on its own?" I asked.

"More often than you'd think," she said. "In this case, I truly can't be sure. I don't know everything."

"I'm starting to think I don't know anything," I muttered.

She smiled. "That's a good place to start."

The Eighth Day

Revelation: Old-fashioned double flowers in deep, dark purple, with velvety petals shading to dark red. Glossy, finely cut foliage contrasts nicely with the superb color. Very fragrant, with a strong scent of clove. The exact history of this heirloom rose is unknown.

CHAPTER 15

I spent another late night with Inspector Lowell and Mr. Boxed Wine, and woke up a little before noon, feeling dreadful. My dreams had been a tangle of rosebushes and hands and my grandmother, and for some reason, my third-grade teacher, because dreams are like that. My head ached dully, but at least I didn't have sleep paralysis.

I stared at the ceiling and thought about ghosts.

I don't believe in ghosts. And if they do exist, they show up in old Gothic manors and crumbling farmhouses, not cookie-cutter tract housing in the middle of a subdivision. No one had died in the house. Gran Mae had died in the hospital, one of those cases where you feel a bit woozy so you go in to get it checked out and the doctor pulls down the charts and says things like "advanced" and "inoperable." She was dead a week later, without ever leaving the hospital again.

Presumably other people had died nearby at some point in the last thousand years. This sort of development was usually on old farmland. I could probably research it, pull up land deeds, see if there had been a house and cross-reference it to an obituary or two . . . or I could just get up and make coffee because *ghosts aren't a thing*.

I got up and made coffee.

Caffeine shocked me awake. But the wakefulness only seemed to bring all the things that I couldn't fix into sharper focus, so I went and buried myself in The Project for the next several hours, because if nothing else, at least I could sort hoverfly photos. Even if everything was terrible and Mom was in some kind of trouble and Gail was—what? enabling her? feeding her delusions?—even if all that was true, at least at the end of the day we'd have a couple hundred correctly labeled hoverflies. Sometimes that's the best that you can hope for in life.

I stopped when the coffeepot was empty, debated making another pot, and decided against it. Instead I stood at the sliding glass door and stared out into the garden. The garden somehow devoid of any life except sporadic outbreaks of ladybugs.

It was still nagging at me. Set ghosts aside, because they aren't real. Set Mom aside because . . . well, honestly because I'm a coward and I couldn't deal with it right this minute. Bugs, though . . . bugs I know. Bugs I could deal with. If I was going to figure out why there weren't any bugs, I was going to go about it methodically.

My first step was to establish that there really weren't any in the backyard. Sure, I hadn't been seeing any insects except the ladybug hordes, but the human eye is notoriously susceptible. Fortunately, entomologists have a secret weapon when it comes to insect collection, namely, the pitfall trap.

First you get something with smooth sides—a yogurt container, a large plastic cup, one of the leftover margarine tubs that your mother is incapable of throwing out, not that I'm naming names, *Mom*—whatever. (I found an elderly note with the margarine tubs that read MATCH WITH LIDS. Some things do not change.) You dig a hole and put your container into it so that the lip is level with the surrounding dirt. Toss a few leaves in so that your victims feel at home, then leave it overnight and check in the morning to see who fell in, then let them go. (Alternately, if you are collecting and require the specimens, add an inch of alcohol and a drop of detergent so that they expire swiftly.)

The hard part is digging the hole, particularly in North Carolina clay. I took my ill-gotten margarine tub and picked a likely spot under the rosebushes.

I got about two inches down, hit a root, swore, moved an inch to the side, hit another root, swore again, moved another inch, and finally got about three inches into the clay.

Clink. My spade hit something, but not a root this time. Also not the septic tank, I was pretty sure, which would have gone *clonk*. (Look, archaeologists get to be very good at determining material composition based on the sound of a spade tapping it. It's a survival skill.)

My first thoughts were that I should go get a toothbrush or a paint-brush to brush away the dirt and cursing myself for not laying out a proper grid. Then the rest of the brain caught up with the archaeologist brain and pointed out that this was my grandmother's backyard, not a midden, and I was not doing a dig. I was making a small hole for bugs to fall into. Totally different.

Mostly different.

Not that people don't do fascinating work in more modern settings, but this was not going to be colonial-era anything, it was going to be, at best, something left over from the developer in the nineties.

I told myself all this but the guilt still got to me, and I got my phone out and took about ten photos, just in case. Then I went back to work with the spade, gingerly loosening the dirt around my discovery.

It was a glass jar. The outside was almost opaque with dirt. I had to be cautious with the spade so that I didn't break it, assuming it wasn't already broken somewhere at the bottom. But after a few minutes of careful levering, it came loose. The resulting hole was more than large enough for my pit trap, which was nice.

I brushed the dirt off my find. An old-fashioned quart mason jar. Not unusual in the South. It was full of small bits of something yellow-white and shaped like lumpy pebbles. The lid was rusted shut, but I didn't need to open it. Any archaeologist worth their salt would have recognized the ivory-colored shapes.

I was holding a jar of human teeth.

CHAPTER 16

I would just like the universe to acknowledge at this point that I didn't scream, or flail, or throw the jar, or scream "What the ever-loving FUCK!?!" or anything like that. I am a professional. I have uncovered teeth before, mostly in digs on the Black Sea, where it's not so fraught if you turn up human remains.

It's just that there's a big difference between teeth in situ at an archaeological dig and discovering a jar with somebody's molars buried in your own backyard.

A lot of molars. *A lot.* Probably close to a hundred of them. I set the jar down very carefully on the patio table, dropped into the chair, and stared at it, overcome with the creeping heebie-jeebies for about five full minutes.

Okay. Okay, I'm cool. There's a logical explanation. There's always a logical explanation. If there's a jar full of teeth here, it's because someone put it here. Probably Gran Mae.

A memory flashed across my brain, so clear that I couldn't believe I'd ever forgotten it. I must have been ten or eleven and one of my baby teeth had come out. I was staring at it in my hand, fascinated and a little disgusted.

"Be sure to put it under your pillow tonight, so the tooth fairy will come."

"I don't believe in the tooth fairy, Gran Mae."

"Oh, I suppose you're all grown up now," she said testily. "Fine. Give it to me." She held out her hand. When I didn't respond quickly enough, she snapped her fingers. "Come on. Give it here, Samantha."

"It's my tooth," I said, closing my fist over it.

"Don't be silly. You'll just lose it."

"I might not, though," I said. I don't know why I was so resistant, but it felt unfair of her to say it. Brad was always losing his retainer. He'd had to have the cafeteria staff fish it out of a trash can once. I wasn't anything like that. The thought of losing my homework or forgetting a permission slip made me want to curl into a ball of anxiety. It wasn't *fair*.

"Give it to me," she said again, and something about her voice made me look up at her face. She was angry. I couldn't figure out why. It was *my* tooth. It wasn't like I'd taken it from her.

I took a step back. From the doorway, Mom said, "It's her tooth, Mother. She can decide what to do with it."

"Don't be ridiculous, Edie," snapped Gran Mae over her shoulder. She reached out and grabbed my wrist, and for all that she was old and delicate-looking, her fingers felt like iron pincers. "Now *give it to me*."

"Hey! Ow!"

"*Mother!*"

Gran Mae ignored us both. She pried open my fist, plucked the little bloody ivory pebble out, then dropped my hand. "There!" she said, sounding satisfied. Then she laughed. "Now don't you all feel silly?" And she swept from the room.

I rubbed my wrist, feeling like I might cry, and Mom said, "Sam . . ." At the time I thought she was mad at me for not being nice to Gran Mae, but now, remembering the whole scene, I recognized that Mom was just as upset as I had been, but she didn't know what to say. She was a single mom and she was stuck and we were stuck with her. If Gran Mae threw us out, we had nowhere to go. We'd lost the house when Dad died. Mom was working two jobs and trying to get enough money to get us into an apartment, and meanwhile we were all at the mercy of Gran Mae's whims. Even the ones that she knew were wrong. Or in the case of the teeth, downright bizarre.

I stared at the jar on the table. Yes. All right. That was a logical explanation. Once Gran Mae had played tooth fairy, she had to do something with the teeth afterward. Maybe it felt wrong to flush them down the toilet or put them in the trash. Lots of cultures have taboos around disposing of body parts, many of them much stricter than the modern American suburbs. She might have put them in the jar and then felt like she needed to bury them.

Right. Okay. Perfectly logical explanation. Except for the fact that there were so damn many of them, and even if you added up me and Brad and my mother, that *still* wouldn't get you a jar half full of teeth!

I turned the jar, staring at the teeth, dozens of them, hundreds, molars and incisors and bicuspids, all strangely small, as human teeth are.

Some of them had been burned. There's a very specific look to burnt teeth. The enamel survives, but the pulp doesn't. The edges of the tooth start to split into little fissures. I could count at least ten that had been through a very hot fire before they ended up in this jar.

A logical, *innocent* explanation.

On a dig in college, on the Black Sea, I was working very carefully on a human skull. I had a toothbrush and a paintbrush and as I moved the dirt away, grain by grain, I kept finding more and more teeth. There seemed to be a second row of them in the skull, like a shark, filling the front of the face from just beneath the nasal cavity. I couldn't believe what I was seeing. I kept brushing and wondering what the hell they had done to this person—buried a skull inside a skull and mashed them together somehow? That didn't make any sense. (I did not think aliens. I *didn't*. I very deliberately did *not* think aliens. You start thinking aliens and then you start believing that ancient people couldn't have made great works without alien help and then you're that guy in the corner at academic conferences who nobody talks to, publishing increasingly racist articles about how the Nazca couldn't possibly have drawn those lines on their own.)

Finally I went and got my advisor and said, in so many words, "What the ever-loving fuck is going on here?"

Dr. Abbot, who was an endless delight, took one look at it and burst out laughing. "They're a kid who still has their baby teeth. The adult teeth all sit right above in the jaw. Looks freaky, doesn't it?"

"Oh Jesus." I exhaled. "I had no idea."

"Yup. Your skull looked like that once too." He grinned at me. "You were thinking aliens, weren't you?"

"I was *not.*"

So there we were. Terribly freaky-looking thing, perfectly innocent explanation. Undoubtedly there was an equally innocent explanation for why there was a jar of hundreds of human teeth buried under my grandmother's roses, and I'd think of it soon.

Very soon.

Any minute now.

. . . fuck.

Honestly, there just aren't that many good reasons for the average homeowner to keep jars of human teeth lying around.

I debated whether or not to tell Mom. On the one hand, she was clearly having problems already, and it couldn't be good for her mental state to have her daughter wander in from the garden with a jar of teeth. On the other hand, I feel like you have a right to know if something like that turns up in your yard.

(I suppose there was a slim chance that Mom herself had put the teeth there, in the same way that there was a slim chance that I might be capable of unaided flight, but it did not seem likely.)

I sat in the chair, staring, until Mom came home. Then I shoved back from the table and went inside. "Mom? Hey, Mom . . . I think there's something you need to see . . ."

⌒

Fifteen minutes later, Mom and I were still sitting in the patio chairs and staring at the jar. Every few minutes, one of us would utter some variation on the phrase, "Well, shit." Mom's newfound prohibition against swearing had not held up to a jar of human teeth in the garden.

"Who could have put it there?" asked Mom. And then, not waiting for an answer, "It must have been there before the house was built."

I frowned. The lot had probably been scraped before then, and while it wasn't impossible, I had a feeling that a glass jar would have been crushed. Earthmoving equipment does damage to artifacts like you would not believe. "I guess that's possible? But I think it's probably more recent."

"*How* recent?"

I had a sick feeling in the pit of my stomach. "Well . . . Gran Mae was the first owner of the house . . ." I remembered the fit she had thrown over my lost tooth. "And she got very weird about our baby teeth."

"No, she didn't," said Mom, almost automatically.

"Yes, she did. Don't you remember when . . . ?"

I looked up. Mom was staring intently into my eyes, shaking her head just a fraction. *Don't say it,* that look said. *Don't say it.*

I stopped. I swallowed. After a long moment, Mom relaxed a little, probably because I'd stopped talking.

She acts like someone can hear us.

"Um," I said. *Is someone listening? Does she think we're being recorded somehow?* Which might be paranoia, but might not be. I thought of Gail saying, "Maybe she's acting completely rationally based on her experience." But what was her experience?

Mom pushed her chair back and stood up. "Well!" she said brightly. "I don't know about you, but I could use something to drink after that. Maybe a really fancy iced coffee. Or just ice cream. What do you say?"

"Uh . . . yeah, that sounds great." The false heartiness in her voice was no less alarming than anything else. I looked over my shoulder involuntarily, as if I might see someone spying.

Nothing there but the roses.

"There's a really good coffee shop in Pondsboro," I offered. "Or we could go into Siler City and get ice cream."

"Maybe there's a Baskin-Robbins," said Mom. "Are those still a thing?"

"I have no idea. Maybe." I picked up my keys. Mom's hands were shaking and there was a brittle light in her eyes that I didn't like at all. "How about I drive?"

We made it about two miles down the road before Mom burst into tears.

"Uh," I said. I am not good with other people having emotions at me. I don't even really like having them myself. "Um. Are you okay?"

"Just drive," said Mom, wiping her eyes.

"Okay."

Siler City was farther away. I took Chicken Bridge Road, which is long and meandering and turns a few times and doesn't have any scenery that requires comment.

"I'm sorry," said Mom, after we'd passed about five barns and a small herd of unimpressed cows.

"You don't have anything to be sorry for," I said. "Or at least, I don't think you do. Can you tell me what this is all about?"

Mom took a deep breath and let it out. "It's Gran Mae," she said, huddled up in the passenger seat. "She's not gone."

CHAPTER 17

I knew it was coming. I'd half-expected it ever since I saw the notes, and certainly since talking to Gail. Still, hearing it out loud felt like a fist to the gut. "Gran Mae is dead," I said, very carefully.

"I *know* that," Mom said, her misery tinged with exasperation. "I didn't say she wasn't dead, I said she wasn't *gone*. She's at the house. Haunting it, or whatever you want to call it. And she watches me. And I know you think I'm crazy."

"I didn't say that."

Her eyes were red-rimmed, but she gave me a wry look nonetheless. "Sam, I'm your mother. I *know* you. You crave rational explanations like I crave carbs."

"Yeah, but . . ."

"Do you remember that time I had to come get you at church camp? Because you made a counselor cry?"

"Oh come on! She tried to tell me that dinosaur fossils were put in the ground by Satan to test the faith of paleontologists. She had it coming."

"You were *eleven*."

"Eleven-year-old me is not proof that adult me thinks you're crazy."

Mom folded her arms and just looked at me. I resolutely kept my hands on the wheel and my eyes on the road, but I could feel that look burning into the side of my head.

"Well, it *is* a little unbelievable," I muttered finally.

"You think I don't know that?" asked Mom wearily. "Believe me, I thought I was cracking for months. But things keep happening."

"What sort of things?" I seized on this hopefully. Maybe there was a rational explanation, and we just had to get there.

"Doors slamming. Pictures falling off the walls. Not just one, so don't start in about the house settling." (Since I had, in fact, been about to say something about the house settling, this felt particularly pointed. I bit my tongue.) "You know all those little pictures I had hanging up along the stairs? The ones from Arizona?"

"Yeah?"

"They all fell off at the same time. I was standing right there and every single one just dropped simultaneously. Scared the crap out of me."

"Some kind of vibration in the wall . . ."

"The heads of the nails had been sheared through. Every single one of them."

". . . oh." We passed another group of cows. They were no more impressed than the previous bunch. "What did you do?"

"Honestly?" Mom snorted. "I freaked the hell out and went to a hotel that night. Didn't even pick up the glass first. She won that one."

"Okay," I said, trying to pick my way through a conversational minefield. "But even if something is doing this—and I'm not saying it's anything but the house settling—how do you know it's Gran Mae? It could just be . . . I dunno, some random ghostly presence."

Mom was already shaking her head. "No. It's her. I know. She gets so angry sometimes. I can feel it, all through the house, just like when she was alive. You'd walk in the door and it was like this weight in the air and you knew it was going to land on you, but you didn't know when." She made a sound, a little half sob. "And it's almost a relief when it does, because at least it's over."

I had known that Mom's childhood was not exactly idyllic, but this made it sound even worse than I'd realized. "And it's like that now?"

"Yeah." She stared out the window. "Yeah. Sometimes I walk in the door and I can feel it all over again, and I know something's going to happen."

"Have you . . . uh . . ." I tried to think how to phrase it diplomatically. "Have you tried talking to a therapist about this?"

"That was the first thing I did," said Mom. "First she told me that it was normal to feel the presence of our dead loved ones sometimes, and to consider it a blessing. I told her it was terrifying and I hated it and I thought the house was haunted. She decided I had unresolved issues with my mother. Which yes, obviously I do, but I've had those since I was born, and the house wasn't haunted until last year."

"What happened last year?"

"I have no idea!" She slapped the dashboard in frustration. "Things just started *happening*. It was fine before that, and then all of a sudden she was back!"

I turned onto the highway. Was it the house? Maybe if I could just get her out of the house, things would resolve themselves. "Have you considered moving?"

"Oh yes," said Mom bitterly. "I considered it. I went so far as to have a Realtor do a walk-through. She kept telling me that it was in great condition but I should repaint because the color scheme was *so* fun and *so* quirky but buyers didn't understand that. Then she opened a cupboard and the shelves flipped up and twenty coffee mugs slid off and hit her in the face."

"Oh my god."

"Yeah. She chipped two teeth. I paid for her dental bills."

I reached for a rational explanation, even though they were getting increasingly hard to come by. "Maybe the screws holding the shelves in—"

"Nails," said Mom. "Cabinet nails. Sheared through, just like the ones on the stairs."

"Okay, I understand that must have been scary, but you can't think that a ghost is out there . . . what, cutting the heads off nails? Maybe someone's trying to scare you out of the house, to get you to move." (Why, I couldn't imagine. Lammergeier Lane wasn't in the way of any oil pipelines, so far as I knew, and developers had long since lost interest in Pondsboro.)

"If so, they're doing a pretty good job targeting Realtors." Mom folded her arms. "The next one who came over had everything on top of the refrigerator fall on him. Cookie jar, kettle, that one big ceramic teapot. He hadn't opened the fridge door or anything. And there's no way that the teapot could have just fallen off. It was at least a foot from the edge." She snorted. "It didn't seem like a good idea to talk to Realtors after that. They kept getting hurt."

"But you repainted anyway."

"I thought maybe she'd calm down," said Mom. "It worked too. At least for a while. The house didn't feel so angry. Then your brother and Maria came to visit."

"That's why you told her it wasn't safe. You thought Gran Mae didn't like her."

"Gran Mae dropped a glass door on her foot. If the glass had shattered, she'd have been cut to ribbons. As it was, it broke her foot in *three places*. Three! God, it's all my fault. I should have realized. She always pretended she wasn't a racist old bitch, but she'd have worn a bedsheet if she thought she could get away with it."

There was more life and anger in her than I'd seen since I came to visit. I wished I could believe that it was a good thing. On the other hand, at least I could stop trying to think of nice things to say about Gran Mae.

"So the jar of teeth . . ." I began, and didn't know how to finish that sentence.

"She could have put it there," said Mom. "No, scratch that. I'm *sure* she put it there. God." She shuddered. "When Dad died, she had him cremated and I saw her that night. I'd stayed overnight to make sure she was okay." She gave a brief, brittle laugh. "Insomuch as she was ever okay. She . . . she dumped out the ashes on the table, and then she dug through them with her bare hands. She pulled out bits. I didn't know what she was doing. I'm pretty sure she didn't know I was there."

I was staring at her so hard that I hit the rumble strip on the side of the highway and had to jerk the car back toward the centerline. "She *what?*"

"Teeth," said Mom wearily. "Teeth don't burn."

"No, I know." (Teeth and bone fragments survive burning pretty well, so these days they usually run the remains through a machine that crushes those bits into powder before they hand you your loved ones. This is going to be very annoying for future archaeologists.) "But you're saying she was picking them out?"

"Yeah. She threw a fit at the funeral home, said that she didn't want him ground up like meat, so they wouldn't do the final bit. I was so embarrassed. I apologized to the funeral director after." Mom shook her head. "He was so nice. He said that grief was strange and it wasn't even the strangest request he'd had that week."

It was just like Mom to remember someone being nice forty years ago. "And she picked the teeth out afterward?"

"I think so. And she was just as obsessed about my baby teeth as she was about yours."

"That must have been awkward," I said, which was incredibly inadequate.

Mom laughed hoarsely. "Oh god! When I had a tooth fall out at school, you'd think I had done it to spite her. I told her that I'd thrown it away and she threw an absolute fit. A scary one. Then she wouldn't speak to me for days." She scrubbed her hands over her face. "She wasn't a great mother," she added after a minute, which was possibly the understatement of the century.

"I'm so sorry," I said, and meant it. "I didn't know. I mean, I know what she was like to Brad and me, and I sort of figured she must not have been, but . . ."

"She mellowed a lot," said Mom.

"Jesus." The thought that we'd had the mellow version was alarming. "How did you come out so well?"

"I went to college," said Mom. "Away from home. Mother wasn't sure about having me live away from home, but if I was going to join a sorority, I had to live on campus, and of course I had to join a sorority, because . . . I don't know, she had some image in her mind that nice

Southern girls did that. And it was the eighties and campus was full of Take Back the Night marches and AIDS activists and everything just clicked. Mother hated it, of course. Right before he died, when he was in the hospital, Dad told me not to move back in with her. 'Don't let her drag you back in,' was what he said." She rubbed her face. "I wish I'd listened."

I swallowed. My grandfather had died of a heart attack long before I was born. I'd never thought there was anything suspicious about it. Probably there wasn't. Heart attacks are perfectly normal.

Nice and normal, even.

"Where do you think she got the rest of the teeth?" I asked.

"The rest of them?"

"There were more than just baby teeth in that jar," I said. "And more than one set of adult teeth." I'd looked at the jar long enough. If I was a good archaeologist, I'd have poured it out and tried to match it to multiple individuals, but I think even good archaeologists get to have the screaming heebie-jeebies for a bit first.

Mom stared at me. I kept my eyes on the road, but I could feel her eyes boring into the side of my head.

"Jesus *fuck*," she said finally, and despite everything, I wanted to cheer. *That* was the Mom I remembered. She'd learned to swear in the eighties too.

The road stretched out. We passed the alpaca farm, still offering trendy weddings and fiber arts classes. Finally Mom said, "She *was* a hospice nurse."

My breath came out in a long sigh. "Yeah," I said. I'd been thinking that too. "Yeah, she was."

"Sometimes old people lose teeth."

"They do."

Mom and I looked at each other, and then I stared at the road and she stared at the alpaca farm. The other alternative did not bear thinking about.

You see so much evil in a small town, Gail had said.

I don't believe in ghosts. I don't.

"I don't know what to do," I said finally. "Do we try to get you a different therapist, or a doctor, or an old priest and a young priest?"

"The Catholics don't do that anymore. I checked. And if I tried to get one of those people out who think they're fighting demons, I'm afraid I'd just make her angrier."

I don't believe in ghosts. But if anyone was going to be too mean to stay dead . . .

I made a noncommittal noise. Mom reached out and touched my shoulder. "Believe me, hon, I hope I'm crazy. I think being crazy would be a lot easier than being right about this."

I had no idea what to say to that. We went and got ice cream and ate it in silence then drove back together, because what else could we do?

When we got home, the jar of teeth was gone.

⇌

I stayed up too late that night. It wasn't exactly insomnia, it was more that I knew that I'd lie awake and think too much if I tried to sleep, so I didn't. I played *Civilization* on my laptop, which was just engrossing enough, combined with the TV, that I didn't have to think. I stared at the screen and let myself think absolutely nothing except how to develop my cities and which one of the other nations was going to declare war on me first.

No great surprise that I fell asleep on the couch. I retained enough presence of mind to put the laptop on the coffee table and then slumped over the arm, not quite watching the TV.

I don't know how much later it was when I started to dream. I was still lying on the couch, but I could see into the backyard, and someone was walking back and forth outside. They went along the line of roses, then back, over and over again. I couldn't move. I just sat and watched them walk, like a soldier patrolling their post. Something white squirmed outside the line of roses, trying to edge through a gap between them. The white things drew back when the person passed, then surged forward again.

Little piggy, hissed the voice. *Look at the mess you've made, little piggy. Who's going to clean this up?*

I tried to turn away, but the owner of the voice had hold of me, pressing my face against cold glass. The white thing was on the other side, dark shadows moving under its skin. I thrashed helplessly, opening my mouth to yell, but dirt fell in and I woke, choking.

Daylight was streaming through the window. My arm was asleep and I had a painful crick in my neck. I'd spent the night on the couch, with my face angled toward the garden.

The Ninth Day

Sunday Dinner: An award-winning climbing rose with one-inch-wide apricot-yellow blooms. Strongly scented, reminiscent of cloves, cinnamon, and nutmeg. Sturdy and disease resistant, extremely thorny, suitable for hedges and animal barriers.

CHAPTER 18

There is probably something more awkward than the morning after you've found a jar of teeth and your mother has admitted she thinks she's being haunted by your dead grandmother, but I couldn't think of it. In the kitchen, Mom and I made coffee, exchanged fraught smiles, and tried to come up with extremely safe conversation topics. There were surprisingly few. She asked how my work was coming and I told her and she agreed that The Project certainly sounded difficult and I asked about her work and she told me and I agreed that clients certainly were something and both of us worked very hard not to scream into our coffee cups.

After about half an hour of this, during which I checked my email eleven times on the laptop and tried unsuccessfully to connect my phone to the internet again, I decided to go for a walk.

I went upstairs to change into my jeans. It wasn't until I sat down on the chair to pull my shoes on that I realized that the chair was empty.

The picture of Elgar was gone too.

I looked around foolishly, as if you could just misplace a two-foot-tall framed picture of a mad sorcerer. Sure. Just like putting your phone down somewhere, or your car keys.

I didn't even think about mentioning it to Mom.

The vulture was back on the mailbox, but I hardly noticed him anymore. Or her. Vultures aren't sexually dimorphic, according to Gail. She'd mentioned at some point that Hermes might actually be a Hermione, but you can't tell without a DNA test. Regardless, Mailbox Vulture was now just part of the yard, like a particularly goth lawn sculpture. Gran

Mae would have considered that very not-classy, but Gran Mae kept jars of human teeth buried in the garden, so she no longer got to have a say in appropriate exterior decorating.

Phil's truck was parked in Mr. Pressley's driveway. He did Mom's yardwork. Oh god, had he found any other jars of teeth in the yard over the years? Should I ask?

I should probably ask. While it was bad to have one jar of human teeth in the garden, somehow having dozens would be much, much worse. At that point we might have to inform the police. Getting cops involved did not seem like it would improve either Mom's anxiety or my own, but surely there's a critical mass of human teeth where you're pretty much required to go to the authorities.

Yes. I should ask Phil. And not when Mom was in earshot.

Which meant going across the street and talking to Phil now.

Which meant . . . braving Mr. Pressley.

I gulped.

I had a doctorate and a job and a car and I was thirty-two years old and still I knocked on Mr. Pressley's door with my heart in my throat.

He probably wouldn't shoot me on sight. He'd never actually shot anyone, so far as I knew. He was more likely to call the police. And I had a perfectly legitimate reason to be there. I was asking if Phil was around. This wasn't like when I'd asked him to buy Girl Scout Cookies as a kid.

And he definitely knew that I was coming. I'm sure he'd spotted me the minute I left the house.

I told myself all this. I could hear the distant sound of a Weedwacker behind the house. Maybe Mr. Pressley wasn't home. Maybe he couldn't hear me. I knocked again.

The door opened half an inch. "The hell d'you want?"

The voice was old and dry and had a crack in the timbre, but there was still plenty of power behind it.

"I was hoping Phil was here," I said. My voice was only a little higher than normal. "I had a question for him."

"Who's asking?"

"Err . . . I'm Samantha Montgomery."

"You with the guvmint?"

"N-no?"

"Who you with, then?"

"I don't think I'm with anyone?" I tried to think of something else to establish my credentials. "My mom lives across the street. Phil is her, uh, handyman."

The door opened another half inch and light winked off a pair of glasses as Mr. Pressley stared at me. "You're her kin?"

"I'm her daughter."

He shook his head impatiently. "Not her. *Her.*"

"Uh . . ."

"The old lady." He was silent for a moment, then added, somewhat helpfully, "She's dead."

"Oh. Her. Yes. That was my grandmother."

"Huh!"

I have been cussed out in traffic with less venom than was packed into that syllable. Good lord, had Gran Mae alienated everyone on the planet? I rubbed my forehead. "Err . . . I didn't like her much either?"

There was a long moment where I expected him to slam the door in my face. Then he made a gruff noise that sounded like a laugh—a laugh? From Mr. Pressley?—and opened the door. "You best come in, then," he said. "Don't touch anything. And don't be telling your friends about what you see in here!"

"I won't," I promised, stepping over the threshold as warily as a swimmer entering deep water.

Mr. Pressley's house was old and musty and smelled like a smoker had lived there since the house was built. The walls were no longer beige or ecru but nicotine-colored. The carpet had been replaced with linoleum at some point, which was certainly a design choice that someone had made.

I followed him through the house. It was a mirrored layout from Mom's and made me feel like I'd slipped into some dimly lit parallel dimension. There was an American flag in one corner and piles of papers and questionable electronics on the coffee table. I could hear a TV coming from somewhere. Whoever was speaking was furious at the liberals, the Democrats, the communists, and, for some reason, the Amish.

Mr. Pressley went to the back door. The sliding glass was covered in blackout curtains that had been duct-taped around the edges. He paused at the door and gave me another suspicious look. "You want to talk to Phil?"

"Yes, please," I said, trying my best not to look liberal, Democratic, communist, or Amish.

"Huh." He unlocked the door, removed the dowel holding it closed, and slid it open just wide enough for a human to pass. "He's in the back. Phil! You got a visitor! Says she's from across the street!"

The sound of the Weedwacker stopped. Phil came around the side of the house, wearing cheap plastic eye protectors. He took them off and wiped his face. Sweat had stuck his T-shirt tightly to his chest, revealing rather more muscle than I had expected to see that morning.

Mr. Pressley stepped back and waved at the door. I went out and heard him close and lock the doors behind me.

"Sam?" Phil twisted to check the Weedwacker's string, which did impressive things to the T-shirt. "Is something wrong? Mrs. M okay?"

"You're kinda ripped," I blurted, which was not even remotely what I had been intending to say.

Smooth. Yup. That's me.

Phil's eyebrows shot up. He smelled like fresh-cut grass. "Um," he said.

"I'm sorry, I didn't mean . . . you're not . . . well, you *are*, but obviously . . ."

It seemed like an excellent time to stop talking. We both carefully avoided eye contact for a moment. I think Phil might have been smiling a little, but I wouldn't swear to it because I was definitely not looking at him.

When it became obvious that the earth was not going to oblige by swallowing me whole, I said, "Mom's fine. I, uh, had a bit of a weird question for you. I'm sorry to bother you."

He glanced at the blacked-out doors behind me. "It's not a bother, but I'm sorry you had to . . ." Phil trailed off delicately, allowing me to fill in the blanks of Mr. Pressley, the house, and the bizarre anti-Amish sentiment.

"No, it's fine. Err." I also looked behind me. It was such a weird question that I didn't want Mr. Pressley hearing it and getting the wrong idea. *Not that I have any idea what the right idea is, when it comes to jars full of teeth buried in the backyard.* "Uh . . ." I lowered my voice. "When you've been working in the backyard, you haven't come across any old jars, have you?"

"Old jars?" His brow furrowed. "Not that I can remember, sorry. I mean, I find a lot of odd junk in people's yards, so unless it was really unusual . . ."

"I suspect you'd remember these," I said dryly. "They've got . . . err . . . some human teeth in them."

Phil dropped the Weedwacker. "*Teeth?*"

"Yeah, uh. Baby teeth, you know . . ." I decided to leave out the bit about all the other, perhaps less innocently collected teeth. It was strange enough already. "Gran Mae, err . . . hoarded them, we think. I found a jar. I just wanted to make sure that it wasn't one of many."

He let out a low whistle. "Jesus Christ."

"I know, I know." I shrugged helplessly. "That's why I asked. I mean, it's not the kind of thing you want somebody to just stumble over and freak out . . ."

"Yeah. Yeah, I can see that. No. I haven't found anything like that."

"Mom is *totally* weirded out," I said, hoping to establish Mom as a fellow victim of the situation and not an accomplice in dental collecting.

"God, I bet. Poor Mrs. M."

"Uh." I rubbed the back of my neck. "She, um, really relies on you as a handyman, so please don't get spooked by this." *Or by the bit where*

I was ogling you. In fact, if we could just forget that completely, I'd appreciate it. "I don't think there's any more around. It's not Mom's fault that Gran Mae was . . . well . . ."

Phil gave me a wry look. "You don't have to explain to me about grandparents."

"No, I guess I don't. Well, uh, I guess I'll get going then. Can I go around the side, or . . . ?"

"No," said Phil. "It's booby-trapped."

I waited a moment to see if he was joking. He did not laugh. "Ah. Of course." Naturally Mr. Pressley's side yard would be booby-trapped. What had I been thinking?

We shared another look of mutual understanding, then Phil banged on the back door twice. Mr. Pressley opened the door a crack. "You done?"

"Yes," I said. "Thanks, Phil."

"No problem."

His grandfather grunted and opened the door far enough for me to squeeze through. In the distance, the TV announced that if God was taken out of the schools, the Devil and communism would take His place, teaching evolution and secular humanism.

Mr. Pressley led me back to the front door and unlocked it. There were multiple dead bolts on this side.

"Thanks for letting me talk to Phil, Mr. Pressley," I said.

He grunted again. I stepped out onto the porch, expecting to hear the door close behind me, but instead Pressley said, "Hey. Girl."

I turned back. "Yes?"

His glasses winked at me. "They're watching the house."

"Who's watching the house?"

"You know."

"The . . . the government?" I hazarded. (For a moment I almost said, "The Amish," but I couldn't imagine that going over well.)

Mr. Pressley pulled his glasses down and looked at me over the tops. "Not the sharpest knife in the drawer, are you, girl?"

"Probably not," I admitted. "Who's watching the house?"

"*Them,*" he said, sounding irritable, and shoved my shoulder, pointing me toward the street.

I blinked. The door shut behind me, but I barely registered the sound of the bolts being thrown.

On neighbors' rooftops, on the mailboxes, in the trees, and even on top of the cars, at least fifty black vultures were perching, and every single one was staring fixedly at my mother's house.

CHAPTER 19

"Every vulture in the neighborhood is staring at Mom's house," I said, opening the gate into Gail's garden.

Gail stood up and frowned, brushing dirt off her hands. "*That's* not good."

"Do they do this often? Stare at something? Is something dead in our attic or on the roof? A possum? Maybe a raccoon?"

She gave me a pitying look. "Vultures are extremely sensitive to the dead. Particularly when the dead are doing things they shouldn't be."

I gritted my teeth. I didn't want ghost stories, I wanted a wildlife rehabilitator's opinion. Obviously the vultures weren't there for ghosts, because *ghosts don't exist.*

Do they?

Of course they don't. There's no scientific literature supporting them at all.

Absence of evidence is not evidence of absence.

Yeah, that's what the Bigfoot hunters all say too. Start believing in ghosts and you might as well throw in aliens and Chupacabras.

And hands under the roses?

"I don't believe in any of that stuff," I said.

Gail folded her arms. "Do you truly not believe in it, or do you not believe that it would happen to your mother?"

"I don't—"

"You're an archaeologist. Do you think every other culture is misguided too?"

She might as well have hit me with a two-by-four upside the head. My mouth sagged open and I didn't have any words to put in it.

Because of course I didn't think that. Not even close. I'd spent my undergrad years reading *Black Elk Speaks* and *Divine Horsemen* and all the other classics and I sure as hell didn't speak up in class and say, "Well, the Ghost Dance wasn't real." If I was attending a Haitian dance with associated spirit possession, I wasn't going to grab anybody by the shoulders and inform them that they weren't *really* being ridden by the divine, or yank the mask off a kachina and say, "Look, there's really a person under here!"

Sure, I *might* think privately that there was probably a specific altered state that was being ritually induced and the results were influenced by the cultural context, but I would keep my damn mouth shut and my mind open, because who was I to come in all high and mighty and tell someone their spirits weren't real? Practitioners of other faiths are just as smart as I am, and they'd spent a helluva lot more time in it than I had. A couple of hours of comparative religions class didn't somehow give me more insight than somebody who'd spent their life experiencing the divine. Maybe there are divine horsemen. Maybe gods walk among us. Who was I to say differently?

Unless, apparently, we were talking about my mother, and Lammergeier Lane.

Never mind that my mother is definitely as smart as I am. Never mind that she was the one who taught me to be skeptical in the first place. I was willing to extend strangers a courtesy that I absolutely was not extending to Mom and Gail, and that was . . . yeah, that was pretty shitty of me, no getting around it.

IT'S REAL YOU'RE NOT IMAGINING THINGS. Hell, I'd probably write myself the same note in the same circumstances.

Gail said, very gently, "If you keep your mouth hanging open like that, I'm going to toss a dead mouse in it. I won't be able to resist."

Hermes came bouncing around the side of a flower bed, apparently having heard the word *mouse.*

I closed my mouth and swallowed hard. "All right," I said. "That's . . . valid. You're right. I'm dismissing this because it's my mom. I shouldn't do that."

"No one is a prophet in their own land," said Gail. She picked up a glass, took a sip, and eyed me over the rim. "There may be hope for you yet."

"Has Mom told you that she thinks my grandmother is haunting her?"

Gail grimaced. "Yes, and I told her to get the hell out of there. Offered to let her stay with me. But she was afraid that the old bat would retaliate, and I can't say that she's wrong. We were never friends, and that's putting it mildly."

"She really didn't approve of your garden," I muttered, looking over the flowers that buzzed with pollinators, unlike the silent roses.

"The garden was only the surface. We belonged to two wildly different schools of thought when it came to the unseen world, and our practices were . . . very different."

I turned this statement around in my head, trying to unpack the meaning. It sounded far too much like some of the things I'd skimmed past in *Thelema in America*. "Practices?" I asked weakly.

"Magic, Sam," said Gail, and tossed Hermes another chunk of mouse.

"You mean like a *witch?*"

"No," said Gail thoughtfully. "I'm a witch. This is different."

I reminded myself that I was going to keep an open mind.

"No," Gail continued, "I'd probably use the word *sorcerer* for your grandmother. It's not a kind power, not at all. But honestly, the semantics are the least important part of this."

MAD WIZARD OF BOONE ARRESTED! flashed through my brain. "It wasn't my grandmother," I said. "It was my great-grandfather. He was a sorcerer. Err . . . thought he was one, anyway. You know." I rubbed my forehead. My open mind was not going to extend to Parsons, Pasadena Antichrist. I had limits. "Apparently he was pretty famous for it."

"Was he, now . . . ?" Gail chewed on her thumbnail. "Now *that's* interesting. That would explain a lot, actually."

"Not to me!"

Gail laughed. "Poor Sam," she said, not entirely unkindly. "This is terribly hard for you, isn't it? Humor me for a minute, will you? Pretend that magic is real and some people can manipulate it. You can argue later."

"Fine," I said.

"There was always something very odd about your grandmother," said Gail.

"You don't know the half of it," I muttered.

She ignored me. "A great cruel power, doing almost nothing. Like a dormant volcano. All she did was grow roses. Not the way that a witch would, growing plants to improve a place, to bring more magic about through hard work and sweat and weeding, but as if she were building a wall of thorns to keep something out. If her father was a sorcerer, that would make a certain sense. Perhaps she inherited his talent but only bits and pieces of his training. All she knew was how to make herself safe, and she bent all that energy and all that malice to putting up that wall."

I stared at her. She took care of vultures and could talk about biodiversity. You don't expect that from people who then tell you, quite calmly, that your grandmother's roses were magic.

"So you're saying my grandmother was an evil wizard."

"More or less, yes."

"*My* grandmother."

"Yes."

I clutched my forehead. I'd promised that I would wait to argue, but this was ridiculous. I could not be having this conversation.

You found a jar full of teeth . . . whispered my brain.

Which means at most that Gran Mae was a very disturbed woman! Not that she was some kind of sorcerer! This is not a game of Dungeons & Dragons!

"Look," I said, "she was difficult and she was definitely racist and she told some really weird stories occasionally, but she was my grandmother! She always had Popsicles in the freezer for me and my brother and she wrapped presents and she . . . she did grandmother stuff! She wasn't going around chanting and drawing pentagrams on the floor!"

Gail was unruffled. "I didn't say she wasn't a grandparent. There are plenty of truly evil people in the world who are also absolutely gaga over their grandchildren and would knife someone at Christmas to get them a Cabbage Patch Kid. Or whatever it is these days, I can't remember. Elmo? Something."

"Buzz Lightyear," I mumbled, thinking of how Gran Mae had got me one for Christmas and had told me that it was the last one in the store and she had fought off two other women for it. At the time I thought she'd used a shopping cart and maybe her elbows. Now I had to worry that she'd been using demons. "This is nuts."

"People are complicated."

"But . . ." I couldn't get all this in my head. "Okay, even assuming it's real, which I am still not granting you, she's dead! Very dead! Years and years dead!"

"The roses aren't," said Gail simply. "And I think maybe she put a lot more of herself into those roses than anyone realized."

"And now Mom's trying to . . . what? Keep the ghost happy?"

"The dead are easier to appease than the living," said Gail, "at least in most cases."

The noise that came out of me was probably a laugh. It startled Hermes and he bounced sideways and gave me a wary look, as if I had done something extremely rude. "Gran Mae couldn't be appeased when she was alive," I said.

"That hasn't stopped Edie from trying, I think."

Appeasement. Yes. Everything was clicking into place. Mom was trying to keep Gran Mae happy. She'd painted over the bright colors that she loved, taken down art that meant something to her, and put up the things that Gran Mae would have wanted. Generic family photos and beige walls and that stupid, *stupid* Confederate wedding. All to keep a dead woman happy.

No, not even happy. To keep her from being angry.

I wanted to scream. I wanted to go buy five gallons of paint in the brightest colors I could and repaint the house. I wanted to burn that racist-ass Lost Cause painting in the backyard.

I turned on my heel and yanked the gate open. Regardless of whether ghosts were real, there was no way in hell that I was letting Mom paint her entire life ecru for a dead woman's approval. Gail called after me, but I didn't hear what she said.

I stepped out of the tree line at the end of the lane and blinked.

The air over Lammergeier Lane was full of wings. A kettle of vultures boiled overhead, dozens of them, forming tight circles over one particular house. As if the house were a dead thing and the vultures were about to land and begin to feed.

I broke into a run.

I never run if I can help it, and definitely not without supportive undergarments, but I ran now. Mr. Pressley was getting a show if he was watching. I locked one hand over my chest to slow the tectonics and put my head down and charged.

The vulture on the mailbox took off, wings flapping. "Sorry," I gasped at it as I ran past.

I flung the door open and found Mom standing in the living room, wringing her hands. I wanted to ask her what was wrong, but I was panting too hard.

"Sam," said Mom. Her voice was painfully sweet, but her eyes darted frantically back and forth, like a trapped animal. "You're back. Gran Mae's come to visit. Isn't that nice?"

". . . what?"

"Now we can have Sunday dinner as a family."

My heart sank. This was it. Whatever was wrong with Mom had finally snapped into full-blown delusion.

"Mom," I said, starting forward, still gasping for breath. "Mom, whatever is wrong, I'm here and we'll sort it ou ..."

My voice died.

My dead grandmother was sitting at the table. "Hello, Samantha," she said. "It's so nice to see you again."

CHAPTER 20

"I don't even get a hello?" said Gran Mae, as I stared at her. "After all these years?"

"I . . . I . . ." I didn't have words. I didn't even have thoughts. It was impossible. Gran Mae was dead. This was someone else. A twin we didn't know about. A different daughter of Elgar Mills.

I took a step forward and realized immediately that this wasn't a twin. She wasn't even a human.

She was made of roses. Her skin was rose petals layered together, white and rose and blush pink, and when she cocked her head, the petals shifted slightly. The edges overlapped like the scales of an enormous serpent.

She blinked at me, and I saw that the irises of her eyes were the tight swirl of tiny rosebuds. When she spoke, her tongue was a seething mass of ladybugs.

I'm hallucinating, I thought with sudden relief. *This isn't real.* I felt weak-kneed, almost giddy at the thought. *This wasn't real. It's the sleep paralysis. Or maybe it's just me. There was nothing wrong with Mom. Everything was wrong with me, all this time.*

Oh, thank god. Because if this was actually happening, then it would be . . . the worst thing . . . ever . . .

"You aren't real," I said.

"What kind of thing is that to say to your grandmother?" she snapped. A ladybug crawled out between her lips and she dabbed at it with a napkin like a drop of blood.

I squeezed my eyes shut and dug my nails into my palms. I knew it wasn't real, so it should go away now, right?

Right?

I opened my eyes again and Gran Mae had pursed her lips in the way she did when I was ten and eating eggs for breakfast.

Mom's hand closed on my wrist. "Isn't this nice?" she said, in her panicked *we-have-company* singsong.

That tone of voice snapped me out of whatever hole I was sinking into. It was a hindbrain function, I think. When Mom talks like that, you're in public and what you say is a reflection on her and you will straighten up and behave *right now* or you will lose your phone privileges for a *week.*

Even decades later, my spine responded to that voice. I straightened up. "Hello, Gran Mae," I said to my hallucination. "It's ... uh ... I was surprised."

"I'll bet you were," said my grandmother. "Seeing as I'm dead and all." She folded her napkin and set it down at the table. There were four places set, with the good china plates from the cabinet. The ladybug climbed out of her napkin and began to trundle across the tablecloth.

"Err," I said. "Yes, that."

"Is that ham cooked yet?" snapped Gran Mae.

"I'll put it in the oven now, Mother. Sam, can you help?"

I backed into the kitchen, not wanting to look away from the rose thing with my grandmother's face. Mom had dragged the fixings for a Sunday dinner out onto the counter, or the closest equivalent she could find. There were cans of green beans and a box of instant mashed potatoes, and, sure enough, a ham. I lifted it into the pan she held out. It was frozen solid.

"You should have started last night," said Gran Mae. "You were never a very good cook, Edith. I tried to teach you, but you had no head for it."

"Yes, Mother." She closed the oven on the frozen ham and caught my hand. Her fingers closed hard over mine and I squeezed back. Both our palms were damp with sweat. It felt real, but so had the sleep-paralysis hallucination.

Leaves moved against the window behind Gran Mae and I realized that the roses were pressed up against it. That should have been the deck, but the leaves were there and the roses and the window was open just a crack and long rose whips poured through and twined around Gran Mae's chair, running up the back and vanishing inside the rose petals.

A puppet, I thought. *A puppet made of roses, with vines instead of strings.* I was almost impressed. I had never suspected that my imagination could come up with a hallucination like this.

"This can't be real," I said to Mom.

Her eyes showed white all around the irises. "It's real," she whispered. "It's all real. I told you she wasn't gone."

"Come here, Samantha," said Gran Mae. "Come sit down here and talk to your grandmother. It's been so long."

Mom's fingers tightened so hard that I felt bones grind together. "I need her to help me cook, Mother," she said.

Something lashed across the counter. Another rose whip, moving like a snake. It knocked the cans onto the floor and sent the silverware flying. Mom and I jerked back. Thorns rasped against the surface of the counter.

"*Now,* Samantha," said Gran Mae, not raising her voice.

"It's all right," I said to Mom, disentangling myself. If I talked to her, maybe I could draw her attention.

(The attention of a hallucination? Did that make any sense at all?)

"Well," said Gran Mae, as I sat down at the table across from her. "Look at you." Her rose lips were pursed again. "Not married, are you?"

"No, Gran Mae."

"Of course you aren't. No one wants to marry a little piggy." She drummed her fingers on the table with a clicking sound. She had no nails, only darker petals. There was something under the rose petals making the clicking. "You've been sticking your nose in where it doesn't belong, haven't you?"

I swallowed. If this was sleep paralysis, it was lasting far longer than the previous times. "What do you mean?"

"Digging things up. Never stopped to think things might be buried for a reason, did you?"

"You mean the jar of teeth?"

"Among other things." She drummed her fingers on the table again. "Edith! Are there collards?"

Mom's voice sounded choked. "I'll . . . I'll have to look in the pantry, Mother . . ."

"Then look! You should think of these things yourself."

"Yes, Mother."

I dug my nails into my palms again. Nobody should make my mom sound like that, but I didn't know how to fix it. *It isn't real*, I told myself again, but I was having a harder and harder time believing it.

"We've got to have collards," said Gran Mae with a sniff. "Father always insisted on collards at the table. Not that I'd ever use *canned*."

"I was reading about your father," I said, hoping to distract her. "Elgar Mills."

Petal lips curved. "Father. Yes. I heard you talking about it. You're always so *busy*, Samantha."

"They called him a sorcerer."

"Oh yes." Her smile widened, showing white petal teeth. "He knew things, Father did. So many things."

"I read some of his letters," I offered.

The smile died. She narrowed her eyes at me. "You shouldn't read other people's letters," she said.

"It was on—" I started to say, and then a hot line etched itself across my forearm. I looked down, shocked, and saw blood welling from a dozen small cuts. A rose whip curled around my right wrist, slick and green and shockingly prehensile.

"What . . . ?" I tried to yank my hand back and the thorns on the whip dug savagely into my skin. "Ow! What the fuck?"

"*Samantha!*" Gran Mae stared at me. "You know what happens to little girls who swear!"

I swallowed. This didn't feel like pain in a dream. This felt like pain right here, right now, and if that was true, this was happening right here, right now.

This is true. This is real. Gran Mae is here.

(But it's impossible!)

It doesn't matter what's possible. It's happening.

(But—)

If it was just you, you could curl into a little ball and scream all you want, but if it's real, Mom's here too.

I took a deep breath and shoved the screaming down. "I'm sorry, Gran Mae," I said, trying to sound contrite, and clamped my left hand over as much of my forearm as I could to try to stop the bleeding.

Gran Mae shook her head and leaned back, looking into the kitchen. "I can't believe you're using instant mashed potatoes."

"I'm afraid I don't have any real ones," said Mom carefully. "I wasn't expecting company."

"Excuses." Gran Mae sniffed. "You should always keep some things on hand, in case company comes by."

"Yes, Mother."

"What is our guest going to think? You know it reflects badly on the way you were raised, Edith."

"I'm sorry."

I had to distract her again. "You must have learned magic from your father," I said.

Gran Mae's rosebud eyes snapped back to me. "Magic. Yes, I suppose you'd call it magic."

"What do you call it?"

"Power," said Gran Mae. "Will. Everything is will. Will and blood. And occasionally teeth."

I nodded as if this made sense. "So your father taught you."

She made an indelicate noise. "Father didn't teach me a blessed thing."

"Err . . ."

"He was much too busy. And so obsessed with his children. His . . . other . . . children. Not me." She narrowed her eyes and the rosebuds compressed, briefly giving her oblong pupils like a goat's. "Never *me*."

"His other children?" I asked weakly.

"Oh yes. The ones he made. The ones who turned against him." She laughed softly. "But I learned anyway. It was easy. He never noticed what I did, as long as his dinner was on the table. All I had to do was pay attention."

I swallowed. It had been twenty years since I had spoken to Gran Mae, and it's very different being an adult than a ten-year-old. Had she always sounded so angry and petty and gloating? Had I just thought it was normal when I was a kid?

"That was very clever of you," I managed.

"Trying to butter me up, Samantha?" She rolled her eyes. "You haven't gotten any more subtle since you were a child. It *was* clever of me, though, not that he noticed." The rose whip tightened again and pain stabbed up my arm. From the kitchen, I heard the clatter of cookware and the beep of the stove.

"Father was like that," said Gran Mae, almost dreamily. "I loved him, but he never realized that other people were just as smart as he was. Rather like you, Samantha. Always thinking he's the smartest one in the room." She shook her head. "Couldn't even pretend to be normal too. Also like you. All I wanted was a nice, normal life, like everyone at school. Like everyone on TV. It's so important to be normal, don't you think?"

"Yes, Gran Mae," I said dutifully. Blood was oozing down the sides of my wrist and staining the tablecloth ladybug red. I hoped that Mom couldn't see it.

"He was sick for a long time, you know," she said. "I took care of him. *Me*. Not any of his freak-show friends. People always asked how I could stand to be a nurse for dying people. Ordinary people are nothing compared to a dying sorcerer. He was never grateful. None of you are *ever* grateful."

"I'm sorry, Gran Mae." The rose thorns felt as if they were burrowing into my skin and sawing along the tendons.

"Mmm. Father was sorry too, when I finally got tired of him. Amazing how easy it was. All that power, all those years, and all I had to do was just let his other children in and walk away." She laughed softly. A single ladybug crawled across her teeth.

I swallowed. This did not seem like a safe line of inquiry. I groped for something else. "Why did you send the ladybugs?"

"Me?" She laughed. "Stupid child. The ladybugs were your fault."

I blinked at her. "What?"

"You gave the roses blood and demanded ladybugs. What did you think was going to happen?"

I didn't have time to do more than gape at her, because the front door opened.

"Mrs. M?" called Phil. "Samantha? Grandad said you left a message for me? Something about nails?"

Oh god.

I twisted in my chair, feeling the thorns tear into my wrist, not caring. "Phil!" I screamed. "*Run!*"

But it was too late. It had been too late, probably, since he passed the gate with the white picket fence and the roses growing in the yard. The door slammed hard enough to rattle the glass in the windows and Phil said, "Wha—?"

Gran Mae's smile grew. She dabbed another ladybug away with a napkin. "I see that our dinner guest has arrived."

CHAPTER 21

The problem, I think, was that Phil was basically a good guy. If he'd been a little more concerned with saving his own skin, he would have run when I yelled, or maybe even broken the door down and fled. I don't know for sure.

But because he was a good guy, he hesitated, and then he came forward into the living room, saying, "Mrs. M? Sam? Are you all..."

He stopped. His eyes traveled over Gran Mae and I don't know if he understood what he was seeing, but clearly he knew that something very strange was going on. He looked down at me and he couldn't have missed the bloody tablecloth, or the way that Mom was cowering in the kitchen.

"Aren't you going to introduce me to your gentleman friend, dear?" asked Gran Mae.

"I...I..."

"What is going on?" he asked. "Sam? What's happened to your hand?"

"Samantha," said Gran Mae warningly, and the rose whip tightened.

"Phil," I gasped, as agony shot through my wrist. "Phil, this is my g-grandmother. Gran Mae. Gran Mae, this is...this is Phil. Pressley."

"Oh, yes," said Gran Mae. She climbed to her feet and extended a rose-petal hand. "I believe I know your grandfather."

Social courtesies were deeply ingrained in Phil. He started to extend his hand automatically, then caught himself, but by then it was too late.

Rose whips lashed out from under the table, coiling around his legs and yanking him forward. Phil yelped. I reached for him involuntarily, trying to catch him, and the stem around my wrist slammed my arm against the table.

"We were waiting for you," said Gran Mae pleasantly, as Phil collapsed into the chair at the head of the table. "How is that ham coming, Edith?"

"It's still cooking, Mother."

"So," said Gran Mae, as the rose stems lashed Phil's ankles to the chair legs. "What do you do for a living?"

"I . . . I . . ." His chest heaved. He tried to grab for the stems at his ankles and pulled his fingers back bloody. Gran Mae clicked her tongue disapprovingly. Phil stared at her. Perhaps he was finally working out what kind of monster was sitting at the table with him. "What *are* you?"

"It's not polite to comment on a lady's appearance, young man."

"Are those roses? What—how—"

"Roses, yes," said Gran Mae. "Aren't they clever?" She patted her petal hair. "Of course, I wouldn't get dressed up like this normally, but Sunday dinner should be special, don't you think?"

My feet were still free. I found Phil's foot and pressed down on it hard, trying to avoid the stems. His eyes shot to me and I shook my head infinitesimally. *Don't make her angry,* I wanted to say. *I know it's a tall order and the number of things that make Gran Mae angry are measured in the thousands, but if we can just get through this, surely she'll go away . . .*

Impossible to convey all that with a look and a foot tap. I did my best.

"Young people these days have no idea how to make conversation. What do you do for a living, Mr. Pressley?"

Maybe some of what I had tried to express got through. He swallowed. "I . . . uh . . . I'm a master gardener, ma'am."

"A gardener!" The rose puppet turned in her chair, pressing her hands together. "How lovely! Do you like roses?"

I suspected that Phil currently hated roses with an undying passion, but he tried to hide it. "Uh, well . . . as I'm sure you know . . . growing roses in the South can be a real challenge . . ."

"You don't have to tell me twice, young man. I lost the most beautiful red rose to black spot the year I moved here."

"Yes, uh...there's...um...a lot of breeding for...um...disease resistance...some new varieties that we're all...err...watching closely..."

"Are there any in orange? It's so hard to get a really lovely orange." She smiled almost coquettishly. "I know they're not particularly classy, but I just can't resist."

"Err..."

"Gran Mae," I interjected, "may I go and help Mom with the cooking?"

She waved her hand negligently. "Yes, go do that, Samantha. You may be excused." The rose shackle around my wrist relaxed. I pushed my chair back, trying not to make any moves that might attract attention, and scurried to the kitchen.

Mom had dumped cans of beans and collards into dishes, and was now pressed against the cupboards, as far away from the roses as she could get. "Sam," she whispered. Tears tracked down her face. "Sam, are you okay?"

"Fine," I lied. I wrapped a dish towel around my wrist and looked around for anything I could use as a weapon. There was water simmering on the stove for the instant mashed potatoes. Would a pot of boiling water be enough?

In the dining room, Phil was stammering something about coral roses and recent Knock Out varieties, and Gran Mae was making well-practiced sounds of interest. I opened the drawers, looking for a knife.

"Edith! It's time to bring out the ham."

Mom took a deep breath. "Yes, Mother." She turned off the stove and pulled out the ham, still frozen. I found the big carving knife and pulled it out. Could I hack through the stems with this?

I didn't get the chance. As soon as Mom set the frozen ham on the table, Gran Mae snapped her fingers, pointed to me, and said, "Give that to Mister Pressley, so that he can carve the ham, Samantha."

I lifted the knife and Gran Mae's rosebud eyes locked on mine. Green stems slithered along the floor.

"You know what happens to children who don't respect their elders, Samantha."

I passed Phil the knife.

"Now let's say grace," said Gran Mae, and bowed her head. "Heavenly Father, thank you for the blessings we are about to receive . . ."

It was like being ten all over again, and looking at Brad, except this time it was Phil. He mouthed, *What the fuck?* at me. I shook my head helplessly. Mom clutched the back of her chair with white-knuckled fingers. Phil took the knife and leaned down, sawing at the stems holding him prisoner. Would Gran Mae feel it?

She didn't seem to. The prayer droned on. I wondered if the knife was having any effect on the stems at all.

"Amen," finished Gran Mae. She looked up and smiled sweetly. Phil snapped upright, knife in hand. "Now where are the collards, Edith?"

Mom grabbed the bowl of green glop and set it on the table. Gran Mae looked at it, lip curling, and poked it with her fork. "These are *cold*," she said.

"I'm sorry, Mother."

"And this ham." She set her fork down with a click. "Edith, this ham is frozen. And you put it in front of a *guest*."

"You told me to—"

"Don't talk back to me, young lady!"

"I am fifty-nine," said Mom. "And I have been cooking for years and—and—I don't care if you are my mother, you can't make a ham cook in five minutes!"

I was torn between the desire to cheer and the desire to jump in front of her and fend off Gran Mae's wrath.

Gran Mae put her hands flat on the table and rose to her feet. "I'm sorry that you had to see this, Phil."

"It's fine," mumbled Phil. He made as if to scratch an itch, continuing to saw the knife against the stems. I worried again if Gran Mae would feel it. Taking a knife to her precious roses would be high on the list of things to make her angry. But plants don't have nerves like people, so maybe she didn't.

"Edith. You are overwrought. Go to your room."

"I am not a child," said Mom. "You are being unreasonable, and you know it, but you can't admit that you're wrong." She swallowed hard. "You never could."

Gran Mae's eyes narrowed. Leaves began to whip against the window. "Is that so?"

Hectic spots of color had risen on Mom's cheeks. "I don't know what you're playing at, Mother, with this ridiculous dinner party—"

"I am trying to *fix* things!" shouted Gran Mae. Her voice was just as cutting as I remembered. "Because none of you could ever do it for yourselves! A perfectly good gentleman caller and none of you even invited him for dinner? Do you *want* Samantha to end up like you?"

I was terrified and miserable and in pain, and it turned out that I could still be embarrassed. How nice.

"All I ever wanted was for my family to be *nice* and *normal*," raged Gran Mae. "We could all be so happy, but you just couldn't do it, could you? Always fighting me, always sulking, never *happy*, no matter what I did!"

Mom had an arm up as if she were fighting against a strong wind. She shook her head but her breathing was short and ragged. "I don't—it wasn't like that—"

"Ungrateful. After everything I did for you, even taking you and your brats in when your man got himself killed, after all that I've done, you're still not happy! It's never enough for you, is it?"

I don't know much in life, and the last few days, it had turned out that half of what I thought I knew was wrong. But the one thing I did know was that *nobody* talked to my mother like that while I was around.

I took a deep breath and yelled, "*Shut the fuck up!*" at the top of my lungs.

Gran Mae whipped around, her rosebud eyes going wide. I shoved Mom behind me as if we were in a fistfight, which maybe we were.

"You!" said Gran Mae. Was I imagining things or did she sound a trifle uncertain? "How dare you talk to me that way?"

"How dare you talk to my mom like that?" I shouted back.

"Would you rather I talked about *you?*"

Bring it, I thought, bracing myself and keeping my eye out for vine whips. I hoped like hell that Phil was making some progress sawing himself free, but I didn't dare look over at him.

"How about we talk about you instead?" I asked. "With your creepy fifties décor and your creepy fifties racism and all your creepy fifties shit? Trying to mold everybody into an episode of *Leave It to Beaver* and throwing a tantrum every time they stepped out of line."

The rose figure whistled like a teakettle. I could see vine whips thrashing outside the sliding glass door.

"You think you're so smart," hissed Gran Mae. "Always did, didn't you? Tit for tat, every time. Nobody could tell you anything, could they? And yet look how you turned out. No husband, no kids, nothing but bones and bugs."

The problem with family is that they know where all the levers are that make you move. They're usually the ones who installed the levers in the first place. But Gran Mae had only known me for a few years as a child, with my mother running interference. Whatever levers were in my head, she hadn't put most of them in. "Don't want kids," I said cheerfully. "Not even sure I want a husband, for that matter."

Gran Mae snorted. "You'd never get one anyway. You're..." She paused dramatically, apparently about to unleash her ultimate cruelty. "...*fat.*"

"Yeah, no shit, Sherlock." I started laughing. I couldn't help it. It was all so ridiculous. Gran Mae thought she could get me about my *weight?* I'd come out of academia. If she wanted to tear me apart, she should have commented on my doctoral thesis.

T. KINGFISHER

Still, she tried. "Look at you," hissed Gran Mae. "You're disgusting. When was the last time a man even looked twice at you?"

"Three months ago," I said. "I dumped him after two weeks because he was super clingy and cried every time we fucked."

(This was true, incidentally, although it may have been more like a year and three months ago, but Gran Mae didn't need to know that.)

I had, momentarily, rendered her speechless.

"You unladylike little . . . little . . ." The rose doll struggled to find a word harsh enough. "You don't use language like that in this house!"

"I'll use any fucking language I please!"

A rose whip reared up like a snake and slapped at my mouth. I fended it off with my arm, feeling thorns catch on my shirtsleeve.

"That's enough of that," said Gail from the doorway.

CHAPTER 22

Her hair was a wild halo of silver. She had on leopard-print leggings and an oversized T-shirt that read OREGON: FIFTY MILLION BANANA SLUGS CAN'T BE WRONG. She was wearing hot-pink Crocs and carrying something in her left hand. I had never been more glad to see another human being in my life.

"You!" screamed Gran Mae. "How are *you* still alive?"

"Clean living," said Gail, coming into the dining room. She took in the scene with a glance. "I'm sorry that it took me so long to get here."

"You can turn right around and go back where you came from, witch."

Gail shook her head. "Go back to the grave, Mae Mills," she said, in a voice like the tolling of a bell. "You have no place here."

The afternoon light blazed through the sliding glass door. It made her shine like an avenging angel. Against the wall behind her, etched starkly against the pale paint, I saw the shadow of a hooked beak and mighty wings.

An hour ago, I'd have thought I was imagining things. Right now, it didn't seem so much normal as inevitable. Of course Gail would cast the shadow of a vulture. In a world where Gran Mae had returned in a body puppeted by rose vines, why wouldn't she?

"This is my house," spat Gran Mae. "You can't order me in my own house!"

"It's Edie's house," said Gail.

Gran Mae looked ready to spit. "Edith is *my* daughter. This is family business, not yours."

She dragged her fingers over the tablecloth and I saw green stems coming from the tips like claws. *Ah,* I thought, very calmly. *That's what was combing my hair.*

I guess it wasn't sleep paralysis after all.

"Edie," said Gail, looking at Mom. "Tell her to leave, and I can force her out."

"You can't." Gran Mae looked contemptuous. "Tell her to *leave,* Edith."

Mom's eyes were huge. She looked from Gail to Gran Mae and back again.

"Do it." Gran Mae's voice cracked like a whip.

Gail didn't speak. She just lifted the thing she carried at her side. It looked like a spray bottle.

I stepped sideways and put my hand on Mom's shoulder. Her hand came up to cover mine and her voice shook but she was still the toughest woman I'd ever known.

"Mother," she said, "I'd like you to leave now." And then, because it was Mom, she added, "Please."

Gail took another step forward, raised the spray bottle, and sprayed Gran Mae directly in the face.

The rose puppet shrieked. Petals dropped away from her cheeks and her hands shot up to cover them.

"Go back where you belong, Mae Mills. Leave the living alone. If you cannot find the way, I will show you."

"You?" hissed the puppet between her hands. "I know the way better than you ever will, you miserable, classless *witch.*"

Something passed between them. It felt like I was standing next to a speaker at a concert and the bass thrummed through my chest, even though there was no sound. Gail staggered, catching herself on the back of the chair, and then sprayed the puppet again.

"Go. Back."

Phil must have finally cut himself free, because he jerked his chair

back and nearly fell over. His sneakers were bloody, but he rose to his feet and pointed the knife at Gran Mae.

"Fine," Gran Mae spat, lowering her hands. "Fine. You know best, all of you. You think you'll do so much better without me, don't you?" Her face twisted into a smile. "You think it'll be so much better if I just butt out? Fine. I'll go." Rose petals drifted down from her hair. She took a step back toward the sliding door.

"Go, then," said Gail, breathing heavily. I wondered what it had cost her, whatever she had done.

Gran Mae laughed softly. The petals were falling in earnest now, flaking away from her face. "I'm going. Maybe you'll learn what happens to people who don't appreciate all the sacrifices that kept them safe." The ladybugs on her tongue began to spread out, crawling out through the gaps in her skin. "The underground children get them."

"The underground children aren't real," I said. "You made them up."

"I can't tell you anything, can I? But you'll wish you listened." There were larger holes opening up in her face now, with only shadow and rose stems behind them. "I didn't make them. My father did . . . and they're very, very angry." Her hands were only rakelike rose stems now, as the petals piled at her feet. "The roses said *stay away.* I put jars of teeth and nails at the roots to keep the children out, but you were so smart, you dug one up and made a gap." Her lips dropped away in rolled pink petals. A ladybug crawled out of her eye socket. "Father's blood wasn't enough. They wanted more. Now I suppose they'll finally get it."

"Get out," grated Gail. "You aren't welcome here."

"Very well," whispered the rose puppet. It was only stem and thorn now, a scaffold of green in human shape. "If that's the way you all want it. This is no longer *my* house."

And she fell apart, very quietly, the stems going brown and weathered gray, and collapsed into a heap of leaf mold on the kitchen floor.

Mom staggered. I moved to catch her. "It's all right, Edie," Gail said. "It's all right. She's gone. I think."

"Really?" asked Mom hoarsely. She steadied on her feet. "Really gone?"

"I think so."

"What did you spray her with?" I asked. "Holy water?"

Gail looked down at the bottle in her left hand as if she'd forgotten it. "Oh," she said. She turned the bottle so that I could see the label.

"Weed killer?"

"Look, I don't approve of industrial herbicides, but in this case . . ." She looked embarrassed. "I try to stay organic, but Japanese honeysuckle really doesn't respond to anything else."

"Excuse me," said Phil, "but can someone tell me what . . . *the fuck* . . . is going on?"

To this day, I don't know what Gail would have said, because at that moment, the floor dropped out from under us and everything went black.

Day or Night
or Nowhere

---

there are no flowers in this place only the roots of roses and the things that move
between them
only roots and runners
only thorns

CHAPTER 23

The air was full of dust and the groaning sounds of wooden boards being badly stressed. Someone said, "Shit," and I agreed wholeheartedly with the sentiment. My head ached. I had fallen over something uncomfortable. It had knobs and rods and hard bits, all of which were placed at precise angles to jab into me. Most of a frozen ham appeared to have landed in my lap. Whatever had happened, it appeared to have affected the whole house, or at least the dining room.

"Is everyone okay?" asked Gail.

"I feel like crap and I seem to be wearing a ham."

"What the fuck is happening?" Phil asked again.

"Edith?" Gail called.

"I'm here," said Mom faintly. "I think I'm stuck under something, though."

"Mom!" I felt enormously relieved, partly because she hadn't been squashed in the fall, partly because I was in the dark and something terrible had happened and on some level, I really just wanted my mommy to tell me everything would be okay.

I heard someone blundering past me. "Where do you keep the flashlights, Mrs. M?"

"Junk drawer . . . in the kitchen . . ."

I sat up, trying to shove the imprisoning rods away, and banged my head on something hard. The sounds of drawers opening came from the kitchen, and a minute later a beam of light shot through the darkness. I realized that I was partly trapped under one of the dining room chairs and managed to push it off me. The ham rolled away, leaving a pineapple ring and a maraschino cherry stuck to my shirt. The bowl of green beans had overturned onto my legs, but fortunately the tablecloth had caught the worst of it. Whenever . . . whatever it was . . . had happened, the table had fallen on its side, spilling everything toward me.

The beam of light was joined by another one as Phil found a second light. I put up a hand to ward off the glare as he came toward me. The dining room was a sea of overturned chairs, and the sideboard had fallen over.

"Mrs. M? Where did you end up?"

"Over here," said Mom from the other side of the table. It was at an angle, as if two of the legs had broken off. I got to my feet and joined Phil, and he silently handed me one of the flashlights.

Mom was trapped under the table and a pile of chairs. She looked very pale, although no one looks particularly healthy in a flashlight beam.

"Are you okay, Mom?"

"I'm not sure. My ankle's stuck."

A heavy wooden table leg had fallen across her shin. Phil and I each grabbed part of the table and heaved. Mom pulled it out and I heard her hiss of pain. I transferred the flashlight to my teeth and began pulling chairs out of the way.

"Was there an earthquake?" asked Phil.

"Not an earthquake," said Gail. Another point of light flared up as she lit a candle. It smelled strongly of plastic. "Dammit, Edith, I've told you not to buy cheap scented candles."

"I am not spending twenty dollars on a candle," said my mother. Phil pulled her to her feet. She was clearly favoring her ankle and had to lean on his arm. "For twenty dollars, it would have to give me an orgasm every time I lit it."

Phil made a small sound of emotional distress. I wanted to cheer. That was the Mom I remembered.

I ran the flashlight toward the sliding glass doors to see if there was glass on the floor. To my surprise, they were intact. I could see dirt on the other side, mixed with pebbles and the thin white threads of roots. It looked almost like a cross section of a dig, complete with a harder layer of orange clay at the bottom. Whatever had happened, it had buried the side of the house completely.

"Did the house fall into a sinkhole?" I asked.

Phil joined me at the door. He frowned. "Do we even have sinkholes in this part of the state?"

"Have you got a better explanation?"

There was enough candlelight for me to catch the look he threw at me. Considering what we'd just lived through, that was probably justified. Still, I was just going to pretend for a few minutes that we had fallen into a real, actual, goddamn sinkhole that just happened to open up in our nice and normal subdivision, rather than a portal to hell or the bowels of the Thelemic Antichrist or whatever the hell else it might conceivably be. If I pretended hard enough, it might even be true.

For one thing, people sometimes *survived* falling into sinkholes.

"I was just tied to a table by a crazy woman who fell apart into rose petals," Phil finally answered. "I don't have an explanation for *anything*."

This was not helpful to my mental state, even if it was true. "Let's assume it's a sinkhole for the moment," I said very carefully. "Maybe we can go upstairs and get out through a window."

Possibly there was something in my tone that made Phil decide not to pursue the matter just yet. "Worth a shot," he said.

Phil and I made our way to the stairs. The steps were littered with broken glass and shattered frames. I pushed my graduation photo aside with my foot and followed Phil up.

We checked my bedroom first. The window was dark, but when I ran the flashlight beam over it, I saw no roots or pebbles. It looked as if the beam was vanishing into the distance, not as if something was pressing against the glass like the dirt downstairs, yet it was pitch black.

It couldn't possibly be dark outside yet, could it? It had been late afternoon just a few minutes ago. I pulled my phone out, the screen bright in the darkness. Five thirty.

This was not the darkness of five thirty.

As impossibilities went, this was minor compared to my grandmother made of rose petals. I had accepted that; surely I could accept this too. This one wasn't trying to kill me. I went up to the window, moving the flashlight beam, trying to see anything. Phil cupped his hands around his eyes and stared into the dark.

"Anything?" He sounded resigned.

My flashlight, angled down, hit the porch roof, lighting up the black asphalt shingles. I felt a sudden wave of relief, although I'm not sure why. Possibly I was just relieved that the laws of physics still seemed to apply. I moved the beam again and encountered . . . earth.

Churned earth, specifically. The wreckage that follows a bulldozer, everything ripped up and mixed together, not the smooth undisturbed layers that archaeologists pray for. Not even the settled dirt and clay of an old development like Lammergeier Lane. This was new and raw, as if someone had dumped hundreds of tons of dirt around the base of the house and then turned off the moon and the stars overhead.

I swallowed. The dirt came up the edge of the porch roof and continued as far as the flashlight beam would go. Where had it come from?

"This looks a bit like a sinkhole," said Phil, with very little hope in his voice. "Doesn't it?" It seemed to be his turn to pretend that this was completely normal.

It was on the tip of my tongue to say that a sinkhole wouldn't take out the sun too, but I knew exactly what he was feeling, so I didn't argue.

Phil gazed out the window for a few minutes. "This is fucked up," he said finally.

"Yes. Yes, it is." I felt oddly calm. Of course there was no sky. Of course there was nothing but dirt and the house. My grandmother had come back from the dead made of roses. If that was possible, why should the world obey any rules at all?

"Let's check out Mom's window," I said finally, turning away. Phil followed me, so close on my heels that he nearly stepped on my feet when I stopped at the door.

"Sorry," he mumbled.

"S'okay." I opened the door. A Post-it note fluttered to the floor like a dying moth.

The floor creaked underfoot as we went to the window. Here again, dirt was piled up past the first story. The deck had vanished completely. Farther back I could just make out a few bedraggled shapes that might have been stones or the tops of the rosebushes, but the flashlight beam didn't reach very far. The darkness outside seemed somehow thicker than the absence of light. Smoke? Dust?

It's like the dark has weight here, I thought, then wished I hadn't. I could hear the house creaking and popping around me, little noises of strain as the house settled. God only knows what it was settling into.

I focused again on the shapes outside the window. Those had to be the rosebushes. They'd been buried in dirt, just like the bottom half of the house, and now only the tops were sticking out. As if we'd been caught in a blizzard, say, except that it was dirt.

"We could probably climb out my window onto the porch roof," I said. "It's only a couple feet down from the window. Then maybe we could jump down from there."

"Yeah," said Phil. "Let's go tell Gail and Mrs. M."

On the way out the door, I saw that the Confederate wedding had fallen and shattered. I took a certain pleasure in putting my foot squarely on the groom's smugly wistful face.

The stairs groaned again as we went down, more loudly than before. *All that weight can't be good for the walls*, I thought. I vaguely wondered how we were going to remove all the dirt and how much it would cost to repair the damage, then snorted at myself. *You know, the resale value of the property may not actually be the biggest concern right now.*

Mom and Gail had found more candles and righted the table. They looked up when we came in. "What's it look like?" asked Gail.

"The first floor is buried," I said. "The upper windows are clear, but it's very dark out." I wondered how on earth to express what we'd seen. "I, uh, don't think we're in Kansas anymore."

Gail let out a long breath. "Yeah," she said. "I was afraid of that."

"But where are we?" asked Mom.

Phil and I shrugged helplessly. "Someplace dark," I said. I didn't think saying "another hellscape plane of existence" would be particularly helpful.

We all looked at Gail, who shook her head. "Don't look at me. I'm just a witch. This is completely beyond my experience."

Mom put her hands on her hips. "Well, how do we get back?"

Gail made a helpless gesture. Phil said, "Um." I did neither. My gaze was riveted on the sliding door.

Behind Mom's head, something white moved on the other side of the glass.

CHAPTER 24

My first thought was that there was a person trapped on the other side of the door. A small white hand touched the pane, moving through the earth as if it were water. It slid along the surface of the glass and it had dirt under its tiny fingernails and I heard myself say, very quietly, "Fuck. Fuck, fuck, fuck."

"Sam?" said Mom. "What's wrong?"

The hand reached the edge of the doorframe. It scrabbled briefly, silently. Dirt filled in the spaces left behind it, and then it began to move downward, toward the latch.

The underground children. I don't know if I said it out loud. I only know that I lunged across the room, tripping and scrambling over the broken furniture, and flung myself at the door, hitting the lock a bare instant before the hand reached it.

I clung to the handle, gasping for breath, lending my weight to hold it closed. The flashlight got wedged between my boob and my arm and shone on the dirt. The hand plucked at the handle and I felt a shudder through the latch.

"Sam . . . ?"

"Something," I gasped. "Out there. Wants in."

In the flashlight beam, the white hand was joined by another. They closed delicately over the door handle and pulled. The door shifted a quarter inch, the length of the latch, and I threw all my weight against it in a panic.

"Check the windows," ordered Gail. Thank god, someone else was

taking charge. I heard Phil sprinting to make sure the front door was
locked.

Dirt shifted sideways. More of the arms came into view, and then a
soft, ribbed body like a giant grub, and then one of the underground
children pressed its face against the glass next to mine.

"Oh god," Mom said behind me. "Oh god."

Its head was shaped like a monstrous fetus, the skull squared off, eyes
set far down on the sides. White skin covered everything, transparent
enough to make out dark shapes underneath. It turned its head so that
an eye faced me and I watched the edge of the flashlight catch it and the
misshapen blue bruise beneath suddenly shrank as the pupil contracted
beneath the skin.

We stared at each other, my great-grandfather's other child and I, and
my mind was empty of everything but horror.

One of the little white hands drifted away from the latch and ran
across the door next to my face. I heard the faintest squeak of flesh
dragging across glass.

"There's one at the kitchen window," Mom said hoarsely. I heard her
limping across the floor, and the snap of the window latch. I turned
my head just in time to see another one squirming through the dirt on
the other side of the door. Its body rubbed against the glass, thick and
segmented like a beetle grub. I watched the ripples pass through the
segments as it wriggled forward. Maggots move the same way, but they
aren't the size of my torso.

"What the hell are they?" yelled Mom from the kitchen.

It reached the other half of the glass door. Dirty nails picked at the
screen, the metal mesh digging into the thing's fingertips, but it showed
no sign of pain.

"Elgar's other kids. The underground children." I could feel a high, hys-
terical laugh in my throat. "Oh god, Mom, they're our aunts and uncles."

"What?"

My great-aunt or whatever it was got through a bit of screen and
pried it back. The weight of the dirt held the bulk of the screen in place,

but it got one hand underneath. Its arm seemed to have no joints and hardly any bones.

"We have a problem!" yelled Phil from the direction of the front door.

I tore my eyes away from the underground children and waved the flashlight beam toward him.

We did indeed have a problem. The front door was wide open and dirt had poured in through it. Phil was trying to dig it out of the way so that he could get the door closed but for every handful he scooped away, another rained down.

"Shit! Shit, shit, shit!" I ran toward him just as a dainty white hand came around the side of the doorframe above his head.

"Phil! Get down!"

Perhaps he'd learned his lesson about not listening to me when I said, "Run!" He flung himself backward, hitting the wall.

The white hand felt up and down the frame. Small, pudgy fingers opened and closed over the doorjamb, then reached farther into the room, grasping at the air. Finding nothing, it withdrew.

Before I could even start to feel relief, dirt clods began to shift and a blunt white head surfaced like a seal breaking through water.

"Gail!" I yelled. "Gail, do something!"

I heard pounding footsteps behind me. The underground child looked around, its skinned-over eyes studying the space before it. It had a tiny toothless mouth, barely an inch wide, and as we watched, its mouth opened and it made a small, mewling cry, like a newborn kitten.

"What do you expect me to do?" snapped Gail. "I've never seen one of these things either!" But she stepped forward anyway, bottle of weed killer at the ready.

A second underground child popped up beside the first and looked back and forth curiously. The first one turned its head sideways to look at Gail through one wide-set eye.

"Go back, unclean things," Gail said. "Go back to the grave. Go back to the earth. O you wardens of the sky, protect us—"

The first underground child launched itself at her.

Gail threw an arm in front of her face and it hit her forearm, hands clutching at her wrist and shoulder. Phil jumped up, grabbing for the thing's body. His fingers sank into it as if he were grabbing wet clay, and it made a tiny sound of distress, then lowered its mouth with surprising speed and latched onto Gail's arm.

"Aaaaa*fuck!*" Gail yelled, and sprayed it full in the face with the weed killer.

It dropped. Phil kicked it like a flabby football and it hit the wall and slid down, leaving a dark, oily smear. Its arms ratcheted for a moment, then fell limp. In the glaring yellow beam of the flashlight, Gail's arm had bloomed black with blood.

The second child lifted its head, small mouth working. It wiggled down the mound of dirt toward the body of the first one.

"Gail," said Phil. "Gail, how bad did it get you?"

"No idea," she said, clutching her arm against her stomach. "Feels like it tore a whole chunk out."

As if to illustrate this point, the underground child had reached the dead one. As I watched, it opened its mouth and set it against the dead one's skin. Despite the seeming lack of teeth, it bit down, then pulled back, leaving a neat circular scoop taken out of the corpse, as precise and bloodless as a melon baller.

"I'm gonna be sick," said Phil.

The child swallowed, its whole body wiggling with a peristaltic motion, and made a happy mew, a small kitten discovering tasty food. It took another bite.

More arms appeared in the doorway.

"I think we should go upstairs," I said. "And put as many doors between us and these things as we can."

"I agree," said Phil.

"Motion carries," said Gail, the three of us backing toward the stairs as more heads crested from the dirt.

I looked around for Mom and found her already hobbling toward us.

I got an arm under her shoulder and half-dragged her to the steps. They weren't wide enough for two of us to go up, so she went first, with Phil grabbing her arm to help pull her up.

I shot a last look at the doorway. There were four underground children feeding on the dead one, and another coming through the door, mouth working as it tasted the air.

I went up the stairs backward, flashlight beam still fixed on the bottom. Would they follow? Maybe the dead one would keep them distracted long enough for us to barricade ourselves in a bedroom. I wasn't actually sure what we'd do after that, but at the moment, barricades seemed like a *really good* idea. I looked over my shoulder and saw that Phil had gotten Mom to the top and was sweeping his flashlight beam back and forth.

I was halfway up when the first underground child crawled into the beam of light. It tilted its head from side to side, skinned-over eyes contracting, and then put its hand on the first step.

CHAPTER 25

The four of us flung ourselves into my bedroom and I slammed the door behind us and locked it. Phil grabbed the dresser and I took the other end, trying to maneuver it around the bed so we could wedge it against the door. I know for a fact that it weighed a ton, but I barely felt it. There was so much adrenaline in my veins that I could probably have lifted the entire bed.

"All right," I gasped when the door was barricaded. "All right. Hopefully that'll keep them out for a little bit."

"Gail!" cried Mom. "What happened to your arm?"

"One bit me," said Gail. Blood soaked the front of her shirt, turning the cartoon banana slug into a grisly horror. "It's pretty bad."

Mom snatched the doily off the dresser. "Give me your arm," she ordered.

Gail held out her arm. I leveled the flashlight on it so that Mom could see what she was doing, caught a sickening glimpse of bone, and had to look away. "Jesus, Gail!"

"Hurts like hell," she admitted. "Was afraid I was going to pass out."

"Well, don't," said Mom.

"I'm working on it."

Mom wrapped it hurriedly. She was halfway through when we heard a noise that echoed as loud as a gunshot.

A small wooden *crunch* came from the door, and then, faintly, a mew of distaste.

Then another crunch.

"Fuck," said Phil, from the bottom of his heart. "What *are* those things?"

"The underground children," I said. "Our grandmother used to threaten us with them, like the boogeyman. You know, that they'd come get us if we were bad. But, uh, they seem to be real. Apparently her father made them." I grabbed the nightstand and began wrestling it on top of the dresser. If they could gnaw through the wood, maybe the extra weight would slow them down. "Remember that bit I read you? About the sorcerer in Pasadena who was trying to make a magic baby? And Elgar kept telling him that it was a terrible idea because he'd tried it and it went bad?" I jerked my head toward the crunching noises. "I'm pretty sure that's them."

"So how do we stop them?"

I spread my hands helplessly. "I don't know! Elgar didn't know! Gran Mae was keeping them out, I guess, with jars of teeth or some shit, but I dug up the jar and it stopped whatever she was doing!"

"A circle of protection," said Gail, leaning against the wall. The white fabric around her arm was only a few shades whiter than her skin. I wondered how much blood she had lost. "The roses and the teeth. It was to keep them out. *The roses said, stay away.* And she poured everything she had into the roses." Her laugh was barely more than a gasp. "So much power that it kept going long after she was dead. And I'd watched her do it for years, and had no idea."

"Was that why she was haunting the place?" Mom asked. "To protect us?"

Gail closed her eyes. "I'm sorry, Edie," she said. I think she was trying to be gentle, but didn't have the strength for it. "I don't think she planned it. I think she just didn't die as completely as she expected. And the circle just kept going all that time."

"Myeeuu?" whispered one of the children at the door, a starving kitten noise. "Meu?"

"Can you do something?" I asked Gail.

"Like what?"

"I don't know! Something magicky!"

"I'm an herb-witch who talks to vultures! I've never dealt with anything like this before!"

I clutched my head. "Can you just put the circle back up?"

"This isn't like rebooting your computer! I can't just turn magic off and back on again!"

"Well, what can you do?"

"Against these things? Do you have a week or two to wait while I research it?"

A splintering crunch heralded the demise of more of the door. I caught a glimpse of something white floundering around at the base as one got an arm through.

"I don't think we've got a week," said Phil, and shoved the screen out of the window.

"Is going outside really the best idea?" asked Mom. "Won't there be more of them out there?"

"If you have a better idea, I'm all ears," Phil said.

The door rattled violently in the frame. A half dozen tiny mews went up from the hallway, as if the underground children were having a conference about how to get inside.

"So, the roof," said Mom.

Phil handed her and Gail out the window, then turned to me. My build was not exactly optimal for climbing out windows three feet off the floor, but it's amazing what you can do when you're hearing the door to the room be eaten away behind you. Phil grabbed me around the hips and lifted and shoved and I half-fell onto the porch roof under the window.

The asphalt shingles were rough and felt like they took half the skin off my arms. I got to my feet and swept the flashlight into the dark, trying to find shapes that I could recognize. It was still black as tar out and the air was close and still.

"Are we in a cave?" asked Mom, as Phil joined us on the roof.

None of us said anything like, "How could we possibly be in a cave?" Phil and I scanned the landscape with our flashlights again. The dirt was only a few feet below us. There were no walls that I could see, but it *felt* like a cave, enclosed somehow.

Perhaps it's just a very small alternate universe, I thought, and fought the urge to giggle.

I looked over at Mom. She was propping up Gail, who had her eyes closed and an expression of deep concentration on her face. Doing something magicky, as I'd asked? Or just trying not to faint? Blood had already soaked through the bandage on her arm.

"Something over there," said Phil.

I followed his beam and saw shapes toward the back of the house. They looked like what I'd seen before, the remains of the buried rose-bushes. With both flashlights on them, I could make out the edges of leaves covered in a thick layer of dirt, as if someone had unceremoniously dumped hundreds of tons of earth into the back garden. *Which, apparently, they did.*

A crash from the room behind us indicated that the underground children had made it through the door.

Phil shoved the window closed, but the locks were on the inside. If they were smart enough to figure that out, we were in trouble. Well. More trouble. The glass seemed to confuse them somehow, or maybe they couldn't get a good grip on it with their toothless little mouths.

"The roses," said Gail suddenly. She opened her eyes and they glittered in her bone-white face. "We need the roses. Sam, can you feel them?"

"What?"

"The roses. They're still there, aren't they?"

"Well, yes, it looks like the whole garden came with us. They're under a lot of dirt, but I can sort of see—"

"Can you feel them?"

"How can I possibly feel them?"

"They're your grandmother's. She was in them. She's gone, but they're still there. Can't you tell?"

A few hours ago, I would have said something sarcastic. But a few hours ago, the world had been a very different place. I looked over the buried remains of the rosebushes. "Feel them?"

Could I?

"The roses said, stay away," said Gail, and I remembered Gran Mae saying that, and then the other things she had said. *You gave the roses blood and demanded ladybugs. What did you think was going to happen?*

Gran Mae thought that I had summoned the ladybugs. But I couldn't have. I'd cut my finger on a thorn, and then I'd said to the ladybug . . . said . . . *There should be a lot more of you.*

And more had come. Hundreds. Crawling into the bedroom and up the sink, trying to get closer to me, to the person who had demanded them.

Had it been the roses responding to me?

But why? How? I wasn't a witch. I didn't know the first thing about ritual magic. I was . . .

. . . the granddaughter of a sorcerer, and the great-granddaughter of the Mad Wizard of Boone.

Some things run in families.

Could I feel the roses now? If I tried?

The window rattled. I spun toward it and saw white palms pressed against the glass. Phil jammed his hands down, trying to hold it down, but there was only a thin ledge to put his weight on, and there were at least five hands on the inside of the window.

On second thought, this might not be the best time to be ruminating about my feelings.

I lunged to help Phil, throwing my weight onto the narrow window ledge. "Mom! Gail! *Move!*"

Mom grabbed Gail and began hauling her along the porch roof, away from the window. It wasn't a wraparound porch, so at some point they would have to get up on the main roof over the garage if they wanted to keep going. How well could the underground children climb? Was it better than two older women, one with a bad ankle and one who was trying not to go into shock?

The window moved up an inch, then slammed back down. The underground children were terrifyingly strong. The only thing saving us was that they didn't seem to understand how windows worked. If they had all pushed up together, Phil and I would have been overpowered, but instead, it seemed as if one would accidentally push up a bit, then get distracted. One of them was gnawing on the windowsill, occasionally spitting out little circles of wood. "Myeeu," it said, clearly annoyed by the inedibility of the frame. "Myeeuu!"

"What do we do?" asked Phil.

"I have no idea!" I risked lifting my hand for half a second and shoved my flashlight into my cleavage. (I couldn't have done it with a Maglite, but with the cheap little flashlight, boobs are a perfectly good holder.) The beam made a bright oval on the window and one of the children rubbed their hand across the glass, apparently fascinated. Its skin glowed like alabaster in the light.

Now that I had full use of both hands, it was a little easier to hold the window down. Unfortunately I couldn't see Mom and Gail very well. There was only a beam of light moving crazily over the porch and the sound of Mom's voice saying, "Stay with me, Gail. Talk to me."

"I'm a little busy!" Gail snapped.

"Doing what?"

"Something magicky! And bleeding."

The window slid up again, farther this time. One of the children got a hand underneath. Its fingers actually brushed my wrist, cool and moist as earth, and I nearly gagged.

Phil and I smashed the window down so hard that the glass cracked. The underground child let out a thin yowl and yanked back, its boneless arm stretching impossibly thin. It thrashed its body against the window and the crack raced across the glass with a high, crystalline chiming.

It was directly in the flashlight beam when the arm began to tear loose from its body. It seemed to have no bones at all in the upper arm, nothing like a socket. Instead, triangular stripes of skin ripped free from the segmented flesh and peeled back, oozing something clear and oily.

The underground child that had been gnawing busily at the window frame stopped, made a curious "Meuu?" sound, and latched onto the oozing wound.

They both dropped from the window. The other children followed immediately, and I heard thrashing and a thin wail of pain nearly drowned out in the satisfied sounds of feeding.

"Now!" I told Phil. "While they're distracted."

We bolted down the porch. Mom had gotten onto the garage roof and was trying to hoist Gail up with minimal success. Phil got both arms under her and heaved, then turned to me. I landed a foot in the rain gutter and nearly tore it off the house, but I got up there, and we all scrambled over the peak of the roof, away from the window, toward the backyard.

It was no different on this side than it had been on the other. Dirt was mounded up past the first floor. There was no breeze. I ran the flashlight along the edge of the yard and saw the buried tips of the roses.

I couldn't feel them. No matter how hard I tried, I wasn't going to be able to feel them in some mystic sense. I was *terrible* at feeling things. Hell, I'd told the school counselor that when I was nine. I was only good with things that I could touch.

"Can almost reach . . ." whispered Gail. Her eyes were closed again. "Almost . . ."

I didn't know what she was trying to reach. I sure as hell couldn't reach the roses from here. The little roses along the side of the house were completely buried, and only the climber and the biggest bushes showed bent and broken twigs above the dirt.

The sound of breaking glass came from the window on the other side of the house. Would they know to climb over the peak of the roof? Were they smart enough to come after us?

"Meeuuuu? Meuoo?"

Maybe I didn't need to *feel* the roses, though. That wasn't how I worked. What I had to do was touch them.

It was stupid and suicidal and if I'd suggested it to any of the others, they'd have tried to talk me out of it. But I could hear the dragging of grublike bodies across the shingles, and I knew we didn't have any more time to talk.

I launched myself off the roof, stumbling when I hit the dirt. It was much looser than it looked, and it compressed under my feet so that I had to lift my knees practically to my chest as I staggered across the remains of the backyard.

"*Sam!*" Mom yelled.

"Stay there!" I yelled back.

A white head lifted from the dirt a few feet away. The underground child turned its skin-eyes on me and mewed inquisitively.

Fuck. I kept moving. My flashlight beam bounced across the soil. I had thought I'd be able to sprint to the roses but this was like wading through mud. I was only halfway across the yard, and I could hear other children calling around me.

Something white squirmed under my foot as I lifted it on the next step. I flung myself forward, nearly losing my footing, and that would be death. I had to stay upright. I had to keep going.

"Meeuuuuu?" asked one of the children, right behind me. "Myeeu?"

I went three more steps and then a white hand reached out of the dirt and grabbed my ankle.

I guess this is it, I thought, as I lost my balance and the ground came at me. *I'm gonna die now.*

Well, shit.

It struck me as funny, as I lay full length on the ground, how casual everything seemed suddenly, as if death were one more minor catastrophe, like dropping a coffee mug and having the handle break off. I would have laughed if my chin hadn't been half-buried in dirt.

The soil was so soft that landing had barely winded me. I pushed myself up, still feeling that small hand curled around my ankle, and rolled sideways.

I really didn't expect it to do any good. I fully expected to feel a sudden flare of pain in my leg and then probably a lot more pain, and then, if I was lucky, I would lose consciousness so that I wouldn't be around for the unpleasant final moments. But it hadn't happened yet and I could still roll, so I rolled.

"Meuu?"

I scraped at my ankle with my other foot, as if the child were a glob of mud I'd stepped in. The soft, grublike body yielded and it spat its displeasure and bit at the sole of my boot.

I rolled again and something jabbed into my cheek. I swatted at it, expecting to connect with more pale flesh, but instead it felt like . . . twigs?

I scrabbled at the dirt, swinging the flashlight beam up, and saw stems and thorns protruding from the earth.

The roses. I'd reached the roses after all.

I plunged my hands into the dirt-encrusted leaves. Thorns stabbed at me and I nearly wept with relief. *You gave the roses blood and demanded ladybugs. What did you think was going to happen?*

This time, I was going to demand something very different.

The underground child prodded my shoe with its boneless hands, plucking curiously at the laces. Perhaps the taste of the rubber sole had confused it. "Meeuu?"

I found a stem and closed my left hand over it. Pain screamed up my arm. I hoped it was enough blood for this . . . whatever it was. Magic? Was magic as primitive as trading blood and pain for hope?

A small, toothless mouth closed over my foot and took away a mouthful of leather and the very edge of my heel. It barely registered as pain compared to the terrible throbbing in my hands.

"Get them away," I hissed to the roses. "Get these monsters away from us."

The roses say . . . stay away . . .

Nothing happened.

"No . . ." I whispered. "No, you were supposed to do something. You have to do something. You *have* to."

No one answered. I put my face against the ground and waited to die. *I'm sorry, Mom. It was a bad idea, but it was the only one I could think of. I'm sorry I couldn't fix this.*

Light touched my eyelids. I opened my eyes, expecting a flashlight beam, but instead I saw a brittle green light streaming away under my fingers.

Under their blanket of earth, the roses had begun to glow.

CHAPTER 26

Green roselight filled the garden, casting hundreds of shadows through the dirt. It reflected from the walls of the house and I saw Mom and Phil holding Gail between them, while the underground children gathered just below their perch.

I turned my head and saw the child holding my foot in its dirty-nailed hands. The blue bruises of its eyes contracted as I watched. My blood stained its mouth where it had bitten into my flesh, looking black in the glow of the roses.

I knew nothing of magic. I barely believed in it. But I felt something well up in the center of my chest, a pressure that mixed with the shooting pain in my hand and my heel, and I *pushed* with it, as hard as I could, at the white horror that clung to my ankle.

It was as if the roses were a battery and by gripping the stems my body had closed the circuit. Roselight twined up my arms and the pressure in my chest grew so strong that I thought my heart would explode out of my chest, smashing my ribs outward as it went. Power arced through me, green and terrible, a power of stem and root and thorn, a power made of my grandmother's life and my great-grandfather's obsession. I could taste the freesia skin powder she wore and feel her bird-claw hands gripping mine, and I heard her voice as if she was standing at my shoulder.

Little piggy.

No one can tell you anything, can they?

Father says . . .

You could be so beautiful.

Little piggy.

Nice and normal.

The underground children will get you . . .

The words flicked by, hundreds of them, thousands of them, the words that had built our life together, but there was one particular set of words that I needed. I sorted for them with all the intensity that I had once used to sort pictures of insects, looking for the words that would save us.

The roses say, stay away . . .

I found them and seized them and curled my hands more tightly around the rose stems, driving the thorns even deeper, and pushed those words out toward the underground children.

The pressure on my ankle was ripped away. I saw the grublike body go tumbling backward, arms flailing. It landed on the earth a dozen feet away and lay still.

The arcing power slowed and the pressure in my chest began to ease. My heart suddenly remembered that it was supposed to be beating and began hammering wildly against my ribs. I took a deep breath and then another.

"*Sam?*" Mom yelled from the roof. "*Sam, are you okay?*"

"Yeah," I croaked. There was no way that she could hear that, so I tried again. "Yeah. I think. Yeah." That was a little better.

"What happened?"

Gail's voice was weak, but it carried across the yard. "She used the roses, Edie."

"I don't know what that means!"

"Yeah," I said. "Yeah, me neither."

I pried one hand loose from the roses and sat up, keeping my left hand wrapped around the stems. Blood was pouring down my fingers. I shoved my hand under my armpit to slow the bleeding and looked around the yard.

The underground children had been pushed back, away from the roses, but none of the others had been killed. Three were already converging on

227

the dead one. I could see more white heads popping out of the soil, reflecting ghostly green in the roselight.

Christ, there were a lot of them.

It was clear already that whatever the roses were doing, it wasn't enough. The clear space around the roses was barely six feet wide, and Mom and Gail and Phil were still trapped on the roof. What had worked when the roses were a circle around the house was useless now that the circle had been breached. The underground children couldn't get to me, but unless I could get the others to the safety of the rosebushes, it wasn't going to help.

Phil might be able to run the distance to me. Mom couldn't, not with her ankle, and Gail's pallor, in the green light, was so ghastly that I was amazed she was still upright. I had to do something else. Otherwise I was going to lie here, bleeding, and eventually the underground children would come over the roof and I would watch my mom and friends die.

What else could I do? No, that was the wrong question. What else could the *roses* do?

The roses say . . . say your prayers . . .

Not helpful.

They'd brought me ladybugs, but it had taken time. Could insects even find us down here, wherever this was? And even if I convinced the roses to bring me a swarm of hornets or something, how did I get them to go after the underground children and not me? Hornets are not exactly a precision weapon. Neither are wasps.

Gran Mae had built a puppet for herself out of rose stems and leaves. Could I build something like that as a decoy?

"Meeuuuu . . . ?" came a thin cry from high up on the roof. Phil and Mom jerked around. Gail's mouth moved, but I couldn't hear anything from this distance.

I didn't have enough time for anything fancy. I didn't have enough time for much of anything.

A small white hand came over the top of the roof, feeling delicately across the shingles. Three more underground children waited in the dirt under the eaves, ready to latch onto Phil or Mom if they tried to run.

"Sam?" called Mom. "Sam, are you still okay?"

"I'm fine," I lied. "Give me just a minute."

And then, knowing that I was about to do something supremely foolish and probably fatal, I buried my left arm to my shoulder in the roses and opened myself up to the power.

Gran Mae's presence filled my ears and my throat and my lungs, wrapping around my rib cage, sinking into my bones. I could hear her spitting words at me, at my brother, at Mom, at the world. It no longer felt as if she was standing at my shoulder or holding my hand. This felt like being possessed.

I don't believe in demons, I thought, and then I laughed at myself because I didn't believe in ghosts either. That was the last coherent thought I had as my grandmother's power poured through me. Malice and the scent of freesia powder. Rage that had festered for so long that it had turned to poison.

And under that, pain.

And under that, loneliness.

Say there was a bright girl who grew up unloved, with a strange, erratic father who saw her as nothing more than someone to cook and clean and get out of his way. Say that that daughter taught herself bits of his magic to try to win his love. Say that it didn't work.

Say that she turned instead to families she saw on TV, to smiling black-and-white patriarchs who dispensed wisdom and loving discipline and tousled their children's hair, to women who vacuumed the house while wearing pearls. Normal families. *Nice and normal.*

Say that she lived her life trying to match that, and when real people failed (as of course they failed) the old rage and loneliness welled up and came out as cruelty.

I understood Gran Mae then, I think. I could not pity the adult she had become, but I could pity the girl she had been.

In the end, she had turned to the roses. She had poured everything she was into them, and they had wrapped around her and kept her alive, a ghost of root and stem, flower and thorn.

And here I was now, gripping the rose stems with blood-slicked hands, and the roselight was all around me, vivid green. I stood at the heart of the roses and my grandmother's power filled me, and all I had to do was utter a command.

I gave them the only order that I could think of.

The roses say . . . BURN . . .

⌒

"Sam!" Mom shouted in my ear. "Sam, that's enough! Sam!"

The smell of smoke and burnt fat filled my nostrils. I wondered if it was me. There's a thing that happens sometimes where you catch fire, but your clothes aren't as flammable as you are, so they act as a wick for your own fat and you burn almost completely. Supposedly that's what happens with spontaneous human combustion, at least in theory.

What little I knew about spontaneous human combustion did not involve Mom yelling in my ear. Maybe I had just overslept. Maybe it was a school day and Mom had made bacon and that's what I was smelling.

I opened one eye blearily. My head throbbed. My fingers throbbed even worse.

"Jesus Christ, Sam," said Mom, "what have you done to your hands?"

What had I done? I lifted my hands in front of my face. They were covered in blisters and black ash. Blood flowed sluggishly from dozens of punctures. I could see the snapped-off ovals of rose thorns embedded in my palms.

The world snapped immediately into focus. The underground children. *Shit.*

I tried to scramble to my feet but my knees buckled. "Where are they? Are they gone?"

"Yeah," said Phil. His laugh was more incredulous than amused. "Oh yeah. Whatever the hell the roses did, they took care of it."

I prodded my memory like a sore tooth. I had given an order, and then the roselight had erupted and my hands had burned and my grandmother had been screaming in my head and the roses had screamed too and green whips had lashed out everywhere, blackening with heat even as they struck. And the underground children . . .

I couldn't lift the flashlight anymore, but Phil swung a beam of light over the dirt for me, and I saw charred shapes wrapped in brittle, ashy stems.

It finally occurred to me what I was smelling. I would have been sick, but it seemed like far too much effort, so I settled for swallowing a few times and feeling queasy, on top of everything else.

When I shifted, more stems fell to ash around me. The leaves had been reduced to charcoal ghosts that shattered at a touch.

"You did it," said Gail. She was sitting down too. She gave me a wan smile. "You used the roses."

Had I? It was what I had meant to do, but it had felt like Gran Mae as much as the roses. It was her voice and her loneliness that had echoed in my head and twisted around my bones.

She was gone now, burned away as thoroughly as the roses. I felt hollowed out, cored, as if a shell of ash was all that remained, and I might fall apart at a touch.

"But how do we get out?" asked Phil. "We're still here. Wherever here is." He swung the flashlight around, the beam vanishing into the darkness that still nevertheless felt like walls.

I shook my head. The roses had burned. There was nothing left of their power, or Gran Mae's. There was barely anything left of me. I couldn't fix this.

"It's all right," said Gail. "I think, now that the roses are gone, it will be easier." She held her hand out to Phil. "Help an old lady up."

He helped her to her feet and she leaned against him, her eyes closed. For a moment, I thought I felt something coming from her, but as I said, I've never been good at feeling things. Probably it was just an aftereffect of the roses.

"Sam," said Mom, wiping her sleeve across my forehead, "Sam, what did you *do?*"

I shook my head again.

"Almost..." murmured Gail. "Almost... *there!*"

Light bloomed in the darkness overhead. Mom gasped. Phil swore, as heartfelt as a prayer. I tilted my head back, trying to push away the darkness that clung to the edges of my vision, and saw a distant shape overhead.

It burned, but with a kinder fire than the roses. Golden as a blaze of sunlight, as the wind off a wheat field, as the stripes on a bumblebee. If I had ever pictured the light at the end of the tunnel, it would have looked something like this.

The fire descended toward us and I wondered if I was dying. Gail reached her hands up toward it, swaying on her feet.

It was Hermes.

Light haloed the vulture like an angel. One outstretched wing was made entirely of golden flame. He turned his head and the discs of skin on either side of his face gleamed like burnished copper, and his beak opened.

The noise that came out sounded like a pigeon cooing with a sore throat. It was completely absurd, for an animal that was currently doing a pretty good imitation of an archangel. As hollowed out as I felt, I laughed, and the laugh filled a little of the empty place in my chest.

"Good boy," said Gail. "Oh, good boy, Hermes! You found me! I wish I had a mouse for you. Now go and open the way."

The glowing vulture tilted his wings and rose on invisible thermals, circling upward. The fire began narrowing to a finer and finer point as he rose into a sky that didn't quite exist. When we could no longer make out individual feathers, only a small, brilliant shape, the light seemed to gather itself, and then it flashed outward, bright and sharp as an explosion.

Afterimages seared across my retinas. I blinked them away, trying to find an undamaged bit of skin on my hands to wipe my eyes.

When I could see again, the world was lighter. I could see gray, gritty light coming from somewhere near the roof. It outlined Gail, who had collapsed against Phil, and lit the tear tracks on Mom's face.

"Are we somewhere now?" Mom asked. I had no idea how to answer her.

A voice came from the patch of gritty light. A familiar voice. Not the voice that I had expected to hear at the end of the world.

"What the hell happened to your house?" shouted Mr. Pressley. "Was it the government?"

Days Later

Coragyps atratus: Black vultures are small, compact vultures with broad tails and strong wings. Easily identified by a silvery patch on the underside of the wing tips, they feed almost exclusively on carrion. These highly social scavenger birds form strong family bonds and will share food with other members of their family flock. In the evening, they will usually gather together at a communal roost to feed the young and reinforce social bonds.

CHAPTER 27

The official word was that Mom's house had fallen into a sinkhole. The insurance company muttered something about there not being any sinkholes in the area, but they paid up anyway. It was hard to argue with the fact that the house was sitting in a big-ass hole in the ground, after all.

Mr. Pressley had been watching the house, he said, when the house was suddenly pulled underground. "Like a duckling yanked down by a snapping turtle," was his exact description. "Swimming along and then boom! Just like that." He called the police, who ignored him as a known crank, and when they didn't show up, he walked over to the Goldbergs' and demanded that Mrs. Goldberg call the police. They listened to her and finally sent somebody.

Meanwhile, Mr. Pressley took one of Phil's ladders, tied a rope to his waist and handed the other end to Mr. Goldberg, and went looking for us himself. He had all four of us out by the time the police arrived and called the fire department, which was just as well, because the dirt cavern collapsed shortly afterward.

Our injuries were attributed to the house having fallen into the sinkhole. Nobody batted an eye at Gail's arm or Mom's ankle. My hands were a little bit trickier, but I said that I'd been cooking on the stove when the house fell and something burning must have hit my hands. The doctor looked like he might press the matter, but by then the painkillers had started to take effect and I just muttered something about having to crawl out through the rosebush and a nurse shooed him away and went back to picking thorns out of my battered hands. About all I remember after that was Phil and I looking at each other and giggling hysterically. They must have given him the good painkillers too.

And that was pretty much that. Mom and I stayed with Gail once we were discharged from the hospital. Hermes was given many dead mice and almost an entire raw liver and told that he was a good and beautiful vulture. He preened. I called Brad and didn't even try to tell him the truth. He insisted on flying out immediately. Mom and Gail and I talked together long enough to get our stories straight, and then we went to bed and didn't wake up until Brad banged on the door eighteen hours later.

Very little was salvageable from the house. It wasn't safe to go in and get anything out. All Mom had was a change of clothes that she'd left in her car, and, ironically, the hellgrammite print, which had been at the framers'.

Mom insisted on buying me a new laptop out of the insurance money. I wasn't looking forward to re-setting up all my software, but since I was strictly forbidden to type with my bandaged hands, that was Future Sam's problem. Brad demanded that Mom move to Arizona again, and this time she surprised him by saying yes. So he ran around taking care of all the important paperwork and whatnot when one is preparing to move a couple states away, and I sat in Gail's garden, drinking lemonade through a straw.

Phil dropped by a couple of times to check on us. "How's your grandad?" I asked him.

"Completely insufferable. They ran an article about him in the *Chatham County Line*. 'Local Hero Saves Family from Collapsing Sinkhole.' I'm getting it framed for him for his birthday."

I lifted my lemonade in salute. Mr. Pressley really had been the hero of the hour, and I didn't begrudge him the attention. Of course, I also didn't have to live with him afterward.

Phil rocked on the balls of his feet, looking across the garden. *Bombus impatiens* worked their way through the flowers, practically purring as the pollen coated their legs.

"So I hear Mrs. M is moving to Arizona with you," he said finally.

"Yeah. I know she'll miss you." I fidgeted with my straw. *I'll miss him too. No, don't be ridiculous, you don't know him well enough to miss him.*

Even if he does look pretty good in a wet T-shirt.

Phil rubbed the back of his neck, then pulled a scrap of paper out of his pocket. "Well, if you find yourself in need of a handyman out there . . ." He held the scrap out to me. It had a number scrawled on it.

"It's my phone number," he said helpfully.

"Yes, I'd figured that much out." I glanced up at him and he flushed and looked away.

That was interesting. When I typed it into my phone and sent him a text, it took a few minutes to send, which meant that we sat in awkward silence for a bit, and then his phone dinged and he looked down at it and smiled.

"Well," he said.

"Yeah," I said.

"I guess . . . uh . . . safe travels."

I got up. He stuck out his hand as I went for a hug, and then I backpedaled and tried to shake his hand instead and he went for the hug and we ended up in a one-armed embrace with our hands wedged between us.

"Anyway," he said when we disentangled, "don't be a stranger. And take care of Mrs. M."

I promised faithfully to do so, and he left the garden with the bumblebees buzzing in his wake.

❧

"So what were they?" I asked Gail, the day before we were set to leave. "The underground children?"

Gail shook her head. "If you want a scientific explanation, you're going to be sorely disappointed. I can't give you a Latin name to pin to a card."

"I'll take any explanation you can give me."

Hermes crept toward me, insomuch as a vulture can creep. It was more of a stealthy bounce. His eyes were fixed on my shoe.

"Hybrids of some sort, as far as I can tell. I read those letters you sent me the link to." She nodded to me. "Elgar wasn't particularly original. Most of the old alchemists dabbled with creating life. It's all blood and semen incubated in dunghills and the like. I imagine he thought that he could do it better. And he was right, so far as that went. He actually did create *something*. If I had to guess, he found something elemental in the earth and bred it with his ... ah ... essence."

I held up a hand. "Are you suggesting that he ... err ... with a ... ?"

"Ritual magicians can get *weird*," said Gail. "Look at Crowley. Or Parsons."

Well. Probably I should just be grateful that it hadn't involved mescaline.

Hermes reached out very cautiously and touched his beak to my shoelace. I contemplated how far I had come since I had sat in this same chair and arrogantly told Gail that I didn't believe in ghosts.

"So he made the children somehow. Did they rebel against him, then?" I asked. "Like he wrote?"

"It's certainly possible. Although they went to cannibalism very quickly at your mom's house, so possibly they were simply hungry. At any rate, he seems to have spent most of his declining years trying to keep them out. And then your grandmother did the same."

"After she fed him to them."

"After that, yes."

Hermes gripped the end of the shoelace and tugged. The neat bow I'd tied unraveled and he bounced backward, pulling the lace with him, clearly delighted.

I frowned, remembering Gran Mae pressing my tiny fingers to the rose stem when I was a child. I would have sworn that magic would not have been nice and normal enough for her, but then again ... "I wonder if she was planning on showing me how to keep it going."

"Could be. Maybe it skipped a generation."

I stared at my lemonade. Gran Mae had believed in Family, with a capital F. She had believed in us all as a reflection on her, not as the people we actually were. I could believe that she would have wanted us to be safe from the underground children, mostly because it would have been hard to have a coming-out party or join sororities or vacuum the house in pearls if we were all dead.

She might have planned to teach me, but she hadn't felt any qualms about letting us all get devoured when Mom and Gail had banished her. Family, like roses, were something she had planted and something she'd yank out again when it didn't do what she wanted.

"If you ever find yourself with a house," Gail added thoughtfully, "you might try growing a garden. I think you'd be surprisingly good at it."

"As long as I don't grow roses?"

"Mmm." She frowned. "I don't know. Maybe you should. They answered to you in the end."

I shuddered at the memory of the feeling that had coursed through me, Gran Mae's soul distilled down to nothing but power and rage and loneliness. It was nothing I ever wanted to feel again.

"Your grandmother was . . . not a good woman. But you're nothing like her. And all that power that she poured into those roses did keep you and your family safe for many years."

"Safe from monsters that her father created."

"I would suggest you avoid creating monsters," she said dryly.

I snorted. Outside the screen, a fat bumblebee found a flower. *Bombus griseocollis,* I think. Brown-belted bumblebee.

Gail snapped her fingers at Hermes and he abandoned his war with my shoelace and hopped up onto his perch.

"Do you think they're gone?" I asked. "The underground children?"

Gail set down her lemonade and took a deep breath. "I think," she said, very carefully, "that it's a good thing your mother is going back to Arizona with you."

I stared at her.

"Most of them are dead," she said. "You were very effective. Maybe you got all of them. I hope it's all of them. But I would be a great deal happier if there were a few rivers and a mountain range between this soil and anyone with Elgar Mills's blood."

"Oh." I rubbed my forehead, feeling the rasp of bandages against my face. "But if they can do that, how were they not grabbing us whenever we left the house?"

Gail shook her head. "I can only guess, but I think that maybe their senses aren't very sharp. The house smelled strongly of your grandmother because it was her place, so it attracted them. You smell much less strongly, so they wouldn't bother you—not when the house was there. Like setting a lure for Japanese beetles using concentrated pheromones. There's plenty of other smells nearby that they could chase, but the lure is so much stronger that it overwhelms everything else."

"Oh," I said again. "And now that the house is gone . . . ?"

"They're slow," said Gail. "And like I said, they may be entirely gone, or at least mostly dead. But I don't think any of you should gamble on that."

Hermes shifted on his perch and settled himself into a more comfortable loaf shape. I eyed him thoughtfully, wondering if he remembered his brief time as an archangel. "Is Hermes your familiar?"

Gail looked at him fondly. "He's my friend."

I suspected that was all the answer that I was going to get. I took another sip through the straw. "You'll look out for Phil, won't you?"

"Of course. I try to look out for everybody on Lammergeier Lane."

She smiled a little as she said it, and I remembered the beaked shadow I had seen on the wall behind her. Just a small thing, really, compared to all the strangeness that followed, but I was certain I hadn't imagined it.

Strange, the powers you find sometimes, in a garden at the end of the road.

Gail sighed. "I'll miss Edie terribly, you know."

I nodded. "Maybe you can come visit sometime. If you can find a vulture-sitter."

She chuckled. I stared into my glass and thought about the underground children slowly crawling westward, inch by inch, burrowing through stone and earth, blindly following the scent of our shared blood.

Oh, what the hell am I worried about? I thought. *It'll take centuries for the little bastards to get across Texas.* I drained my glass and stood up and went to go find Mom. Behind me, I heard Hermes make a small, tragic vulture noise, and Gail laughed and tossed him another mouse.

ACKNOWLEDGMENTS

Good heavens, here we are at the end of another book. You'd think that I'd see it coming, given that I'm the one writing the things, but somehow they always seem to creep up on me and leave me wrung out and flattened in their wake.

A House With Good Bones came about primarily because of my long-standing feud with roses. I am an avid gardener, but I do not actually like roses very much. They seem to be either finicky or murderous, without any real middle ground. Nor can you always tell which are which. I have several that I planted because I felt sorry for the poor plant on the discount table, and without exception, they have grown into gigantic murder bushes that require gauntlets to prune. The native swamp rose tried to eat the foundation and sent up runners in all directions, and I eventually had to pry it out of the ground with a pickaxe.

Thing is, I had already written a book about evil roses. It was a retelling of "Beauty and the Beast" called *Bryony and Roses*, and I thought I'd gotten all of my anti-rose sentiment out there.

Nevertheless, I had this mental image that wouldn't quite leave me of a family sitting down to dinner, lashed in place by rose stems, and the matriarch of the family saying, "Isn't this nice?"

It was just a scene. It certainly wasn't a story. I didn't know anyone in it, or how they got there. But it stuck with me, and it kept sticking. For *years.* And one day the lovely people at Nightfire asked if I had anything that might turn into a horror novel, and I found myself trying to explain this scene and also rambling about vultures, and the next thing I knew, I was writing about Sam and her mom and the house on Lammergeier Lane.

I can't say that I went too far afield for much of the material here. I live in a subdivision of exactly the sort described, I am obsessed with bugs, gardening, and archaeology—yes, archaeoentomologist is a real job that you can have, and I envy it a little—and you've already heard about my relationship with roses.

Which mostly leaves the vultures.

Black vultures are, in fact, wonderful birds. They're found all over the American Southeast, and they are highly social animals, with complex family bonds. This makes them different from many other raptors, who tend to be—charitably—extremely single-minded. (The joke is that people who go into raptor rehabilitation start out excited to work with eagles and end up being passionate about vultures.) I own a little piece of land that contains a black vulture roost, and I feel honored to be allowed to host them.

A buddy of mine, Foxfeather Zenkova, has been building a vulture center in Minnesota for several years now. I was fortunate enough to travel to the Himalayas with her as part of a group of artists, and we saw a number of different vultures, including the lammergeier, also known as the bearded vulture. They're the ones who eat bones. They are *magnificent.*

Fox also has a house vulture named Sev, who was the most wonderful, inquisitive ball of floof and is now a wonderful, charming adult who does not understand why humans do not want a vulture to, say, help them cook dinner. The character of Hermes is based largely on Sev, and Fox herself was incredibly helpful with all the questions about vulture habits that came up over the course of writing. Anything I got right was because of her help; anything I got wrong is on me for not asking.

Similarly, most of the good bits are probably because Lindsey Hall at Tor poked them at some point and made them better, as well as Kelly Lonesome and the rest of the Nightfire crew, who have done such an amazing job bringing these books to life. Thanks also go to my agent, without whom it would be much harder to *keep* writing these books.

Big thanks to my Twitter crew of entomologists, who were so helpful in volunteering bug information to round out Sam's experience. I hope I did them proud. The ladybug swarm in England was a real event, which many people remember, generally not fondly.

Jack Parsons is also real, and his story is, if anything, even weirder than I make it out to be in the book. (Aleister Crowley told him to take it down a notch, that's how far out he was.)

My mom is also real, and very sweet, and pretty darn cool. One of my grandmothers was awesome. The other one . . . Well, anyway, did I mention that one of them was awesome?

Finally, thanks to my husband, Kevin, who often has a manuscript shoved in his face at the halfway mark while I wail, *"Tell me if this shames my ancestors!"* He is a good person and probably should not have to put up with that, but I greatly appreciate that he does.

The next time you're out driving and you see the vultures at the side of the road, acting as nature's cleanup crew, give them a nod. They're doing vital work, and we would miss them very, very much if they were gone.

T. Kingfisher
March 2022
Pittsboro, NC

Turn the page for a sneak peek of

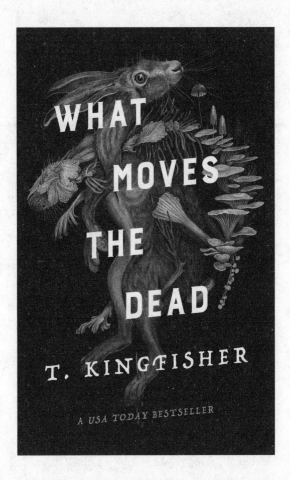

Available now from Tor Nightfire

CHAPTER 1

The mushroom's gills were the deep-red color of severed muscle, the almost-violet shade that contrasts so dreadfully with the pale pink of viscera. I had seen it any number of times in dead deer and dying soldiers, but it startled me to see it here.

Perhaps it would not have been so unsettling if the mushrooms had not looked so much like flesh. The caps were clammy, swollen beige, puffed up against the dark-red gills. They grew out of the gaps in the stones of the tarn like tumors growing from diseased skin. I had a strong urge to step back from them, and an even stronger urge to poke them with a stick.

I felt vaguely guilty about pausing in my trip to dismount and look at mushrooms, but I was tired. More importantly, my horse was tired. Madeline's letter had taken over a week to reach me, and no matter how urgently worded it had been, five minutes more or less would not matter.

Hob, my horse, was grateful for the rest, but seemed

annoyed by the surroundings. He looked at the grass and then up at me, indicating that this was not the quality to which he was accustomed.

"You could have a drink," I said. "A small one, perhaps."

We both looked into the water of the tarn. It lay dark and very still, reflecting the grotesque mushrooms and the limp gray sedges along the edge of the shore. It could have been five feet deep or fifty-five.

"Perhaps not," I said. I found that I didn't have much urge to drink the water either.

Hob sighed in the manner of horses who find the world not to their liking and gazed off into the distance.

I looked across the tarn to the house and sighed myself.

It was not a promising sight. It was an old gloomy manor house in the old gloomy style, a stone monstrosity that the richest man in Europe would be hard-pressed to keep up. One wing had collapsed into a pile of stone and jutting rafters. Madeline lived there with her twin brother, Roderick Usher, who was nothing like the richest man in Europe. Even by Ruravia's small, rather backward standards, the Ushers were genteelly impoverished. By the standards of the rest of Europe's nobility, they were as poor as church mice, and the house showed it.

There were no gardens that I could see. I could smell a faint sweetness in the air, probably from something flowering in the grass, but it wasn't enough to dispel the sense of gloom.

"I shouldn't touch that if I were you," called a voice behind me.

I turned. Hob lifted his head, found the visitor as disappointing as the grass and the tarn, and dropped it again.

She was, as my mother would say, "a woman of a certain

age." In this case, that age was about sixty. She was wearing men's boots and a tweed riding habit that may have predated the manor.

She was tall and broad and had a gigantic hat that made her even taller and broader. She was carrying a notebook and a large leather knapsack.

"Pardon?" I said.

"The mushroom," she said, stopping in front of me. Her accent was British but not London—somewhere off in the countryside, perhaps. "The mushroom, young . . ." Her gaze swept down, touched the military pins on my jacket collar, and I saw a flash of recognition across her face: *Aha!*

No, *recognition* is the wrong term. *Classification,* rather. I waited to see if she would cut the conversation short or carry on.

"I shouldn't touch it if I were you, officer," she said again, pointing to the mushroom.

I looked down at the stick in my hand, as if it belonged to someone else. "Ah—no? Are they poisonous?"

She had a rubbery, mobile face. Her lips pursed together dramatically. "They're stinking redgills. *A. foetida,* not to be confused with *A. foetidissima*—but that's not likely in this part of the world, is it?"

"No?" I guessed.

"No. The *foetidissima* are found in Africa. This one is endemic to this part of Europe. They aren't poisonous, exactly, but—well—"

She put out her hand. I set my stick in it, bemused. Clearly a naturalist. The feeling of being classified made more sense now. I had been categorized, placed into the correct clade, and the proper courtesies could now be deployed, while we went on to more critical matters like mushroom taxonomy.

"I suggest you hold your horse," she said. "And perhaps your nose." Reaching into her knapsack, she fished out a handkerchief, held it to her nose, and then flicked the stinking redgill mushroom with the very end of the stick.

It was a very light tap indeed, but the mushroom's cap immediately bruised the same visceral red-violet as the gills. A moment later, we were struck by an indescribable smell— rotting flesh with a tongue-coating glaze of spoiled milk and, rather horribly, an undertone of fresh-baked bread. It wiped out any sweetness to the air and made my stomach lurch.

Hob snorted and yanked at his reins. I didn't blame him. "Gahh!"

"That was a little one," said the woman of a certain age. "And not fully ripe yet, thank heavens. The big ones will knock your socks off and curl your hair." She set the stick down, keeping the handkerchief over her mouth with her free hand. "Hence the 'stinking' part of the common name. The 'redgill,' I trust, is self-explanatory."

"Vile!" I said, holding my arm over my face. "Are you a mycologist, then?"

I could not see her mouth through the handkerchief, but her eyebrows were wry. "An amateur only, I fear, as supposedly befits my sex."

She bit off each word, and we shared a look of wary understanding. England has no sworn soldiers, I am told, and even if it had, she might have chosen a different way. It was none of my business, as I was none of hers. We all make our own way in the world, or don't. Still, I could guess at the shape of some of the obstacles she had faced.

"Professionally, I am an illustrator," she said crisply. "But the study of fungi has intrigued me all my life."

"And it brought you here?"

"Ah!" She gestured with the handkerchief. "I do not know what you know of fungi, but this place is extraordinary! So many unusual forms! I have found boletes that previously were unknown outside of Italy, and one *Amanita* that appears to be entirely new. When I have finished my drawings, amateur or no, the Mycology Society will have no choice but to recognize it."

"And what will you call it?" I asked. I am delighted by obscure passions, no matter how unusual. During the war, I was once holed up in a shepherd's cottage, listening for the enemy to come up the hillside, when the shepherd launched into an impassioned diatribe on the finer points of sheep breeding that rivaled any sermon I have ever heard in my life. By the end, I was nodding along and willing to launch a crusade against all weak, overbred flocks, prone to scours and fly-strike, crowding out the honest sheep of the world.

"Maggots!" he'd said, shaking his finger at me. "Maggots 'n piss in t' flaps o' they hides!"

I think of him often.

"I shall call it *A. potteri*," said my new acquaintance, who fortunately did not know where my thoughts were trending. "I am Eugenia Potter, and I shall have my name writ in the books of the Mycology Society one way or another."

"I believe that you shall," I said gravely. "I am Alex Easton." I bowed.

She nodded. A lesser spirit might have been embarrassed to have blurted her passions aloud in such a fashion, but clearly Miss Potter was beyond such weaknesses—or perhaps she simply assumed that anyone would recognize the importance of leaving one's mark in the annals of mycology.

"These stinking redgills," I said, "they are not new to science?"

She shook her head. "Described years ago," she said. "From this very stretch of countryside, I believe, or one near to it. The Ushers were great supporters of the arts long ago, and one commissioned a botanical work. Mostly of *flowers*"—her contempt was a glorious thing to hear—"but a few mushrooms as well. And even a botanist could not overlook *A. foetida*. I fear that I cannot tell you its common name in Gallacian, though."

"It may not have one." If you have never met a Gallacian, the first thing you must know is that Gallacia is home to a stubborn, proud, fierce people who are also absolutely piss-poor warriors. My ancestors roamed Europe, picking fights and having the tar beaten out of them by virtually every other people they ran across. They finally settled in Gallacia, which is near Moldavia and even smaller. Presumably they settled there because nobody else wanted it. The Ottoman Empire didn't even bother to make us a vassal state, if that tells you anything. It's cold and poor and if you don't die from falling in a hole or starving to death, a wolf eats you. The one thing going for it is that we aren't invaded often, or at least we weren't, until the previous war.

In the course of all that wandering around losing fights, we developed our own language, Gallacian. I am told it is worse than Finnish, which is impressive. Every time we lost a fight, we made off with a few more loan words from our enemies. The upshot of all of this is that the Gallacian language is intensely idiosyncratic. (We have seven sets of pronouns, for example, one of which is for inanimate objects and one of which is used only for God. It's probably a miracle that we don't have one just for mushrooms.)

Miss Potter nodded. "That is the Usher house on the other side of the tarn, if you were curious."

"Indeed," I said, "it is where I am headed. Madeline Usher was a friend of my youth."

"Oh," said Miss Potter, sounding hesitant for the first time. She looked away. "I have heard she is very ill. I am sorry."

"It has been a number of years," I said, instinctively touching the pocket with Madeline's letter tucked into it.

"Perhaps it is not so bad as they say," she said, in what was undoubtedly meant to be a jollying tone. "You know how bad news grows in villages. Sneeze at noon and by sundown the gravedigger will be taking your measurements."

"We can but hope." I looked down again into the tarn. A faint wind stirred up ripples, which lapped at the edges. As we watched, a stone dropped from somewhere on the house and plummeted into the water. Even the splash seemed muted.

Eugenia Potter shook herself. "Well, I have sketching to do. Good luck to you, Officer Easton."

"And to you, Miss Potter. I shall look forward to word of your *Amanitas.*"

Her lips twitched. "If not the *Amanitas,* I have great hopes for some of these boletes." She waved to me and strode out across the field, leaving silver boot prints in the damp grass.

I led Hob back to the road, which skirted the edge of the lake. It was a joyless scene, even with the end of the journey in sight. There were more of the pale sedges and a few dead trees, too gray and decayed for me to identify. (Miss Potter presumably knew what they were, although I would never ask her to lower herself to identifying mere vegetation.) Mosses coated the edges of the stones and more of the stinking redgills pushed up in obscene little lumps. The house squatted over it like the largest mushroom of them all.

My tinnitus chose that moment to strike, a high-pitched

whine ringing through my ears and drowning out even the soft lapping of the tarn. I stopped and waited for it to pass. It's not dangerous, but sometimes my balance becomes a trifle questionable, and I had no desire to stumble into the lake. Hob is used to this and waited with the stoic air of a martyr undergoing torture.

Sadly, while my ears sorted themselves out, I had nothing to look at but the building. God, but it was a depressing scene.

It is a cliché to say that a building's windows look like eyes because humans will find faces in anything and of course the windows would be the eyes. The house of Usher had dozens of eyes, so either it was a great many faces lined up together or it was the face of some creature belonging to a different order of life—a spider, perhaps, with rows of eyes along its head.

I'm not, for the most part, an imaginative soul. Put me in the most haunted house in Europe for a night, and I shall sleep soundly and wake in the morning with a good appetite. I lack any psychic sensitivities whatsoever. Animals like me, but I occasionally think they must find me frustrating, as they stare and twitch at unknown spirits and I say inane things like "Who's a good fellow, then?" and "Does kitty want a treat?" (Look, if you don't make a fool of yourself over animals, at least in private, you aren't to be trusted. That was one of my father's maxims, and it's never failed me yet.)

Given that lack of imagination, perhaps you will forgive me when I say that the whole place felt like a hangover.

What was it about the house and the tarn that was so depressing? Battlefields are grim, of course, but no one questions why. This was just another gloomy lake, with a gloomy house and some gloomy plants. It shouldn't have affected my spirits so strongly.

Granted, the plants all looked dead or dying. Granted, the windows of the house stared down like eye sockets in a row of skulls, yes, but so what? Actual rows of skulls wouldn't affect me so strongly. I knew a collector in Paris . . . well, never mind the details. He was the gentlest of souls, though he did collect rather odd things. But he used to put festive hats on his skulls depending on the season, and they all looked rather jolly.

Usher's house was going to require more than festive hats. I mounted Hob and urged him into a trot, the sooner to get to the house and put the scene behind me.

ABOUT THE AUTHOR

JR Blackwell

T. KINGFISHER writes fantasy, horror, and occasional oddities, including *Nettle & Bone* and *What Moves the Dead*. Under a pen name, she also writes bestselling children's books. She lives in North Carolina with her husband, dogs, and a garden with several rose bushes that she keeps a very careful eye on.